PRAISE FOR

★ "As the boys take tentative steps to salvage their friendship, they navigate high-stakes choices and consider the value of loyalty, integrity, and sacrifice in a story driven by fast-paced drama on and off the court." —*PUBLISHERS WEEKLY*, starred review

★ "A real winner for its heartbeat, compassion, and integrity."
—*KIRKUS REVIEWS*, starred review

"Readers will race through the intrigue and volatile basketball action to the explosive conclusion." —*HORN BOOK*

"*After the Shot Drops* is both a pulse-pounding sports book and a sophisticated exploration of identity, loyalty, and home. It sings with heart and stays with you long after you've turned its last page. Nothing but net." —I. W. GREGORIO, author of *None of the Above*

"The tangled lives of Ribay's players are even more riveting than the thrilling action on the court. A basketball novel that is so much more than the final score. Terrific."
—CARL DEUKER, author of *Payback Time*

"An honest, riveting story full of integrity about what it takes to save a friendship—this buzzer-beater of a book makes your heart roar from tip-off to the final second." —BRENDAN KIELY, coauthor of the *New York Times* best-selling *All American Boys*

AFTER THE SHOT DROPS

RANDY RIBAY

Clarion Books
An Imprint of HarperCollins*Publishers*
Boston   New York

Clarion Books
An Imprint of HarperCollins Publishers, registered in the United States of America
and/or other jurisdictions.

www.clarionbooks.com

The text was set in Amasis MT Std.

The Library of Congress has cataloged the hardcover edition as follows:
Names: Ribay, Randy, author.
Title: After the shot drops / by Randy Ribay.
Description: Boston ; New York : HarperCollins Publishers, [2018] |
Summary: Told from alternating perspectives, Bunny takes a
basketball scholarship to an elite private school to help his family,
leaving behind Nasir, his best friend, in their tough Philadelphia neighborhood.
Identifiers: LCCN 2017006800
Subjects: | CYAC: Best friends—Fiction. | Friendship—Fiction. |
Basketball—Fiction. | Scholarships—Fiction. | Family life—
Pennsylvania—Philadelphia—Fiction. | Philadelphia (Pa.)—Fiction.
Classification: LCC PZ7.1.R5 Aft 2018 | DDC [Fic]—dc23
LC record available at https://lccn.loc.gov/2017006800

ISBN: 978-1-328-70227-2 hardcover
ISBN: 978-0-358-10806-1 paperback

Manufactured in the United States of America
23 24 25 26 27 LBC 13 12 11 10 9

For those who hurt.

The world is before you
and you need not take it or leave it
as it was when you came in.

—James Baldwin

1
BUNNY

'm never sure what to write for the dead. I mean, most of the time when someone hands me the marker at one of these vigils, I just end up laying down something vague and comforting. You know:

See you in heaven.

We'll miss you.

Rest in peace, bro.

Something like that. But it never feels right. Never feels like your words will make a difference, like they'll make his family feel better or stop anyone else from dying for no reason. The person they're meant for won't ever read them, so you're just wasting ink.

But the small, silent crowd shuffles forward, the girl ahead of me passes me a marker, and it's my turn. I've got to write something.

I step up to the big oak tree that stands in the middle of Virgilio Square, its bare branches spread out overhead like skeletal fingers. A white sheet's been wrapped around its trunk, with TE QUEREMOS, GABE, airbrushed across the middle in big blue letters. I know enough Spanish to know that means "we love you." Everyone's notes and signatures are scrawled in the spaces all around it. A bunch of teddy bears and candles sit at the base of the tree in front of a framed photo of Gabe smiling big, all nestled in a nook formed by the roots.

This is where Gabe and his friends were hanging when the shots were fired. Word is the bullet was meant for someone else. Too bad the bullet didn't know that.

I'm tall, so I decide to add my message up high on the sheet where there's only a couple others. I take off my glove and shake my hand to try to warm it up, then I lean against the tree and press the tip of the marker against the white cotton. The black ink bleeds into it.

I stay like that for a few moments, adding nothing but a black dot because I still don't know what to write. I want to put down something meaningful. Gabe lived three streets over and was only a year ahead of me in school. We weren't real tight, but coming up, he was part of the group of kids we'd always play football or manhunt or whatever with. For some reason, I keep thinking about how he used to eat apples whole, core and all. The rest of us would tell him a tree was going to grow in his stomach if he drank too much water. Funny how your mind picks something small like that to replay.

But I also think about last summer, when I announced that I was transferring from Whitman High, our neighborhood school, to St. Sebastian's, a private school in the suburbs. Pride in Whitman High's basketball team runs real deep around our way, so a lot of people didn't like that one bit. My main man, Nasir, straight up stopped talking to me. But Gabe was cool about it. I was shooting around at the courts one day shortly after the announcement, and some guys started getting in my face about it. Gabe stepped in, calmed them down, and sent them on their way. Then he told me to keep my head up, to not let it get to me. Maybe it's because he was good at football and so understood what I was trying to do with basketball, but whatever the reason, it meant a lot. Only, I don't know how to express all this on a bed sheet wrapped around a tree.

I feel the line behind me growing restless, since I'm taking forever, so I give up trying to find the perfect words. I settle for *i won't forget you*, and sign my name. Don't know what happens to us after we die, but if there's some way he can read this, I know he'll understand the words I feel but can't find.

After handing the marker to the woman behind me, I step aside, slip my glove back on, and dig my hands into my coat pockets. I go back to the rear of the crowd that's gathered in the blocked-off street, bundled up in their winter gear and waiting for his pastor or his parents or whoever to take the mic that's set up in the patch of grass next to the tree. After a bit, one of the local politicians gets up there and starts going on about how we can't let something like this happen again. I've heard this song before, so my mind drifts.

It's overcast and frigid. Late February and still hasn't snowed more than a dusting all winter. Looking up, I wonder if today's the day. The gray clouds feel heavy as my heart, like they're about to dump two feet of snow on us at any moment. An airplane crawls across the sky on its way to Philly on the other side of the river, the drone of its engines getting louder as it approaches. A lot of people hate that we've got these jets flying past every few minutes, but I don't mind. It's like God's constant reminder that there's more out there than this. Besides, I kind of like how they make the sun blink when they pass by on a clear day. Of course, right now the sun's hidden behind the clouds, so the plane passes and then it's quiet again except for boots shifting, people sniffling, cars passing on the side streets. Some hushed conversations. Quiet, sad laughter. Every now and then someone breaking down.

The politician at the mic is still carrying on, for some reason talking about one of her new initiatives. I stay tuned out, letting my eyes wander across the crowd. There are a lot of families from the neighborhood out here, as well as what seems like most of the kids from Whitman High. The girls hold each other and dab at their eyes while the guys stand around like they've got faces cut from stone. A few nod at me, but I hang back.

I mostly stay to myself these days. My interactions in the neighborhood usually go one of two ways: either people try to start something like I betrayed them personally by transferring to St. Sebastian's, or they try to put all this pressure on me to go back to Whitman High. Either way, I'm not feeling like dealing with any of it, so I turn to leave, even though the memorial's still going.

That's when I see Nasir. He's off to the side with his cousin

Wallace. Easy to spot them, what with Wallace's height making Nasir look even shorter than he would by himself. Both have their hoods up. Nasir stares at the teddy bears at the foot of the tree while Wallace looks all around like he's got somewhere else to be. I'll see them on the court tomorrow since they both still play for Whitman, but I consider walking over to say what's up to Nas. It's stupid we're still not talking because I want something more than what Whitman can offer. Out of everyone, I expected him to get that.

But as I'm about take a step toward them, Wallace catches sight of me. I nod at him, but he doesn't nod back. He holds my gaze for a beat and then nudges Nas. Nas lifts his eyes and they meet mine for a moment. Then he turns his back to me and walks away.

2
NASIR

Everyone's hanging their head as we trudge toward the bus, headphones on and bags slung over shoulders. Got our asses handed to us by St. Sebastian's, 29–65, and now back we go to Whitman. We might argue we weren't feeling it, what with Gabe's death hanging over us and all, and, yeah, maybe that was part of it. But the main reason we lost tonight?

Bunny Thompson.

Bunny tore us apart at both ends of the court. You think he'd at least have the decency to pull back a bit against his old teammates, but no. Put up a double-double—his, like, fifteenth consecutive one this season. Not that I'm keeping track of his numbers or anything.

And with that, our season's finished. We're teammates but not a team. Players out of game.

The sun is setting behind us, and the air smells like snow. I'm last in line, and before I step through the narrow door, I look over my shoulder at St. Sebastian's one last time.

The school sits there with its fancy stonework, a statue

of its patron saint perched above the main entrance. Dude's hands are bound behind his back, and he's wearing nothing but a loincloth. Five or six arrows stick out of his body, but he's got this smug look on his face like he's about to say something.

The driver starts the engine, and its low rumble calls me back to reality. I turn around and climb onto the bus. Wallace waves for me to join him in the back, but I pretend like I don't notice and slide into an empty seat a couple rows behind Coach Campbell and Coach J. They don't even bother to take attendance. Coach Campbell tells the driver we're all set and then leans back, folds his arms over his broad chest, and closes his eyes. Even Coach J — who's usually so positive you want to slap him — just flips open the scorebook and shakes his head. They didn't say a word about the whole Bunny thing tonight, but they must have been as sore as we were seeing him suited up in St. Sebastian's red and white instead of Whitman's purple and gold.

But whatever. The bus rolls out.

I readjust my earbuds and turn up my music. I consider finishing this book we've been taking forever to read in English class, *Of Mice and Men,* but I decide I'm not feeling it. So instead, I gaze out the window and watch the rich suburbs surrounding St. Sebastian's slide past. My parents always taught me to be content with what I have, to value people over stuff. But still, these are some big-ass houses.

I also try not to think of the game. I mean, it's not like

ball's my life—I'm not even a starter. But my brain keeps pushing it into my thoughts. This loss hurts more than most. Not that anyone expected us to win tonight. St. S was a powerhouse even before this season, before they stole Bunny. That didn't stop me from fantasizing that we'd destroy them and Bunny would realize he made the wrong decision.

Last year, when he was still on our team, we went twenty and nine. Even made it to the semifinals of sectionals. This season: ten and seventeen. Didn't even qualify for the postseason. Unforgivable for a team that's produced its share of all-Americans in its day. I mean, we even lost to William H. Harrison High this year.

William H. freaking Harrison.

Maybe I won't play next season. It's not like I'm that good. Main reason I tried out freshman year was because Bunny wanted me to.

But the worst part? He didn't even talk to me about all this. Went away for a week to DC with his AAU team for nationals in July and came back with the news that he was headed to St. S in the fall.

I realize I'm clenching my jaw and tensing my shoulders. So I take a deep breath, try to let it out real slow and even. Bunny doesn't care about me anymore, so why should I care about him?

Wallace comes up from the back of the bus and drops heavily onto the seat across from me. I sigh on the inside, because I'm not up for pretending to laugh at the dumb jokes I'm sure he's about to crack. But all he says is "You cool?"

I nod, then he nods and turns to look out his window, like all he means to do is keep me company.

Grateful and exhausted, I close my eyes. The track I'm listening to ends, and the next one begins.

3
—————— BUNNY ——————

My hands are so cold the warm water hurts. I clench my teeth and count down from thirty. The pain will pass. Always does.

Sure enough, by the time I get to zero, my fingers feel like fingers again instead of icicles. I shut off the faucet, pat my hands dry on my hoodie, and then head back into the living room.

Jess is on the couch wearing a big sweatshirt and winter cap because the heat's broken again. She's got a fat textbook open on her lap and a yellow highlighter in her gloved hand. But her eyes are on the TV, where the news is playing real quiet. Justine and Ashley, our little twin sisters, are curled up against her on either side under a pile of blankets, asleep like they had a real hard day in the second grade.

I pick up the ball from the other end of the couch.

"You really going back out there?" Jess asks. Her eyes are locked onto the old guy on the screen going on about politics or something.

It's tempting not to. Trust me. It'd be real nice to unlace my sneakers and take it easy the rest of the night. Maybe play *2K* or plop down on the couch right here or go over to Keyona's place. I mean, I did have a full day of school and a hard workout at practice.

But then I think of the playoffs. We'll start with a bye since we were seeded first, so we'll play on Friday for the quarterfinals. Four more days to get ready.

I also think of Mom busting her butt working the graveyard shift at the hospital right this very moment and Dad's bookstore not doing so hot. I think of Jess sitting in front of me studying hard but still racking up student loan debt. I think of the twins buried in blankets because our landlord doesn't bother getting anybody over here to fix the heat like he claims he will and leaving the oven open doesn't warm the whole place.

I know there are people out there who got it worse than we do, but there's people who got it better, too. A lot better, and they're probably not even working as hard.

"Yup," I say. "Right back at it."

"Isn't it cold?"

I shrug, pull my own knit cap from the front pocket of my hoodie, yank it down over my head, and then flip my hood up. "Like it's summertime in here?"

"You're crazy," she says, though I'm thinking the same thing about her spending all that time studying to become an underpaid social worker someday. If I'm going to work hard for something, you better believe it's going to pay the bills. "Aaron said he called someone about the furnace."

"Right," I say. Aaron's our landlord, who lives in the

suburbs. "In the meantime, feel free to burn those to keep warm." I gesture toward the kitchen table at the stack of college brochures that've been flooding our mailbox for the last few months. Schools can't send me specific recruiting stuff until June 15, when I officially become a junior, but until then they can send me all the junk mail they want, apparently.

"Mom and Dad would kill you," Jess says, laughing.

I laugh, too, because it's true. They're collecting each and every one so that we can go over them together when they have time. They won't let me toss one until we've read it all the way through and discussed the pros and cons, even if it's from some small school nobody's ever heard of before, like the University of Chicago in Nebraska or something wack like that. But the problem is they both work so much that that pile of brochures will probably reach the ceiling before long.

I say goodbye to Jess one more time and then head back outside, careful not to make too much noise as I close the door behind me. Out of habit, I glance up at Nasir's window across the street. His light's on, so I think about rapping on his door and asking if he wants to come with me. But then I think of him turning his back on me at the vigil the other day and then him acting like I didn't even exist during our game, so I roll out by my lonesome.

The streets are empty. The houses are dark. Don't want to wake anyone, since it's a Monday night, so I hold the ball on my hip with one hand and bury the other in my pocket as I make my way to the courts. I walk quickly, with my breath puffing out in front of my face.

Nasir and I must have made this walk together a million times throughout the years. One of us would play offense and the other defense as we went up the sidewalk. If the defender could steal the ball, then we'd switch. Most of the time I was the one dribbling. Not that Nasir was that bad, but I knew him well enough to know that his eyes would flick downward right before he'd lunge for the steal, and that's when I'd cross over and spin, slipping past him to run the rest of the way to the court, laughing as he trailed behind. But sometimes I'd let him swipe the ball away just because.

That was how it used to be, though. Now I'm always making this walk alone, putting my moves on ghost defenders. Wondering if I made a mistake.

After a few blocks, I reach the park. It's behind the community center on the other side of the soccer and baseball fields, far enough away from any houses that I don't feel bad dribbling once my feet hit the blacktop.

There's an empty forty at center court. At least whoever left it didn't bust it and leave the blacktop littered with shards of glass like they sometimes do. I go over and pick up the bottle with my right while dribbling with my left. Toss it into a trash can and then turn back to the hoops.

It's not as nice as St. Sebastian's gym, but this is my home court. This is where I started really playing ball with Nasir once we graduated from the low-hanging crate nailed to a telephone pole on our block. I know every crack and dip like the back of my hand. I know if the shot's going to drop by the sound of the clang when it hits the steel rim. I know the lights click off at ten but you can still see enough to keep shooting if the moon is bright.

This is where I've lost and won a thousand games. Where I drained that half-court shot as a sixth-grader to beat the high school kids. Where I broke my nose catching an elbow on a drive and didn't get the foul shots. Where I dunked for the first time and nobody was around to see—except for Nasir.

This is my home court. *Our* home court.

I toss up a rainbow, which sails through the netless hoop.

But I'm not here for three-pointers. I'm here for fadeaway, midrange jumpers—the shot I blew three times during tonight's game. If I'm going to lead St. Sebastian's to another state title, I can't be missing that action every time.

After grabbing the rebound, I reset at the top of the key. Lower my dribble and visualize my man crouching low, hands up like they teach in basketball camp. I start counting down from ten. At five, I fake right and then cross over to the left. At four, I turn and back the dude down, and at three, we're a few feet inside the arc. At two, I pivot and leap. At one, I release the shot at the peak of my vertical. At zero, I fall backwards . . .

The shot falls short and glances off the front of the rim.

I chase it down, return to the top of the key, and restart. Dribble, cross over, back down, pivot, fade away, and release. Another brick. Another rebound.

I keep repeating the motions. Each dribble echoes across the night. The soles of my sneakers scrape over the concrete with each motion. The wind picks up, frigid and stinging. My fingers and toes start to feel numb again, begging me to quit, to save it for practice tomorrow.

But I don't.

I dribble, cross over, back down, pivot, fade away, release.

Rebound.

Reset.

4
NASIR

I finish *Of Mice and Men,* and I'm sitting there with my legs up on my bed, turning it over in my mind, when my phone starts buzzing. I try to ignore it since I'm still lost in the story, but I don't know if there's anything more irritating than that thing buzzing over and over again. For some reason, instead of silencing it, I take a deep breath, set down the book, and pick up my phone from the nightstand to find several texts from Wallace.

The first five or six messages are him carrying on about how the Sixers are playing like ass tonight. I don't watch basketball too often, but even I know that's nothing new. Then there's a couple asking about if I did the chemistry homework and if I'd send him a pic so he can copy it. Then there's a picture of him flashing me the middle finger. A blurry shot of a dark, hairy body part that I don't even want to try to identify. And then a few messages about how bored he is and if I want to go over to some girl's apartment with him.

It's pretty late, and I don't have the energy to figure out how to respond to all the disparate threads of conversation he's laying down. So I set my phone back on my nightstand.

But a second later, it buzzes with another insightful message from Wallace.

Where u at? Stp touching yrself.

I sigh. My cousin, the next Steinbeck. Technically, he's like a second or third cousin. I don't really know how that terminology works past a certain point. He's the son of one of my dad's cousins, so whatever that makes us.

Yo we got 2 talk, Wallace's next message says. Got a prob.

Just one? I finally text back, ignoring his scattershot slew of previous messages. Good thing he's got the memory of a goldfish.

There's nothing from Wallace for a minute and then he shoots back, Shut up miget for real.

Sorry, I text, you have a problem. This is a special occasion. What's up?

I read his next message, and my breath catches: Me and g gettin evicted.

G's his grandma. Now I feel like a dick for joking a second ago. You serious?

Yeah letter says we got till the end of next month.

I'm feeling so bad for Wallace that I don't even know how to reply. He's the kind of kid who's had to deal with more than anyone should have to deal with. Dad's in prison. Mom's a drug addict lost in the wind. He was mostly brought up by his grandma. She's a nice enough lady and does what she can, but she was already old when she first took him in years ago. You wish the world would throw him a break. Instead it keeps on trying to break him.

Why? I ask.

They raised the rent awhile back, he texts. We fell behind.

Why? I ask again.

Why you think? $$$!

Wallace and his grandma live in downtown Whitman right between the university and the main hospital. Seems like it would be a great place to live, what with the view of the Philly skyline right on the other side of the Delaware, but prices keep going up along with the new dorms or parking structures or whatever.

By how much? I text.

To much. lol.

Maybe my parents can help you out, I reply.

Nah i got this.

I know he doesn't. Otherwise, he wouldn't have texted me about it in the first place. Still, I feel like I should offer something, so I message back, I'm sure it'd be cool if you two stayed here if worse comes to worst.

After my phone remains quiet for a couple minutes, I set it down and sit on the edge of the bed contemplating Wallace's situation. *Would* my parents be willing to let them stay with us if they couldn't come up with the rent or find another place to live? My dad grew up right here in the city, and even though his family always had enough to eat, he knows what it can be like for some. And from all the stories I've heard, my mom was living real poor in the Philippines before she met my dad while he was stationed there with the air force. She still sends money back to aunts and uncles I've never met.

I remember when I was, like, eight or nine, I walked into the kitchen to find her and my dad talking about how much to send that month. One of her nephews was sick, so they were trying to figure out how much extra they could afford to give.

"Why do we give them anything?" I remember asking, angry that earlier that day they had refused to buy me the newest Halo game. "It's our money."

I remember she had turned to me. Sad, like I was a disappointment. She said, *"Matibay ang walis, palibhasa'y magkabigkis."* Then she translated it for me, since I can't speak Tagalog: "A broom is sturdy because its strands are tightly bound." Wouldn't be the last time I heard that.

The only reason I think they might say no to the whole Wallace thing is on account of the fact they don't like Wallace. Think he's a bad influence on me, and all that. True, my grades have slipped since we started hanging again, but I'm still pulling A's and B's. Mostly. But given Wallace and his grandma's situation, maybe they'd understand.

I go ahead and send Wallace a pic of my chem homework, then I start hearing this steady thumping outside. It's a familiar beat—the dribbling of a ball against concrete. Even before I peek out the window, I know who I'm going to see.

Just as I thought—it's Bunny.

Probably back from the courts. I mean, I know he's got playoffs starting in a few days, but as if he needed more practice. As if he didn't drop thirty-something points on us last night without breaking a sweat.

I watch him make his lonely way down the block. Past the

sleepy row homes, their doors and windows shut like teeth clenched against the night. Past the first empty lot where people dump their trash. Past the second empty lot, which is used as a community garden in the summer but is a patch of frozen dirt right now. Past my door.

And I know he'll be up in a few hours making this same walk in the opposite direction. On his way to his bus or train or whatever carries him off to fancy-ass St. Sebastian's. Off to his shiny new friends.

Speaking of loose strands.

I think I see him glance toward my window, but I'm not sure because his hood's up so his face is lost in shadow. Either way, I let the curtain fall back and drop my head onto my pillow. I try to fall asleep, but an unsettled feeling has seeped into my bones, keeping me wide awake. Maybe it's because I've been thinking about Bunny, or maybe it's because I'm racking my brain trying to figure out how to help Wallace avoid his impending eviction, or maybe it's because of the ending of that book, which was, like, the saddest goddamn thing in the world.

5
BUNNY

I scan the dining hall, tray in hand, for a place to sit. Took me a few weeks to figure out that even though the kids here at St. S look different from the ones at Whitman, they pretty much split themselves up in the same ways. The popular crew, the nerds, the athletes, the theater kids, and so on. It really is like a cliché from a teen movie, but I guess there's a reason something becomes a cliché.

Same as most days, I sit with Drew, our team's center, and Eric, our point guard. They're talking about this monster dunk Drew had against Whitman. I don't say anything, because even though it was a win, it didn't feel like one to me. Besides, it's Tuesday. We've got sectional quarterfinals coming up on Friday and should be thinking ahead to that, not looking back.

Noticing my silence, Drew runs a hand through his shaggy brown hair. "You feeling okay, Bunny?"

But before I can answer, Eric's pale blue eyes shift to the hamburger on my plate. "That's not going to help." He pokes a finger into the top bun. "Ugh. Looks like a ratburger."

I know Eric's playing, so I shrug it off. The girls giggle. At the other end of the table, I notice Clay, our second-string power forward, smirk. Dude's been salty all season, since it was his starting spot I took. Whatever. I take a bite. You ask me, it's decent. At Whitman they do things like put liquid cheese, greasy ground beef, and stringy lettuce on top of some Fritos and call it a "taco salad." So, yeah, I go ahead and take a second bite of my hamburger, even though Eric poked his finger through the middle.

"Let's go get some real food," Eric says, standing up along with Drew. A couple of the girls rise to follow them, a bubbly blonde named Brooke and a brunette with a lot of freckles named Stacy who's always asking questions in my history class.

"Bunny, you coming?" Drew asks, gesturing for me to follow.

"Nah, I'm cool with my ratburger," I say, because my wallet's empty. One of the assistant coaches might hook me up if I asked, but I'm not trying to get in trouble for a few bucks. There's this rule that you can't accept money or anything to be on the team—you lose your amateur status and can't play in the NCAA. It's what happened to LeBron when he accepted some expensive jerseys from some store in a mall, except he was skipping straight to the NBA, so it didn't matter to him. But I want that college degree, and I want to make sure my parents don't have to pay a dime for it. If that means I'm hungry every now and then, so be it.

Brooke starts tugging me by the wrist. "Please?" she says like she's purring. Stacy joins her.

I look at my burger. Look at Brooke. I notice everyone else around the table watching. "All right," I say, giving in. But it's not like that. I got a girl. Mostly I want everyone to stop looking at me.

I grab my burger and toss everything else. I eat it as the five of us walk right outside, because St. Sebastian's is an open campus and students can leave in the middle of the day. Not that the kids at Whitman don't do the same, but here it's allowed.

The weather's warmed up pretty nice, and as we make our way through the parking lot, I hang back and let the others lead the way past the rows of student cars gleaming in the sunlight. I'm thinking about how there's no student parking lot at Whitman, which gets me wondering if I'll ever be able to stop comparing everything here to how it is back home. If I'll ever stop feeling like someone's going to call me down to the office to say they made a mistake and I really don't belong here.

Eric's black SUV—which he calls the Ballermobile—chirps as he unlocks it with his keychain remote. The vanity plate reads 1BALLR. I laugh a little, remembering how one time Drew cracked on Eric, saying that it probably made people think he was a testicular cancer survivor.

Drew takes shotgun, because even though I'm tall, he's a giant. Closer to seven feet than six. A little slow, but overall a decent center. Could probably play D-II ball somewhere, but he's a senior and already committed to going to school out in the Midwest. He won't be on their team, but I guess that's where his boyfriend's going, so that's where he wants to go.

I climb in the back behind Eric because he's short, so my legs can have at least some space. The car smells like leather until Brooke and Stacy slide in, filling the air with that clean and sweet girl smell.

Before starting the engine, Eric pulls out a joint. I'm not even sure where it comes from. It's like a magic trick. *POOF: Weed!*

"Want some?" he asks, looking at me first for some reason, even though I've never smoked with him. I decided a long time ago that if I wanted to make it, then I couldn't be putting junk in my body.

"Nah, I'm cool," I say.

Eric shrugs, offers it to Drew, who takes a deep hit, and then passes it behind his head to Stacy.

The dank, sour smell fills the car. I slide down my window expecting a teacher or the dean to start chasing us like the Terminator. My anxiety only fades a little as we pull away from the school.

My stomach rumbles. "So where we going?"

Brooke shakes her head when Stacy tries to hand her the joint, so she passes it back to Eric. "Burritos," he says.

Drew nods like Eric laid down some deep truth. "Nice."

Eric turns on the stereo and rock music blasts from the

speakers. But then he hits a button and old-school hip-hop comes on. "Mo' Money" by Biggie. Eric's got a nice system, so the bass thumps for real, not all rattling the car like it does in most rides.

Eric and the girls start rapping along, probably feeling real gangster, rolling with a blunt and a Black guy. Drew looks out the window and bobs his head with the beat. And I get this feeling that I get a lot, like I'm here but I'm not. Like I'm watching all of this from outer space or something.

We pull up to the burrito place a few minutes later. Stacy takes one more hit and then passes the joint back to Eric. He licks his fingers, snuffs it out, and tucks it away in the center console. We step out of his car and join the line, which stretches out the door.

"I'm starving," Eric says, rubbing his belly as he checks out some girls ahead of us in line. They look young, but they're all dressed up like they're on lunch break from some corporate job. "What are you guys getting?"

"Steak and potato," Drew says, without thinking about it.

"Cheese quesadilla!" says Stacy, with more excitement than seems necessary.

Brooke brushes a strand of hair out of her eyes. "Oh, I'm not hungry."

"What about you, B?" Eric says. I don't like that he calls me B, since we don't know each other like that. But I let it go. Chalk it up to his high.

I shrug. "I'm good."

Eric peels his eyes away from the girls to look at me. "Really?"

"Real rap," I say. "I had that burger."

He laughs, and I realize my mistake too late. I usually try to keep my talk kind of white around these guys, but sometimes words slip out.

"Real rap," Eric echoes, testing it out. "I like that. I'll have to start using it."

The line shuffles forward, and we enter the restaurant proper. Drew's still looking at me like I've got a second head on my shoulders. "You're really not hungry, man?"

I laugh for some reason. "Yeah, I'm cool." But the aroma of all that sizzling spiced meat hits my nose and sets my stomach rumbling again like it's ready to eat itself. When you're tall as I am, your body needs more food, I guess. "I'll wait outside."

"If you say so," Drew says.

Brooke sidles up next to me, all smelling like shampoo. "I'll keep you company."

"Um, thanks."

We head outside and then sit down on a bench out front of the place. The metal feels nice, since it's warmed by the sunlight. Brooke extends her legs out in front of her. She smoothes the front of her plaid skirt and tugs up her white knee-high socks. She looks from her legs to mine.

"You're so big," she says.

"Um, I guess." I straighten my tie and adjust my blazer,

more out of the need to do something than because they need to be fixed.

"Still not used to wearing a school uniform?" Brooke asks.

"We had uniforms at Whitman."

"Really?"

"Yeah, khakis and these butt-ugly, purple polo shirts."

"Why?"

"I guess they want to make sure nobody's wearing gang colors at school or something."

She laughs like that was a joke and brushes her hair out of her eyes again. "Can I ask you a question?"

"Sure."

"Why do they call you Bunny?"

I lift my feet off the ground. "Because I got hops."

She looks confused for a moment, then it clicks. "Oh. Like you can jump?"

"Yeah," I say, putting my feet back down. "My friend Nasir came up with it when we were kids. Just kind of stuck."

"I like it," she says, and bumps her shoulder against me. "It's cute. How'd he get his nickname — Nasir, right?"

"Um," I say. "That's his real name."

"Oh."

Something buzzes in my pants. My phone. I slide it out to see that I've got a new text.

"Nice phone." She pulls hers out of her back pocket. The case is covered in diamond-looking stickers that catch the sunlight and nearly blind me. "I have the same one."

"Oh, really?" I say, as if ten million other people don't.

Brooke peers over at my screen and bumps me again with her shoulder. "That your *girlfriend?*" She says the word all singsongy like people used to back in grade school.

I hesitate for a moment. "Yeah."

She nods, and suddenly things feel weird. I text Keyona and then slide my phone back into my pocket.

"Are you nervous?" she asks.

"Huh?" I ask.

"For Friday?"

"Right. The playoffs," I say, looking at my hands. "Not really."

"Really?" she says, smiling like she doesn't believe me. "Even with all those people talking about how good you are and how you're definitely going to help us win another state title? God, I'd be so nervous. That's so much pressure, you know? Like, you'll be letting so many people down if you fail. Not that I'm saying you're going to fail—it's just . . ."

But she doesn't even know the half of it. She's probably thinking about the game.

"Nah," I say. "I don't get nervous when I play."

"Shut up," she says in that playful way girls say it. "I don't believe you."

"Truth. The court's the only place where I feel like I've got control over everything."

"Hmm," she says. "I think I know what you mean. I feel that way when I dance."

"You mean when you cheer?" I ask.

She shakes her head. "It's separate. I joined the cheer team at school for fun. I dance outside of school with a company. We put on recitals and stuff. They're usually really good. We've got a show coming up in April—you should totally come."

Like I have no control over them, my eyes slide down to her dancer's legs. But I'm not trying to be sketchy, so I force myself to look up at some clouds as if they're the most interesting thing in the world.

"Maybe," I say. Then my stomach growls real loud again. Traitor.

Brooke is nice enough to pretend not to notice. But not nice enough to offer to hook me up with a burrito.

6
NASIR

Kim Kardashian's skilled hands rub the sunblock into my shoulders. I close my eyes, enjoying the tickle of her fingers against my skin. The warmth of the sun. The infinite crashing of the rolling waves. My shoulders relax. I lean back before she's finished and feel her boobs press against me. She laughs, kisses the side of my head, rests her chin on my shoulder.

"Want to go back to the room?" I mumble.

"What room, Mr. Blake?"

My eyes fly open.

Instead of the beach and a beautiful woman and the sun, I remember it's Tuesday in the middle of the winter and I'm in chemistry. Ms. Martinez stands over me, arms folded over her chest, giving me that teacher death glare.

With everyone's eyes on me, I wipe the drool from the corner of my mouth and sit up. "Sorry."

"Forgive him, miss," some senior says from the other side of the room. "Being a loser's probably real tiring."

Yeah, everyone's got jokes now that our season's over.

But whatever. At least I'm not trying to pass chem for a third time like that kid is.

Ms. Martinez rolls her eyes and turns back to writing on the board. As her words dissolve into white noise, I turn to Keyona a few seats over to see if she's laughing. She's not. Just copying the notes.

I start doing the same, but a couple minutes later, the bell rings. Ms. Martinez shouts the pages for the equations we have to balance for homework, but I can't hear her over the noise of everyone trying to get the hell out of there as if they were going somewhere cool instead of to another class.

I'm almost finished getting down the last of the notes when someone swats at my writing hand, making my pen drag down the page. Wallace, of course. He's standing next to my desk, towering over me with his big-for-nothing self and his lopsided fade. Speaking of kids trying to pass this class for a third time. He flashes a grin and slaps down his homework from a couple nights ago, which I also let him copy off me. There's a check plus at the top.

"You're welcome," I say.

He crumples his homework into a ball and tosses it toward the trash can as if he were putting up a three. Misses by about a mile. "It's windy," he says by way of excuse, and doesn't bother to pick it up.

"So what'd your grandma say about . . ." I hesitate, not wanting to put his business out there for everyone to hear. "About that letter?"

But boundaries aren't really Wallace's thing. "G shouldn't be paying the landlord all that money for some broke-down apartment. You know the roaches are back?"

"What are you all going to do, then?" I ask, packing up my stuff. "Find another place somewhere in Whitman?"

Wallace is dancing in place like he's listening to some song in his head, as if we aren't talking about him getting evicted. "We've got people all over, man. Philly. Baltimore. New York. I'll find a place for G somewhere in one of those spots with one of my uncles."

"They could take care of her?" I ask, because I know it's a lot of work. Wallace hardly ever complains about it, but since we've been tight these last few months, I've seen all he does for her. Cleaning up around their apartment. Running all kinds of errands. Reminding her about her meds. Hanging and watching TV with her. Small stuff like that.

"I'd make sure they'd know how," he says.

"And what about you?"

Wallace shrugs. Doesn't meet my eyes as he answers, "I'm a grown-ass man, man. I don't need to be living with my grandma or anyone else anymore. I'll figure something out. Maybe get a place over by Broadway or something. Worst comes to worst, I've got Nisha."

Nisha is his car.

"Really?" I ask. "What about school? You're almost finished."

He laughs. "Man, I'm not worried about school. Need to get a job. Start making money."

"Maybe you could stay with us until June. I'll talk to my parents tonight," I say, because I know if he doesn't finish this year, he probably won't ever get his high school degree.

"You going to the game on Friday?" he asks.

I know he's changing the subject, but I don't want to fight him on this. Arguing with Wallace usually makes him more stubborn, no matter how stupid the idea is. I slip on my backpack and start walking out of the classroom, and he follows. "What game?"

"You know what game."

Of course I do. I just don't want to say his name aloud. "Why would I?" I ask.

"To cheer against his Oreo ass. See him cry when they lose."

"Nah, I'm good," I say as we step into the hallway. Obviously, I'm not happy about Bunny switching schools, but I don't actively seek out ways to make his life miserable. I prefer to pretend he doesn't exist.

He shrugs. "Let me know if you change your mind. I'll holla later—looks like someone's waiting for you."

Sure enough, Keyona's in the hallway, her books pressed to her chest. Her athletic body is poised with perfect posture, looking real good. If this were one of those teen movies, there'd be a heavenly light shining behind her as her hair wafted gently in the breeze. Except this is real life. She's wearing her tight curls in an updo, and the lighting is those forever-flickering fluorescents in the ceiling. She's not even smiling. Just glaring at me with her intelligent, deep brown eyes, like I'm a collection of data points for her to analyze.

"Take care of my man." Wallace winks at her, doinks my head, and then peaces out down the hallway in the opposite direction of us, the opposite direction of his next class.

"Did you let him copy off you again?" she asks.

"Huh?"

"Be straight with me, Nas."

I shrug. "Trying to help my man."

"You're not doing him any favors," she says. We begin walking *together* toward our next class, which we haven't done in months. She and I used to hang out a lot with Bunny, but turns out he was the glue that held the three of us together.

"Not your problem," I say. And I realize I'm being kind of a dick, but I don't even know why she's sweating one small assignment like that.

She sighs, like I'm a lost cause.

We turn the corner, walk in silence past a couple making out against the lockers. Keyona rolls her eyes and mutters, "Have some self-respect." Then she turns to me. "You know *why* you're not actually being helpful, right?"

I hate it when she does this. Creates arguments by asking questions until I have to say it myself like I'm some big fool for not seeing the Truth in the first place. But whatever. I play along.

"Right," I say. "That whole give-a-man-a-fish rap."

She nods. "Does Wallace know chemistry any better after you giving him all the answers? Is he any smarter?"

"No," I mumble.

"That's what I thought. And you know what else he didn't learn?"

"No. What?"

"That he needs to work hard to accomplish something. I bet Wallace is going to drop out or barely graduate and become another lazy fool hanging out on the corner."

She's not wrong, but if this were anyone but Keyona, I'd walk away, because I hate it when people talk about Wallace that way. Instead, I hook my thumbs under my shoulder straps and mentally weigh the benefit of her talking to me against the subject of our conversation. I mean, she doesn't have any idea what's going on in Wallace's life. People always assume they know what others are going through, that they know what's best for them. But they almost never do.

"It's not so simple," I say.

"It is. My father grew up with nothing," she says. "He started his own business and made something out of himself. So, yeah, it kind of is."

I don't want to make her angrier, so I hold my tongue. She neglected to mention that her father did have a family to support him along the way. It's not like he crawled out of some shantytown alone wearing a soiled burlap sack. She also neglects to mention that his business—an auto body shop—isn't doing so hot. But lockers slam closed up and down the hall, so I know the late bell's probably about to ring. No point in continuing this argument.

"I mean, look at Bunny—" she starts to say, but I interrupt her.

"How'd y'all do last night?" I ask, referring to the girls' basketball team. She's a point guard like me. Unlike me, she's good and has a starting spot.

Keyona hesitates for a moment, probably deciding if she's going to let me change subjects like that. I know she knows that's what I'm doing. Finally, she says, "We won."

"Nice," I say. "The school should make some announcement about that."

"They did."

"Oh."

The bell blares. Keyona looks at me for a second like there's something else she wants to say about Wallace or Bunny or hard work, but she shakes her head and dips into class without waiting for me.

Yeah, I'm smooth like that.

7
BUNNY

School lets out at noon on Wednesdays at St. S so teachers can have meetings, so I'm out of practice by four. Drew gives me a ride to the train, and I take it all the way downtown and head to Word Up, the bookstore my dad owns with his friend Zaire.

The bell above the door jingles as I step inside, and the scent that hits me is the smell of my childhood: old books and incense. Eartha Kitt's singing quietly in French from the speakers mounted in the ceiling, but there's nobody in sight except for Zaire's black cat, Damba, lounging on top of one of the bookshelves. I don't even see my dad in his usual place behind the register.

"Hello?" I call as I drop my bags and step farther inside. "Dad?"

Damba meows at me from his place on high, but that's the only response I get.

"Nice to see you, too, Your Majesty," I say.

I've been so busy with school and basketball that I haven't stopped by in a minute. The place looks exactly the same as always, though. Shelves crammed with books as well as lots stacked in piles on the floor. There's a small stage near the front with a few café tables and old couches around it. The walls are covered in words in all different handwritings, favorite quotes written by the customers.

Coming up, Nasir and I used to spend some time here after school and on the weekends when the weather kept us off the courts, but Jess basically lived here.

Back then, it seemed like there were always people wandering these aisles. Older folks, college students, younger kids — you name it. There'd be some event or another nearly every night like an open mic, a book launch, or a community meeting. Word Up even put out their own neighborhood newsletter for a long time that you could pick up by the register for fifty cents.

But nowadays it's real quiet every time I come by here.

"Dad?" I call again as I pass the end of the African history section.

This time I hear some movement from the back. There's the muffled sound of the toilet flushing behind the bathroom door, and then Dad walks out, drying his hands on his pants. He smiles when he sees me, though I know he's probably disappointed I'm not a paying customer.

"Bunny!" he says, wrapping me in a hug.

"What's up, Dad?" I say.

We separate, and he pushes his glasses up on his nose and looks me up and down like he hasn't seen me in a few years. Which, between my late practices and his evening shifts, doesn't feel far from the truth. I try to remember if he's always had that many gray hairs in his dreadlocks, if the wrinkles at the corners of his eyes have always been this deep.

"You good?" he asks.

"Yeah, I'm good," I say.

"Cool, cool," he says, and then we kind of stand there not saying anything for a few moments. "Any particular reason you stopped by?"

I shrug. Take a seat. "Not really."

He sits across from me. "How's school?"

"School is school," I say. "How's business?"

He sighs. "It is what it is."

I feel like there's a lot more to say about these things, but neither of us knows how to say it. We sit there listening to Eartha Kitt, and it's like we're on opposite sides of a river with no idea how to cross.

"You coming to my game Friday?" I ask after some time.

Dad rubs his forehead. "I'm trying to get Zaire to switch up with me that day, but you know how that fool is about working nights."

"Yeah, I know," I say, all quiet. Zaire got robbed when he was working a closing shift in the first few months after they opened the store. After that, he demanded the day shift as his permanent responsibility. They couldn't afford to hire any other employees, so my dad agreed. It's all right during the summer since it means we get to spend all day with him, but during the school year, it's rough, since we barely ever see him unless we drop by the store. It also means he hardly makes it to any of my games. He always watches the video my mom or whoever records, but it's not the same.

He's not saying anything, and I don't know what else to say, so eventually I make up some excuse for needing to leave, and say goodbye.

8
NASIR

I t's Wednesday night. My mom's leaning back in her recliner reading. My dad's in the kitchen, drinking a beer while he cooks dinner, filling the house with the scent of sautéed onions as he plays some Tupac from his phone's speaker. I'm standing in front of the table in the dining room, which is between the kitchen and the living room. We've got a small enough place that it's basically like we're all in the same room.

I tell them I need to talk, then I explain Wallace and his grandma's situation. When I finish, my mom lowers her book and marks her page. My dad takes a sip from his beer and pulls this face like it's gone bad.

He says, "I thought she owned the place."

"Guess not," my mom says.

"You think there's anything we can do for them?" I ask.

My dad gives the frying pan a shake, and the onions sizzle in the hot oil. "We don't have that kind of extra money lying around right now, Nasir."

"But he's family," I say. "I thought we help family."

He sets the pan back down on the burner. "We do. When we can. But we've got a lot of family, and we can't help all of them. His grandma's survived this long—she'll figure something out. You know she marched in Selma with Dr. King?"

I'm not trying to hear about Selma right now. "Wallace said his grandma might move in with some other family, but he doesn't know where he'll go." I shift my weight. "What if he stays with us?"

My mom and dad exchange a look.

Then my mom says, "I wish we could, honey. But where would he sleep?"

I know this is an excuse. We have three bedrooms in our row house. Mine, theirs, and a smaller one my mom uses as a studio for her painting. I know she'd say no to him using the studio, since that's her space, but there's always the couch or the floor of my room. I offer these two as possibilities.

"Do you really think he'd be comfortable?" she asks.

"More comfortable than he'd be sleeping in his car," I say.

"Nasir, Wallace is . . ." My dad searches for the right word as he picks up the cutting board and uses his knife to scrape sliced pieces of raw chicken into the frying pan. The oil sizzles and starts popping again. "He's independent. I'm sure he doesn't want to be under someone else's roof, following their rules."

I don't say anything, because I know he's right. Wallace told me as much himself. Still, I know it's not as simple as Wallace finding a job and getting a place, so I hate feeling like there's nothing I can do but watch his life fall apart. I feel like I'm in one of those movies where I can see the future coming from miles away but I can't do a damn thing about it.

"I'm glad you want to help," my mom says. "You have a good heart. Your dad and I will take a look at our budget. Maybe we can find enough to help them put a deposit on a place."

But I know from experience her *maybe* is basically a *no,* and my heart feels a long way from good. Anger courses through me. Anger at Wallace's landlord. Anger at his shitty parents. Anger at my own parents, my own small house. Anger at Bunny, St. Sebastian's, and the unfairness of this world that tells us to help each other but thrives on us not helping each other.

"Whatever," I say, and turn away. I start setting the table, slamming the plates and silverware down hard enough to express my frustration but not hard enough to get yelled at.

"I'm all for helping others," my dad says a couple minutes later, adding some spices to the chicken, "but people also have to help themselves to a certain extent. Wallace's grandma isn't in any state to be holding down a job, but Wallace sure is. So why isn't he working?"

"He goes to school," I say.

"And what's to stop him from getting something part-time? He's over eighteen. He should be contributing instead of living off her Social Security checks. The woman took him in and raised him like her own. Least he could do is help out with rent. When I was his age, I'd catch the bus after my last class and put in five or six hours bagging groceries a few nights a week."

"I don't have a job," I point out.

"Your job is to be a student. Me and your mom work hard to make sure that's all you have to worry about right now, and you're doing good at it."

"It's not fair for Wallace."

"No, it's not. But that's the hand he was dealt." He takes a sip from his beer and shakes the pan.

"So then shouldn't we do more for people in situations like that?"

My dad takes a deep breath. "Sometimes you think you're helping someone when you're doing the exact opposite. Sometimes the best thing to do is let them figure it out on their own. Now, dinner will be ready in a few minutes. Go wash up."

"So Wallace can't stay with us?" I ask, just to make him say it aloud.

"No," he says.

My mom stares at me like she wants to say something, but she doesn't. I turn and head upstairs, taking the steps two at a time. Instead of washing my hands, I sit on the floor in my room with the lights off like a little kid.

9
BUNNY

After practice on Thursday, Coach Baum makes us stay for film. We're in the classroom off the gym, the one where he teaches his health class. The lights are off, and the St. Mary's vs. Bishop Jackson game from last night is projected onto the whiteboard, the sound muted. Bishop won, 47–46 in OT, so we've got them tomorrow.

During the season, we beat them 68–36. They've got a decent squad of shooters but no height. Eric is taller than most of their guys, and he's our point guard. Based on what we're seeing in the film, their players didn't magically grow a foot taller, so me and Drew shouldn't have any problems in the paint.

Coach stands up there narrating and analyzing both teams' plays. Every now and then, he pauses it, steps in front of the projector so the images are over top of him, and draws X's and O's and lines on the board to illustrate some point. To my left, Drew's passed out, but with his face propped in his hand, so it's not as obvious. To my right, Eric's eyes are on his phone, which he's holding under the desk.

I'm sitting up straight and paying attention. Just because

you crushed a team once doesn't mean they're going to roll over the next time you see them. Never underestimate anybody. They come back hungrier each time, since they've got nothing to lose.

Coach gradually notices the team's attention drifting, so he stops talking. "Hey!" he shouts, and slaps the board, making everyone jump. But it works. Everyone sits up and puts their eyes on Coach. "Why is Bunny the only one paying attention?"

Now everyone's eyes shift to me. I look down at my hands and sink low in my seat.

"Eric," Coach says.

"Yes, sir?"

"Answer my question."

"What question?"

Coach takes a deep breath. "Why. Is. Bunny. The only one. Paying attention."

"Oh," Eric says, glancing at me one more time. "I don't know. Maybe he got more sleep than the rest of us last night?"

Coach glares at the team with a look of disgust on his face, daring someone to laugh. I can sense a few of the guys holding it in. After a few seconds that feel like forever, he shakes his head and says, "Incorrect. Bunny is the only one paying attention because he wants to win. So maybe you should pay attention and learn from him so we can put another banner up on that wall."

With that, Coach continues with dissecting the game tape. Everyone seems to be paying attention now, but I feel like all their eyes are on me still. My mind's floating away as I imagine what they must be thinking. Every time Coach calls me out like that—and he does it a lot—it makes me feel more out of place here, more different than I already do.

And since I'm only a sophomore, I'm in the calm before the storm. Not being arrogant, but recruiters already have their eyes on me—lots of people made that clear at every AAU game I played last summer. As soon as they can, schools will be talking to me left and right. I know that'll make some of the guys resent me even more.

10

NASIR

It's a strange sight: Wallace in the library. *After* school. On a Friday.

As for me, I'd rather be at Word Up, but that's not really an option these days.

I mark my page. "You lost?"

Wallace gazes around like he might be and then takes the seat across the table from me smelling for all the world like he just smoked up. Great, he and his grandma are about to get evicted, and this is how he deals with it.

The only other students in here are a group of nerdy kids sitting at a table in the far corner playing some game that involves rolling a lot of weird-shaped dice over and over again.

"That's some big-ass book you're reading, cuz," Wallace says. He pushes the book up so he can read the cover. *"Landlord–Tenant Laws."* He raises an eyebrow.

"I know you said you didn't even want to stay in that apartment, but here." I turn the book so he can see, and point to the second paragraph. "Read this. The book's a few years old, but most of these probably still apply."

He pushes it away. "Man, I'm not trying to read outside of class."

I spin it back around and start reading the passage aloud. I stop a couple sentences in because Wallace is doing that thing where he lets his eyelids droop and head bob forward like he's falling asleep.

"Wallace."

He fake jolts awake. "Did I nod off? Sorry about that, man. I'm real tired, and that was boring as fuck."

The librarian shushes us as if there were anyone in here actually studying.

Sorry, I mouth to her, and then start to pack up my stuff. To Wallace I say, "I'm only trying to help."

He leans way back in his chair, balancing himself by propping his foot against one of the table legs. "I told you, I'm cool, cuz. You don't have to worry about me, all right?"

"Do you have any money saved up?"

He chuckles.

"Maybe you should look for a job," I say.

"Nah, I was planning on dropping by Bunny's game. You down? It's an early one."

I zip up my bag. "Not even a little. Why do you want to go?"

"I got some action on Bishop, so I wouldn't mind seeing how it turns out."

"You bet *against* Bunny?"

He nods.

"With who?"

He lets his chair drop back to the floor with a loud thud. "Some white kids from St. S."

"How do you know anyone over at St. S?" I ask.

"Man, you know I know everyone all over everywhere."

"How much?" I ask.

"A hundred," Wallace answers.

"You bet a hundred dollars *against* Bunny? I'm no fan of his right now, but that's a dumb-ass bet." I stand up, return the book to its shelf, and then head for the exit. I stop at the door. "Where'd you get that much money from?"

He shrugs.

"You don't have it, do you?"

He grins, pushes the crossbar on the door a little too hard, and I follow him out into the quiet hallway, which is littered with those black plastic bags from the corner store, crumpled-up worksheets, and candy wrappers.

"What happens when St. S wins?" I ask. "Because you know they're going to. You're going to lose that bet and won't have the money to pay up."

"What are their preppy asses going to do about it? Come to the city and shake me down?" He laughs. "But they gave me real nice odds, so if St. S loses and I win that bet, I'm going to have to carry my money in some of those sacks with the dollar signs on them."

Wallace is always trying to get me to wager on things like if he can throw a piece of trash into the garbage can from the other side of the room. I'll take him up on some of those small bets, but I've never been into it beyond that. He may not try in school, but he has a good handle on numbers. After a Sixers game or something, he won't read the article about it, but he'll study the stats for a while. Then he's got some connections with people who give him odds and take his bets when he has the cash to make any.

"Anyway, you can check the score online. Why would you need me to go to the game with you?"

"So I can collect my winnings. And if St. Sebastian's loses, I can take some video of your boy crying. Put that shit up on WorldStar."

"He's not my boy."

"Fine. If you don't want to hit up the game with me, then want to see this movie after?"

"What movie?"

"I forget what it's called. That scary one."

"No way."

"Why not?" he asks. "You afraid?"

"Nah, it's a waste of money. Those horror movies are always terrible."

"So?" he says. "What else you have going on tonight?"

"I've got plans."

"What? Are you going to make a bubble bath and light some candles, read that boring-ass book aloud to your balls?"

I shake my head. "All out of candles."

Wallace starts rapping some lines from some track I don't recognize and acting like he's running a football. Every now and then, he pretends I'm the defense and pulls a spin move around me. I keep on walking.

We eventually make our way outside, where it's cold as hell. I zip up my coat, slip on my gloves and hat, and turtle my head as much as possible. Wallace does none of this, like he doesn't feel the cold at all, but he does stop acting like he's running for the end zone as we walk down the stone steps away from Whitman.

"Real rap, man," he says, his voice more serious than before, "this ain't right."

"True," I say. "It's almost March. Shouldn't be below freezing anymore."

"Nah, not that." He spits. "I'm talking about Bunny transferring and shit. He should be here. The odds should be in our favor. Not theirs."

We reach the bottom of the steps and turn right along Park Street. "Yeah, I feel you. But it is what it is. There's nothing to do about it."

He thinks for a moment. "You think so, huh?"

I laugh, but Wallace doesn't. Instead, he digs his hands into his pockets, lowers his head, and gets real quiet like he does on those days after he comes back from visiting his dad at County. I feel like I should say something, continue the conversation a bit so can he can work through what's eating him and return to his clowning self. But I don't want to talk about Bunny, and I don't know how to tell him my parents aren't willing to let him stay with us. So I let the silence build until it's like a third person walking between us.

We don't say a word the rest of the way to Nisha, who's parked pretty far down the street. She's an old beat-up Buick Electra, the kind of ride you'd expect someone with a wide collar and bell-bottoms to be driving. He slides in behind the wheel, but when I go to pull the door handle, it's locked. I knock on the glass with my gloved hand, and from within, Wallace mouths, *What?*

"It's locked," I say.

What? he mouths again. Then he cups his ear, shaking his head and gesturing like he can't hear me.

I wait for the joke to end. A few cars pass. A muscular dude puffing on a cigarette as he walks a Chihuahua on the opposite side of the street glances at me. A flock of birds flies across the sky, making me think about how they should've stayed in the south a little bit longer.

Finally, Wallace leans over and rolls down the passenger-side window—and like I said, it's an old car, so he actually has to turn some crank. "Oh, you want a ride home?" he asks.

I try the door again, but it's still locked. I reach through the open window to unlock it myself, but he slaps my hand away and holds out his palm. "Two dollars."

"Ha. Ha."

But he doesn't put his hand down.

He's running this joke a little past funny, but I play along if only to see him slide back to his regular self. I dig a couple of singles out of my wallet and slap them into his palm. He grins, unlocks the door, and pushes it open. I throw some broken Chewbacca action figure he has on the front seat for some reason into the back along with my bookbag and take a seat on the ice-cold, cracked upholstery. I wait for him to laugh and hand the money back, but he starts the engine, turns up the radio, and pulls away from the curb.

"I'll go see that movie with you tonight if you promise to start looking for a job this weekend," I say after we've driven a couple of blocks.

"Deal," he says.

I don't call him out on the two bucks, because I'm thinking about how he might be living in Nisha come next month.

11
BUNNY

A s everyone expected, we crush Bishop Jackson. 60–41, to be exact. We were ahead by thirty going into the fourth, so Coach Baum sat me for most of it to rest up for the sectional semifinals on Sunday.

After the game, Drew tries to convince me to go with him and the rest of the team to some senior's house party, but that's not my scene, and I don't really hang with anyone from St. S like that. Instead, me and Keyona head to the movies.

It's Friday night, so the place is packed with kids from the city and the suburbs. We all stay separate, divided by the color of our skin like the civil rights movement never happened. I wonder if I'm the only person who thinks that's messed up. Never used to. But when you're suddenly one of six Black kids in a school of about a thousand, you start to feel some type of way about these things.

But what can you do?

I recount the money Jess gave me to take Keyona out and do the math. After the tickets, I'm pretty sure I've got enough to buy her some popcorn and a soda, but I'm still kind of nervous. Sometimes things cost more than you think.

I shuffle forward with the line and then glance toward the restrooms. Keyona's standing in a line that goes out the door. She notices me looking and flashes her smile, showing that small gap between her two front teeth that I love. I start thinking about this and everything else about her, and I start cheesing. I'm not even the type of dude who smiles like that for no reason.

But a moment later, her line moves forward. She winks and then disappears through the door. My smile fades.

"Sir, can I help you?" the kid behind the register asks.

"Huh?" I say, noticing that I'm at the front of my own line. "Oh, sorry."

I tell him what I want and eye the total, sweating that I'll have to tell him I changed my mind about something. But I have enough to cover it.

While I'm waiting for the food, some tall white kid comes over. "Hey, you're Bunny Thompson, right?"

I nod, keeping my eyes on the menu board.

"Awesome," he says. "Man, I wish I had my copy of *ESPN* magazine for you to sign."

I scratch the back of my head, not knowing what to say. He's talking about the issue that came out last April, which ranked the top fifty high school basketball players in the country. For some reason, they put me at forty-eight. Not that impressive of a spot, but since I was only a freshman at the time, people started paying real close attention to me after that.

He starts patting down his pockets. A moment later he

pulls out a pen and his ticket stub, and holds them out to me. "Mind signing this?"

I feel other people start to turn and look, probably wondering if I'm someone legit famous. My face warms up. I shift my weight to the other foot. "Sure," I say. I know it's dumb, but if I said no, I'd look like a jerk. I quickly scribble my fifth-grader-looking signature and make a mental note to practice it later so it looks more professional.

"Thanks," he says. "Good luck in the playoffs."

It's kind of cool being recognized like this, even though it's also kind of weird. I mean, I had a good freshman season, but it's not like I've won any championships yet or anything. I guess people love trying to find the next Kobe or LeBron or Jordan so they can say that they knew me when. It's a lot to live up to, though. Impossible, even. People are real quick to turn on you soon as you don't drop over thirty in a game. So I keep working hard and try to ignore all that noise.

The dude behind the counter hands me my food, but Keyona's not back yet. I wander over to the video games and check out the prizes in the claw machine game. There's a stuffed panda bear I think she'd like, because she has a thing for panda bears, so I place the drink and popcorn on top of the machine, slip in my second-to-last dollar, and grab the joystick. I position the claw, and with three seconds left, I punch the button. It drops, closes around the panda bear. And even though everything's lined up perfect, the claw slips over the panda and comes up empty. It moves back over the prize hole and drops nothing. The machine makes that sad, digital *whomp whomp* kind of sound, and I can't help but feel the game is rigged.

I'm standing there trying to decide if I want to sink my last dollar into this dumb machine when I hear a voice behind me that I recognize. Deep. Mumbly. Loud enough to rise over the sound of dozens of other people chatting.

"Yo, pay the man, Nas," the voice says.

Without turning around, I use the mirror set in the back of the claw machine to check it out. Sure enough, there's Wallace at one of the registers. And next to him, Nasir.

I continue watching in the mirror as the dude behind the register passes Wallace a bag of popcorn. He stuffs a handful into his mouth right away and then starts to walk away. I pray he doesn't catch sight of me, because he's one of the people who have given me the most shit about transferring. Plus, I don't want Nasir to see me with Keyona. When the three of us used to hang, before Keyona and I were a thing, it was painfully obvious that Nasir liked her and even more painfully obvious that she didn't feel him like that.

I drop my eyes to the collection of stuffed animals crammed inside the machine, but I don't go anywhere. Just put my hand over the joystick and listen.

"It's your popcorn," I hear Nasir say. "You pay." He's not nearly as loud as Wallace, so I kind of have to strain to make out his words.

"I'm good for it, cuz. You know me."

"Yeah, I do know you—that's the problem. You forget you don't have that job yet?"

"Being your friend is my job. And bringing you to the movies is overtime. Shit. You should be paying me time and a half."

There's a few beats of silence. Probably Nas paying.

"Yooooo," Wallace says. I tense up because his voice is louder, closer. Did he spot me? "Check them out," I hear him say.

"They look like middle-schoolers, Wallace."

"Yo, can I get your number?" I hear Wallace call and then laugh. Except his voice sounds farther away now. The girls must be walking away.

I stay in front of the machine for a few more minutes, thinking on things. Eventually, Keyona returns and wraps her arms around me from behind, which is always kind of funny, because I've got, like, a foot and a half on her. "You okay?" she says, peeking out from under my arm. "You look like you're trying to free these little animals with your mind."

I knock on the glass and point at the panda bear. "I wanted to win that for you."

"Machine's probably rigged." She gives it a small kick and then takes my hand and pulls me toward the theater. "Come on. I don't want to miss the previews," she says, as if she's been the one waiting for me. But I'm feeling her so much that I don't point that out. I snag the popcorn and soda and let her lead me away, glancing over my shoulder one last time to where Nas used to be.

12

NASIR

The lights fade out. In the beat of silence before the previews begin, Wallace calls out, "'Bout fucking time," through a mouthful of popcorn. A few people laugh. More shush him. His face lit by the glow of the screen, he grins at me across the open seat between us. The "buffer zone," as he calls it.

About halfway through the third or fourth preview, just as I'm on the verge of forgetting what movie we're even seeing, the horror movie starts early: Bunny and Keyona walk in— holding hands. I pull my hood up and sink down in my chair. They cross in front of the screen and then walk to a row, like, five or six down from us. They scoot past everyone until they reach a pair of seats directly in my line of sight. They sit down without noticing Wallace and me, and then Keyona leans her head against Bunny's shoulder and he wraps his long arm around her.

Wallace doesn't notice. His eyes are glued to his phone now, feet up on the seat back in front of him. The guy in the seat turns like he's going to say something, but then takes in the sight of Wallace and gets intimidated, I guess, because he swivels back around, pretending like he was stretching. Wallace picks up the soda I forced him to pay for himself and slurps until there's the sound of air sucking through the straw.

I think about telling Wallace I'm not feeling well and we should leave, but I know this is a nice distraction for him. He tries to act like the lost bet and that eviction stuff don't bother him, but they have to.

Anyway, the movie begins. My eyes keep flicking down to where Bunny and Keyona are sitting, though, so it's hard for me to focus on the story. But from what I see, it's a typical teen slasher. The counselors are hanging out around a bonfire on the beach after lights out. They're drinking and having a good time at this place that's evidently named Camp Murder Lake. Not sure why any parent would send their kid to a place like that, but whatever. Two of them sneak away from the group and decide to go skinny-dipping farther down the beach. My gaze drifts to Bunny and Keyona. I wonder if they ever go skinny-dipping.

I force my eyes back to the screen. The couple is now lying on the shore together. A ragged-looking guy, face hidden in shadows, skulks toward them. Startled, the couple try to cover their naked bodies. The boy yells at the stranger to go away, but the stranger creeps closer. I glance down a few rows to see Keyona bury her head in Bunny's chest. Back to the screen. The boy stands and yells at the stranger to leave. Suddenly, there's a flash of metal, and a red ribbon appears across the boy's throat. A look of realization crosses his face as blood pours from the opening in his neck. His body collapses. The girl screams. The movie cuts to the opening credits as Bunny pulls Keyona even closer.

An hour and a half later, the lights come up, phones come out, and chatter fills the air. People rise and start leaving, probably having already forgotten the movie. I'm trying to slip out of here fast as I can, but as I pass Wallace's seat, I notice that he's left his empty popcorn and soda in the cup holders and some candy wrappers on the floor. I want to ignore it all, but my parents taught me too well.

"Wallace, come on, man," I say.

But he keeps walking. I sigh and cast a quick glance at Bunny and Keyona, who are still in their seats watching the credits roll. Seems I have time, so I gather the trash. Only, once I step into the exit aisle, I get stuck behind this large family moving real slow. I try to pass them on the left and then on the right, but they're blocking the way like a defensive line in the NFL.

The music cuts off. I sneak a glance over my shoulder and see Bunny and Keyona getting out of their seats. I turn back around, and I'm about to slide past this wall of a family when one of them drops something, and they all stop to wait for him to pick it up, trapping me.

"Nasir?" I hear Keyona say from right behind me, voice laced with surprise and something else — guilt, maybe.

I take a deep breath, mentally make the sign of the cross, and turn around. "Keyona? What's up! Wild seeing you here."

I look up at Bunny standing next to her. Maybe it's a trick of the light, but he seems taller and more muscular than he did a few months ago. I force a smile. "And, oh, hey, Bunny. What's good, man?"

"Hey, Nas!" Bunny says. His smile looks real as he gives me dap that turns out mighty awkward since he goes in with the open hand and I go in with the closed fist.

I go along with it, trying to play it cool. No big deal that this is the first time we've spoken in months or that he's with the girl he knew I had feelings for, right? Right.

Inside, my heart withers and curls in on itself like one of those dying plants in a time-lapse.

"So you here with someone?" Keyona asks, peering around.

"Yeah," I lie. "Some girl I've been talking to. She's in the bathroom, though."

"Good for you," Keyona says, like she's genuinely happy for me.

Having lost the thin thread of conversation, we turn and continue toward the exit, Keyona walking between Bunny and me.

Bunny clears his throat. "Look, we were going to grab some food. Y'all want to join us?"

"Sorry, B. Got to get her home. Her old man's the real protective type, you know," I say, wanting to plow through the wall of slow-moving moviegoers and burst through the main doors so I can take a deep breath or scream or kick over a trash can or punch something.

"Yeah, I feel you," he says.

Again, nobody knows what to say next. We continue inching our way forward.

"I didn't get to say it the other night, since you left pretty fast," Bunny says, "but good game."

"Was it?"

"Yeah, man. You did good. For real, for real. Your outside shot's really coming along."

I look down at the floor, hating how good that makes me feel. I kick an empty cup out of my way. I feel like I should return the compliment, but instead I say, "True. One for six *is* a pretty damn good shooting percentage. Someone call the NBA."

"Good enough for the Sixers," Bunny says.

A laugh almost slips through my lips, but I shut it down.

When we finally come out of the theater, we find Wallace leaning against the wall. "There you are, Nas. Shit, thought you abandoned my ass." A smirk creeps across his lips as he notices Keyona and Bunny walking next to me. "And look who we got here: the Savior of St. Sebastian's!"

My face burns, and I keep my eyes on my feet now that my lie is exposed like a cockroach crushed on the kitchen floor. Bunny and Keyona don't call me out on it or even cast a sideways glance, though. They greet Wallace like they're all long-lost friends. Wallace is acting all extra, as if he's the friendliest guy in the world.

"Look at you two," he says. I can kind of forgive him for putting it out there like that. I mean, I've never told Wallace how I feel about Keyona, and he's not exactly the perceptive type. But I'm still trying to wrap my mind around how Bunny could go on and do this.

"Yup" is all Keyona says.

I imagine she looks into Bunny's eyes as she says this, but I don't know, since I'm still gazing hard at the worn red carpet under our feet.

"That's nice, that's real nice," Wallace says, grinning. "Isn't that real nice and romantical, Nasir?"

"Super romantical," I say.

And so it is in a sphere of awkwardness that we walk out.

It's late, so most of the showings for the evening have ended, and the parking lot is almost empty. People drift to their cars in quiet clumps. An old man sits on a bench, either waiting for a ride or lost.

Before we step off the curb, Bunny stops to zip up his coat. "It was good seeing y'all again."

"For real," says Wallace.

"Get at me later, Nas, all right?" Bunny says. "We should catch up."

"Yeah, for sure," I lie.

Wallace flashes the peace sign.

"See you guys at school," Keyona says over her shoulder as she and Bunny walk away. After a few feet, Bunny leans into her and says something I can't hear. She hooks her arm through his, and they laugh together.

Wallace and I linger on the curb, because he doesn't re-member where he parked and my head's still reeling too much to recall either. Instead, he fishes a blunt from his pocket and lights up right there in front of the theater. After taking a hit, he heads into the parking lot in what I think is the exact opposite direction from where he parked.

"Yo, you want to hit up this party I heard about?" he asks.

I shake my head. "We should go home. You've got some job-hunting to do in the morning."

Wallace steps off the curb and over his shoulder says, "Man, any place that's open in the morning ain't no place I want to work."

13
BUNNY

After Saturday morning practice, I come home to a cold but quiet house. No TV blaring. No little sisters shouting. Not even any music blasting on the block.

I drop my bag by the door and go to the kitchen counter, where I find a note from my mom saying that she and my dad took Justine and Ashley to the aquarium. There's no sign of Jess anywhere, so I'm guessing she's studying at the library or at Word Up, somewhere with working heat.

I notice a couple new college brochures in the pile of mail next to my mom's note on the counter. One's for a small school in New Hampshire. Division III, probably. There's a photo of a smiling Black dude on the front, but you know he's probably the only brother at the school. I look at it real close to see if they Photoshopped him into the shot, but I can't tell. The other brochure is for Temple University, which is where my dad went for his business degree. There are a lot better teams out there than Temple, but it would be cool to go to the same school that he did. I throw the Temple brochure into the stack with the others and stick the one for the New Hampshire school in the trash, pushing it down so it's not all obvious on top. I flip through the rest of the mail idly and come across a couple of unpaid bills. I set them down and run my hand over the top of my head, a sinking feeling settling into my stomach.

My parents tell me all the time to let them worry about the bills, but I know closing my eyes isn't going to fix our problems.

Money isn't everything, but only people who've never lacked think it's nothing. If I could play in the League for just a few years, I'd earn enough to wipe away a lot of our family's worries.

And that's why, even though I have the house to myself — which happens, like, once a year — I don't take a nap or play video games or text Keyona to come over. I eat a granola bar, head back outside, and start jogging.

I hop over uneven slabs of the sidewalk, sidestep broken glass, and duck under low-hanging branches. I fly past Ms. Tran, who's out doing some yard work to prep her garden for the spring, and past a child's birthday party a few houses down. I dodge the Colemans' busted gate that's always swinging open and pick up the pace when I pass a yard where two snarling Chihuahuas follow me until the end of their fence.

Falling into a rhythm, I try to think about tomorrow's playoff game against St. Cyprian, to review Coach's strategy in my mind. But my brain won't let me. My thoughts keep flipping to last night, to seeing Nasir while I was out with Keyona.

I don't want to think about Nasir or Keyona. I need more pain.

I lower my head and run faster. The cold air stings my face in a way that feels good. I jog off the curb and run in the middle of the street where there's more space. I take a corner faster than I should, not even checking for oncoming cars, since the streets are pretty empty. It's like the whole neighborhood partied too hard last night and slept in.

After a few more blocks, I reach the bottom of the hill. I sprint to gain some momentum and then pump my legs hard as I can. The hill's about two blocks long, a real steep incline the entire way. Halfway up, my lungs and legs start burning. It's a familiar feeling that makes me remember how when we were kids, this seemed like a mountain. In the summer, Nas and I raced up it by foot or on bike.

I usually won, but that never mattered. It was always about making it to the top together. And now here I am without him. Ignoring the ache blossoming in my calves, I make it all the way up. I do ten burpees, and then I turn around and jog in place for a few seconds while I catch my breath.

Then I think on how this place's packed with neighborhood kids whenever it snows. Someone blocks off the street at the top and the bottom with some lawn chairs so people can sled without getting run over. Nas and I used to get in on that right up until a couple years ago when we graduated middle school.

Shaking off the memory, I start down the hill. My legs

going like crazy, the soles of my shoes slapping against the concrete almost too fast for me to keep up with. My breath comes out in jagged puffs. I feel like I'm flying. Or falling.

I slow down when I reach the bottom. I put my hands over my head and try to catch my breath. My skin stings from the cold air hitting the heat coming off my body. I do another ten burpees, put my head down, and climb again.

As I push upward, my brain goes back to last night. This time I let it, welcoming it as much as I'm welcoming the pain in my legs. Like Coach Baum says, that's weakness leaving the body.

So I face the truth: I did my man wrong.

There's no way around it.

I guess I could keep telling myself that I thought Nasir was over Keyona. That if he really did have a thing for her, then he would've made a move by now. We hadn't talked in months, after all, so how was I supposed to know he still felt the same way?

But I need to be honest with myself. Like Mom always says, the worst lie is the one we tell ourselves.

I knew it was wrong the moment me and Keyona first hooked up. I felt it deep in my bones, the same way I can feel the momentum's about to shift from one team to another on the court. Seeing the hurt in his eyes last night only reminded me of that.

I mean, he's been hung up on her since the day she beat me one-on-one during recess back when we were in grade school. I still remember in the seventh grade when she started talking to Kyle Brown, Nas came to my house crying in a way guys never let other guys see. Like he was a little boy. Like he was broken. Sure, he seemed to get over it, but I always knew he hadn't. Nobody ever really gets over falling hard like that for the first time, I think.

So, yeah, I knew.

And still.

When I reach the top of the hill, I wish it kept going, that I could run uphill to the sky and then disappear in the clouds. But it doesn't and I can't, so I do another ten burpees, turn, and race back down. I run the hill a few more times, until my leg muscles are screaming, until I feel stronger, until I've made up my mind.

If I want to be cool with Nas again, I need to break up with Keyona.

14

NASIR

After I spent all day Saturday helping Wallace fill out applications at places like McDonald's and Walmart, he comes over Sunday morning for day two of his job search. He uses our shower since his hot water isn't working, we down the Filipino breakfast my mom cooks for us—rice and eggs with a sweet fried sausage called *longanisa*—and then my dad tries unsuccessfully to convince Wallace to wear one of his old suits.

Our first stop is over at Justin's, where Wallace claims he's got a lead. Justin's is this corner store bodega a few blocks down from my place. It's owned by this Vietnamese dude not that much older than us whose dad handed the place to him a couple years ago when he got tired of America and decided to move back to Vietnam.

We push through the door, past the handwritten sign at eye level that says in big, bold letters NO HOODIES. The bell overhead jingles as we step inside the claustrophobic store. The place is empty except for us and Justin, who's in his usual spot behind a thick pane of bulletproof glass. His arms are folded over his chest as he watches the Weather Channel on the small TV behind the counter, surrounded by cigarettes, condoms, and batteries. I guess he'd be all set for the zombie apocalypse.

He greets us without taking his eyes off the screen. "No hoodies, *amigos*."

"My bad." I lower mine and smooth my hand over my hair.

Wallace leaves his hood up and saunters to the counter. He knocks on the glass, even though Justin's already acknowledged our presence. "Yo, Teddy here?"

Justin nods his head toward the rear of the store.

"I'll be back," Wallace says to me over his shoulder as he walks away, leaving me to wonder who the hell Teddy is.

"No hoodies, Wallace!" Justin calls after him.

"Yeah, okay," Wallace calls back, and then disappears down the narrow aisle, past shelves stocked with all the chips and candy and Cup Noodles. He turns out of sight, and a moment later, there's the sound of a door opening and then slamming at the back of the store.

I try not to think about how sketchy that is.

"Sorry about my cousin," I say to Justin, because I'm pretty much always sorry about my cousin. I should go ahead and get that tattooed on my forehead. Or maybe printed on a T-shirt.

Justin shrugs and continues watching the weather report.

I scan the candy bar rack that's in front of the counter, and my eyes land on the Necco Wafers. I can't believe the dude still stocks them. They're basically the worst candy in the world, and Bunny was the only person I knew who ever ate them willingly. Always had a roll of those chalky-ass medicinal tablets in his pocket growing up. I remember when we were, like, six or seven, I asked why he liked them, and he said that since nobody else did, he never had to share.

I wonder if he still likes them, and I realize that's one more thing I don't know about Bunny Thompson. Didn't know he was going to transfer to St. S, and definitely didn't know he was with Keyona until that awkward as hell run-in at the movies.

I pick up a Snickers bar and place it on the counter. As I pull out some cash, I raise my eyes to the TV, which is showing the weather radar.

"Spring coming?" I ask.

"I wish, man." Justin rings me up. "They're talking about a 'polar vortex' on the way."

"Yay," I say, and slide a couple of dollars through the tray that dips under the bulletproof glass.

Justin passes me my change. "Where's your friend been? Haven't seen him around in a while."

"Huh?" I look toward the back of the store, wondering why Justin would ask after Wallace when he saw him walk by a couple minutes ago. Then I realize he's talking about Bunny. "Oh," I say. "Busy." *With Keyona,* my idiot brain adds inside my head.

Justin nods like he understands what I mean and then goes back to watching the TV. I slip the Snickers into my back pocket and wander into the next aisle looking for that rear door I heard Wallace walk through. There's only three aisles in the place, so it doesn't take me long to find the door. It's gray and heavy-looking, every inch covered with stickers advertising various cigarette and liquor brands.

I imagine the seedy dealings going on back there. Dice games? Dogfights? Russian roulette? Whatever it is, I'm sure it's full of sweaty men with fistfuls of cash, half lit by a single bulb dangling from the ceiling.

As I'm trying to decide whether I want to see for myself, the door bursts open and Wallace emerges, stuffing something inside his jacket pocket.

"We out," he says.

He walks toward the exit, and the aisle is so narrow I have to squish up against the shelves so he can pass. I start to follow him out, but he stops and doubles back, making me squish up against the shelves one more time. He goes over to the refrigerator cases and pulls out a carton of eggs.

"You baking a cake?" I ask.

"Huh?" he says.

He misses the joke. Maybe he doesn't know that a cake requires eggs. "What's with the eggs?"

He grins, placing them on the counter. "Easter's coming early this year."

"What's that supposed to mean?"

"You'll see, cuz."

"Four dollars," Justin says.

Wallace reaches into a pocket inside his jacket and pulls out a crisp twenty. He slides it under the glass to Justin.

"Where'd you get that?" I ask.

Wallace shrugs, takes his change, and leaves. I follow.

As soon as we step outside, I turn to the sky. A few thin clouds moving fast across the blue up there beyond the tangle of wires and bare branches.

"So what was that all about?" I ask as we walk back toward my house, where Wallace's car is parked. There's a few people out on the streets, mostly families in their Sunday best headed to church.

"Made a little deal," he says, cradling the egg carton under his left arm.

"With who?"

He spits. "Some dudes who like to make little deals."

"What kind of deal?" I ask.

Wallace lets out an exasperated sigh. "Man, who are you? The police?"

I put my hands up in mock surrender. "Sorry. Just wondering." Maybe it's for the best I don't know exactly what Wallace is doing. I decide to let it go but stay somewhat on topic. "So where do you want to go today? The mall? There must be at least a few stores hiring there. Get that employee discount action."

"Nah, man, I don't need to put in any more applications." He pats the chest of his jacket where that inside pocket is. "I'm cool. For a couple weeks, at least."

"And then what?" I push.

"Then I'll figure out something else."

I almost leave it at that so I don't make him mad. But then I think about what Keyona said after class a few days ago, about how I think I'm helping Wallace when I'm not. I take a deep breath and ask the question I think she would want me to ask him right now. "You slinging?"

"Slinging?" He laughs for a few moments and then gets serious. "Nah, man." He spits. "You think I want to end up in jail, sharing a cell with my old man?"

"Sorry," I say. "You were talking about making a deal . . . I just . . . I just want to help you. The right way."

He stops and looks me in the eye. "You serious about that, cuz?"

"Of course, Wallace."

"Cool, cool. Then here." He flips open the top of the egg carton and holds them out to me.

"Huh?"

He gestures with his chin toward the eggs and then toward a house a little way down the street. It clicks—he wants me to egg someone's house. I look over and realize he wants me to egg not just anyone's place, but Bunny's. I was so lost in trying to figure out what was going on with Wallace that I didn't even notice we were back on my block.

And I can't believe he wants me to do this.

"I can't believe you want me to do this," I say, head swiveling up and down the street for witnesses. There isn't anyone out, but we're standing in broad daylight. Who knows who's peeping out their windows? Not to mention my parents are right inside my house.

"I told you we've got to make things right," he says.

"By egging Bunny's house? How's that going to help you out?"

He chuckles and grabs one of the eggs. He cradles it in the palm of his right hand while still holding the rest of the carton in his left. Its white shell practically glows like something holy. "I was awake in English class for a couple minutes the other day," he says, feeling the weight of the egg, "and Mr. Okoye started talking about something called catharsis. You know what that means?"

I nod.

He cocks his arm back and chucks the egg. It hits the brick of the Thompsons' row home with a small but oddly satisfying *splat*. "Catharsis," he declares.

Bunny's parents are both probably working, but a rush of guilt floods through me as I imagine them coming home from a long day to find a splatter of yolk cemented onto the side of their house like dried puke.

I pull my hood over my face and say, "Glad you got that out of your system, man. Can we go now?"

But he's already launching a second egg. This time it smashes against the front door, the sound more *thud* than *splat*. The urge to duck inside my house courses through me. I'm waiting for one of the neighbors or even Bunny himself to pop his head out the window to see me out here standing next to big-ass Wallace and his carton of eggs. My parents will straight up kill me.

All right, maybe Wallace isn't such a great influence on me.

He holds out an egg. "You got some feelings about Bunny I think you need to deal with, cuz."

"Nah, I'm cool," I say, even though deep down I know he's right about something for once.

"Get this shit out of your system, or I'll empty the rest of this carton on his house myself."

"Ha. Ha."

I turn to go, but his free hand grips my wrist like a vise. I try to pull away, but I think I've mentioned he's a second-year-senior center and I'm a second-string sophomore point guard.

"Damn, Wallace. Let me go."

"Catharsis, cuz." He's still grinning, but his tone's gotten real serious. And for a moment, it's like he's no longer my goofy cousin, but already another ghost on the corner.

"He's still my friend, Wallace."

Wallace lets out a sarcastic laugh. "He ain't your friend. He up and left to go play ball with some rich-ass white boys. He doesn't care about you. Bunny Thompson's looking out for Bunny Thompson. That's it, Nas. That's fucking it. If you didn't know it before, I know you knew it when you saw him with Keyona. And you know what? Someday he's gonna peace out and walk away from this whole goddamn city like it's a toilet full of shit he just flushed."

And suddenly there's a lump in my throat and I feel like a little boy about to start bawling in the middle of the street, because maybe Wallace is right. I always knew Bunny was on his way to the top. But I always thought he was going to take me with him.

"Fine," I say. Wallace releases my wrist, so I take an egg and fling it toward Bunny's house just to get the whole thing over with. It hits low on the brick.

Wallace makes a stink face. He hands me another egg. "You can do better than that."

"I'm done, man."

"That first one was for him transferring. Make this one for him taking your girl."

"Fine." I take the egg and throw it higher and harder this time. It hits Bunny's window dead center, more of a *thunk* than a *thud* or a *splat*.

"See, cuz? Don't you feel awfully catharted?" he asks.

"That's not really how—" I start to say, but we both notice a curtain move behind one of the windows and hoof it around the nearest corner.

15
BUNNY

omething hits the window.

"What was that?" asks Keyona, from her spot on the floor where her homework's scattered all around.

"Maybe a secret admirer," I say from my bed, where I was thinking about the semifinals later this afternoon.

She gets up and pulls back the curtain. "Ugh." She steps aside so I can see the egg yolk oozing down the windowpane real slow, probably because it's so cold out. She peers into the street and sucks her teeth. "They're gone. What the hell's wrong with people?"

"Probably some bored kids," I say. "Be right back."

I disappear and then return a moment later with a handful of toilet paper. I pull the window up a few inches, and a rush of cold air pours into the room, which is a shame since the landlord finally got the heat fixed. Keyona wraps her arms around herself and moves to the corner farthest from the window. I reach my arm up and around to wipe as much of the egg as I can.

Of course, I don't really think it was some bored kids. I

know it was meant for me, and as I clean it off, I think of all the people who called me Oreo or Sellout, all the shit people posted online that made me stop going online so much, all the side-eyeing I got whenever I walked around the city ever since switching schools. I hoped that stuff would die down as time went on and people got over it—and it looked like it was starting to—but here we are.

I clear off some of the egg, but mostly I end up spreading the smear around. I give up, close the window, and dump the soggy bunched-up toilet paper into the small trash can in my room.

Keyona's moved to the bed, where she sits with her legs drawn up to her chest and her back against the wall. I notice she put on my St. Sebastian's hoodie while I stepped away. I love it when she wears it, because then it smells like her for days. Maybe I should open up the window more often.

"I'm sorry," she says.

"Why? You throw it?" I sit on the edge of the bed, facing away from her.

She moves so we're back to back. Then she starts pushing against the wall with her feet, trying to shove me off the bed. "You know what I mean. I'm sorry that people can't let it go. That you still have to deal with this ignorant shit. I mean, it's only high school."

I shrug, starting to laugh as she keeps pushing. But I'm holding my own.

"Anyway." She gives up, puts her feet down, and flips

around so she's sitting right next me. "You said you wanted to talk about something?"

Did I mention that I love her smell? Not the shampoo or perfume, I mean, but her natural scent, what she smells like underneath all that stuff. Breathing it in makes me want to bury my head in her shoulder and fall asleep. But I don't.

I've got to do this.

"Um," I say. My heart's racing. I think my palms start sweating, and I can't even look at her. But this seems as good a time as any.

"Well?"

I practiced this a thousand times, saying it over and over again in my head so I'd remember the right words. But when I reach for them, it's like air-balling a shot I thought I'd drop.

"Um," I say again.

"You breaking up with me, Bunny Thompson?" Keyona asks. I don't know how to answer that, especially with how she says it all flat. Like she's asking for the time. She laughs. "If you're breaking up with me, you need to tell me why." Again, her voice is calm.

I lean forward and rest my elbows on my knees. I take a deep breath and keep my eyes on my hands, regretting not doing this over a text or a phone call. It would have been wrong, for sure, but it would have been mad easy.

"It's just . . ." I start, not knowing where to go. "I don't know. It's like . . . I don't know. You know?"

She laughs again. "You have to do better than that."

"Sorry, Key. I guess . . . I'm not feeling it anymore. Us, I mean."

"Why not?"

I clench my jaw. I love Keyona, but I hate how she's always trying to make me talk like this. I know how I feel, and I wish she'd just believe me. Why's everything got to be all drawn out?

"Because," I say. "I'm just not."

She nods, as if working this out in her mind.

"When did this start?" she finally asks. "You 'not feeling this anymore.'" She puts air quotes around that last part.

I think of lying, but I decide against it. "I don't know . . . I guess, you know, when we went to the movies Friday."

She nods. "Ah."

"'Ah,' what?"

"I thought this might have something to do with you seeing Nasir again. What? You feel like you betrayed your boy by getting with me?"

"What? Nah," I say. But, yeah, that's pretty much it.

"I know he's had a crush on me forever, Bunny."

"Oh?" I say.

"So what?"

I shrug. I don't want to say anything else, but she keeps on staring at me. I try to stay strong, but I give in. "I guess I still see you as *his* girl," I say. "Since he's liked you for so long, you know. Way before I did."

As soon as the words leave my mouth, I wish I could

hit Rewind. I know better than to say something like that to Keyona.

"Excuse me?" she says. "What makes me *his?* You know I've never been into him like that."

I hold up my hands. "That came out wrong. But you know what I mean."

"No. I don't."

Again, I try to plead the Fifth. But she keeps her eyes fixed on me. Like she's actually trying to make my head explode with her mind. It seems as though it might work, so after a couple of minutes, I give in again and plow ahead. It's kind of like when you're down by twenty points in the last quarter, so you start chucking bad shots hoping something will find the bottom of the net. "It's just . . . I don't know. He told me he had a thing for you a while ago. So I always respected that, since he's my boy. But then he stopped talking to me, and me and you started hanging . . . You're not supposed to get with your boy's girl is all."

She rests her chin on her fist and knots her brow like she's deep in thought. "So let me get this straight: I belong to Nasir because he called dibs?"

"I don't know," I say. "It's not like that."

She moves over to the floor and starts scooping all her books and papers back into her bag. "Do you even know how offensive that is?" She lets out a short, angry laugh. "Of course not. You're a boy." She zips up her bag extra hard, then stands up and glares at me, her hoop earrings still swaying from her sudden movements. "Just because someone likes me doesn't mean I have to like them back. I choose who I want to be with, and I chose you. And nobody, *nobody* gets to claim me like I'm some piece of meat."

When she puts it like that, I can't disagree. I'm not even mad. That's the thing about Keyona: she'll lay the truth down whether you want to hear it or not. And after you do, it's like you just put on some new glasses that you never even knew you needed.

Realizing this makes me want to stop right now and forget that I even started this conversation. Go back to the way things were, because it's not about this anyway. It's much simpler: I miss my friend. I want us to be cool again, and it seemed like this might help us get there. But for some reason, I don't say this out loud.

Keyona starts for the door. "Good luck at your game tonight. And make sure you finish your homework."

"I'm sorry, Key."

"For what?"

"That we're ending like his."

She laughs, and it's genuine again. "Do you *actually* want to break up with me?"

I scratch the back of my head. "Of course not. But—"

"Okay. Then we're not breaking up."

I turn this over in my mind. "You sure?"

She steps forward and gives me a long kiss before disappearing, still wearing my hoodie, still blessing it with her scent.

16

NASIR

After dinner Sunday night, I'm up in my room on my laptop doing research for this history essay that's due next week. But I keep checking the state high school basketball website and clicking Refresh. The game should be over by now, but the results still aren't posted. Not that I really care if St. Sebastian's wins or not—I'm just curious.

Maybe the dude from the newspaper whose job it is to type in those scores forgot to do it tonight. So on my phone, I do a round through Bunny's social media pages to see if maybe he posted something about the game. I'm not surprised to find he hasn't. He's one of the few kids I know who can go weeks without posting anything, even though he has, like, a billion followers now.

I turn my attention back to the New Jersey state basketball website. While I wait for the score to appear, I study the brackets. If St. Sebastian's wins tonight, they'll play for the group championship on Wednesday. If they win that, then they'll play for the state private school title next Sunday. And if they win there, they'll have to play against the public school regional champs in the Tournament of Champions. So not counting tonight, St. Sebastian's needs to win five more games over the next two weeks to take the overall state title.

Easy enough.

Ha. Yeah, right.

But there's enough scouts with eyes on Bunny already that if he can lead his team through the best in the state as a sophomore, without a doubt he'll have his pick of D-I schools come senior year.

We'd always planned on going to the same college someday and rooming together. But I don't have a clue what school he's got his sights on anymore. Things change, I guess.

I click Refresh one more time, and the score finally appears.

St. Cyprian 38, St. Sebastian 70.

Even though I'm somewhat relieved that Bunny got the W, most of me wanted St. Sebastian's to lose. Maybe they'd learn you can't siphon the city of its best talent to make your team any better. If you're butt, you're butt.

I click to see the stats, and as soon as they come up, I say, "Damn," aloud to myself. Bunny's line is ridiculous. Twenty-eight points and fifteen rebounds. Another double-double —that makes sixteen games in a row, I think. I shut my laptop, done for the night.

A moment later, my phone buzzes with a text. It's Wallace.

U c the score, it says, no question mark.

Yeah, I reply. They crushed St. C.

My phone's quiet for a couple of minutes, and then I get another text from Wallace. **We should hack b's facebook.**

Why? I ask.

Catharsis, he replies. He's really proud of himself for knowing that word. A moment later, my phone buzzes with another message from him. **We should post some stupid shit like we're him. U kno his pw?**

LOL, I write back, along with a few laughing-so-hard-I'm-crying emojis. Whatever Wallace would write would be completely immature, but that doesn't mean it wouldn't be funny. Like the time a teacher called him stupid in front of the class so he hacked the dude's Facebook profile and wrote a post pretending to be the teacher confessing that he was one of those people really into feet in a sexual way. Before the teacher deleted the post and wrote a new one explaining his account had been hacked, it had accumulated its fair share of comments. In the end, nobody was hurt, Wallace didn't get caught, and I hear kids still hide their feet in that teacher's class.

But we already egged Bunny's house, so I'm not sure we need to do anything else. Even though I do know his password—assuming he hasn't changed it in the last few months—I text back, **No clue.**

Cool ill just hack urs then.

I laugh.

But in case he's serious, I change my password.

17
BUNNY

After practice on Tuesday, I end up on Nasir's stoop. Don't know why. Maybe 'cause I'm sick of things being weird between us, or maybe 'cause the world feels different since the sun's still up. Warmer. It's that time of year when spring feels like it's on the tip of your tongue.

I'm about to lose courage and duck back into my own house across the street when I hear someone call my name. I turn around to find Mr. Blake walking up, smiling. He's got his work bag slung over his shoulder and the knot of his tie loosened. Long day with the kindergartners, I guess.

"Bunny Thompson? How's it going, son?" he asks, and shakes my hand.

"Good, good, Mr. Blake."

He backs up a step, holds me at arm's length, and looks me up and down like my own dad did when I dropped by the store a few days ago. "You shrink a foot or two these last few months? You look tiny."

"Maybe," I say, returning his smile. It catches me off-guard how good it feels to see him again, to be joking around as if nothing's happened. But if I think about it, it shouldn't surprise me. Even though he was in the military, Nasir's dad has always been overwhelmingly nice in that way people who work with small children seem to be.

"Good work getting that W the other night," he says. "You got the championship tomorrow, right?"

I nod. "For the private schools."

"Immaculate Heart, right?"

"Yeah," I say, kind of surprised he's been following the tournament. "Should be a pretty tough game."

"All right, all right. Maybe I'll swing by. It's been a while since I've seen you play."

"How are your students?" I ask, trying to change the subject.

He laughs. "Little monsters. But I love every one of them." He falls quiet for a couple beats, then asks, "You looking for Nasir?"

I hesitate, nod. Shift my weight to my other foot.

"He's out right now." He looks down the street as if he expects to see him walking up any moment. "With Wallace. But he should be back soon."

Starting down the stoop, I say, "All right. I'll come back—"

"You eat yet?" He interrupts me.

"Not yet," I say, stopping on the last step.

"Stay for dinner, then," he says as he unlocks the door. "It's my night to cook, and I'm making chicken adobo. Is that still your favorite?"

I want to say yes and yes. Mr. Blake cooks Filipino food almost as well as Nasir's mom. But I'm not sure Nasir even wants to see me in the first place, so I say, "Wish I could, but Jess is expecting me. And you know how she is about having all of us siblings sit down and eat together even if our parents are out working. But I can hang out until Nasir comes home."

"I respect that. Don't want to mess with family." He pushes open the door and holds it open for me. I step inside.

Nasir's place doesn't look like anything's changed. Same art on the walls. Same couches and flat-screen TV in the living room. Same bookshelves crammed with paperbacks from Word Up. Same table off the kitchen. And all of it perfectly neat and orderly like always, like they clean every day. My house isn't exactly dirty, but it feels more lived in. We've always got toys or mail or books lying around all over the place, except for the first Saturday of the month, when our parents make us clean from top to bottom. But that clean never lasts more than a couple days.

"Mind helping me start dinner?" Mr. Blake asks, hanging his coat.

"Sure," I say, because what else am I going to say?

We walk over to the kitchen, and as he digs through the freezer, I stand at the counter that separates the kitchen from the dining room. After popping a couple frozen chicken breasts into the microwave to defrost, he grabs some garlic and tosses it to me. I catch it, and he smiles.

"Two cloves. Minced."

I pull one of the cutting boards out from the cabinet where they keep them and slide a knife from their little knife holder thing. I set to mincing the garlic like Mr. Blake taught me when I was younger as he gets the rice pot.

"So how's your mom doing?" Mr. Blake asks over the sound of the grains of rice clinking into the metal.

"She's all right," I say.

"Still on the graveyard shift?" he asks.

"Unfortunately."

Mr. Blake runs the water and rinses the raw rice. "Must be rough."

I shrug. "Pays better. And she gets to be home with my dad all day."

He chuckles. "Bet they like that."

I don't say anything.

He clears his throat. "Anyway, how are the twins?"

I finish with the garlic and wipe the blade. "Good. Justine's still quiet, and Ashley's still loud."

"And Jessica? Doing all right with those college classes?"

"Yeah. Always stressing about some test or paper, though."

"That's how it's supposed to be," he says. "It'll be worth it in the end."

We settle into a comfortable silence as Mr. Blake starts pulling out some spices, and this feels like it's supposed to. Like it used to. The hum of the microwave. The rice quietly simmering on the stovetop. Only thing missing is Nasir.

"Teenage boys aren't so good at talking about how they feel," Mr. Blake says, making it pretty clear we're thinking about the same thing. "I know. I was one a long time ago. Boys tend to keep everything inside and let it out in other ways."

I don't say anything.

"That's why I try to get them talking and processing when they're young. In my class, we start and end every day sitting in a circle on the rug. The Sharing Circle, we call it. We go around, and the kids share how they're feeling."

"That's nice," I say.

"You want to try it right now?"

"Try what?"

"Sharing how you're feeling?" Mr. Blake asks.

But before I can answer, the front door bursts open. Nasir tumbles inside the house, letting in a rush of cold air. His eyes land on me, and he stops short. "Bunny."

I can't tell if it's a question, a statement, or a greeting. And I can't read if he's happy to see me or not, just like I don't know how I would have answered Mr. Blake's question. "Hey, Nas."

His eyes dart to his dad. "You invite him for dinner?" he asks, like I'm not even there.

The microwave stops whirring and beeps a few times.

"Nah," I answer for myself, and start washing my hands. "Just wanted to say what's up."

"Oh," he says. I hear the door shut, his bag thud onto the floor, and his coat rustle as he slips it off.

Mr. Blake pulls the chicken from the microwave. The edges are cooked through, but the rest is still pink. Probably still frozen on the inside. "Thanks for your help, Bunny, but I got it from here. Why don't you all go on and hang out in the living room?"

Nasir kicks off his shoes and picks up his bag from where he dropped it a second ago. He runs a hand over the top of his head and looks away. "Sorry, Bunny, but I've got a history paper to write. You understand, right?"

"Yeah," I say. "It's cool. Another time."

"For sure." And then Nasir dips. I listen to the sound of his feet stomping up the stairs until it fades away.

Mr. Blake sighs. "He'll come around."

I shrug.

"Sure you don't want to stay to eat? You're a teenager —you'd probably still have room for Jess's meal, too."

"Yeah," I say, "I'm sure. Thanks, though."

"Good luck tomorrow. As if you'll need it."

"Thanks," I say. "Always do."

18
NASIR

When I reach the top of the steps, my mom's waiting in the open doorway of her studio, arms folded over her chest. Her smock's smeared with paint streaks, and her hair's up in a bun with a thin brush stuck into it. She doesn't look happy, but she doesn't say anything. Only glares.

"What?" I say.

"You know what," she says.

A moment later, I hear the front door open and shut.

I slip into my room, and she shifts from her studio doorway to mine, death gaze following after me like a dark cloud.

"I think you should go to his game tomorrow," she says.

I drop my bag to the floor next to my desk and start searching through it even though anything I need for my history essay would be on the laptop that sits on my desk. "No, thanks."

She sighs. "Why not?"

"We're not tight like that anymore, Mom."

"Why not?" she asks again.

"Because." I'm still rummaging through the folders in my bag, but it's getting obvious I'm stalling.

"Because why?"

"Because I don't want to." I zip up my bag and move over to my desk chair. I start slowly spinning around, rotating away from her.

"I think it would mean a lot to Bunny," she says.

I shrug, the world still turning. Everyone's so worried about helping Bunny. Why's nobody but me sweating Wallace's situation? Bunny's fine. Everyone's handing him the future on a silver platter.

"When I first came to this country with your father, it was very difficult. My English wasn't very good. I didn't know how to drive yet, so I couldn't get anywhere by myself. And nobody wanted to hire me to be anything except a maid, even though I had a degree in civil engineering. But do you know what was the most difficult thing?"

I'm starting to feel a little dizzy and nauseated, but I keep pushing my feet off the floor to spin myself. "What, Mom?"

"No longer having a good friend close by."

"Bunny changed schools, Mom. He didn't move to a different country."

She thinks for a moment. "I think in a way he did. But I was talking about you."

I roll my eyes. "Yeah, okay."

"You know that your father and I try to allow you to make your own mistakes," she says, "but we know the pain this is causing you to not have a friend anymore."

Great. My parents think I don't have any friends. I stop spinning. The room continues, though. "I'm all right, Mom.

For real. I can't speak for Bunny, but whatever he's feeling is his own fault. He chose this. As for me, I've got other friends."

"Like Wallace?"

"Like Wallace," I say, looking down at my feet.

She starts to say something else but stops herself. An awkward silence settles between us as I wait for her to speak or leave, and in that space I start thinking about whether or not I can really call Wallace a friend. But I don't want to think about that. Because for some reason, soon as I do, sadness rises around me like I'm stepping in water. I spin my chair a bit more so I'm facing away from my mom and looking out the window.

"Will you please go to Bunny's game tomorrow?" she asks after a few moments. "If not for him, then for me."

I spin around once in the opposite direction I had been going in, hoping to undo the lingering dizziness. I sigh. *"Opo,"* I say, which basically means "yes, ma'am." It's one of the few Tagalog words I know.

My mom walks over, wraps her arms around my shoulders from over the back of my chair, and kisses me on the cheek. She smells of acrylic paint and citrus. *"Salamat,"* she says. "Thank you." And then she finally leaves.

I sit there for some time afterward, staring out the window at the electrical wires tangled in the bare branches of the tree that stands between my house and Bunny's.

19
BUNNY

I wake up in the dark and realize someone's sitting on the foot of my bed.

"Bunny?" my dad's voice asks. I feel him place a hand over my blankets on top of my legs like he used to do when he read me bedtime stories when I was little. "You okay?"

"Huh? Dad?" I rub my eyes and sit up, relieved it's not some murderer. I reach for my phone, figuring I woke up late for school. The screen comes on, casting away a bit of the darkness with its blue glow. It reads 1:26 a.m. I leave it face-up like a night-light. My next thought is that something real bad has happened. I remember when Grandma died a few years back, my parents woke me in the middle of the night to deliver the news. "What's going on? Everyone all right?"

"Yeah," he says. "But you shouted—are you okay?"

"I did?"

He nods. "Just a moment ago. Bad dream, maybe?"

I try to remember. There's something there. Fragmented images. Missed shots. People in the crowd booing. Wallace and Nas trapping me in a double team and snatching the ball.

Nas standing on the bleachers in an empty gym. But I feel the details slipping away as my mind reaches for them, tries to connect them. It's like how when you're a little kid at the beach, you chase the receding water, except that next wave's never coming.

"Yeah," I say, rubbing my eyes again. "Bad dream, I think. We won tonight, right?"

"Sure did," he says. "Sixty-two to forty-four."

"Were you there?" I know he wasn't even as I ask. Guess I'm still out of it.

He shakes his head. "Sorry, Bunny."

"Oh, yeah. It's cool."

"But I'll be at the next one."

"Cool," I say again.

As he rises and starts to walk out, another image slips into my head: Nasir's face in the crowd, watching like he wanted me to win, watching like he wanted to be out there with me.

"Dad?" I call after him.

He stops, silhouetted in my door frame. "Yeah, Bunny?"

"Was Nasir at my game tonight?"

"I don't know, son. You can ask him tomorrow. Get some rest now."

"Thanks for checking in on me," I say, like I'm still a little boy.

"That's my job."

He leaves, closing the door behind him. My phone's screen goes dark.

20

NASIR

After school on Thursday, Wallace and I decide to walk down to the courts before heading home. Clouds hang overhead like they're ready to dump some snow on us for real, but it's not happening yet. It's not even that cold. Maybe thirty-something degrees. Which I know is barely above freezing, but it's like spring compared to the single digits we've been getting. And everybody else must feel the same because people are walking down the streets and posting up on the corners like it's July.

"You want to try to run a game, or you want to watch?" I ask. Neither of us is dressed to ball. Under our winter coats, we're still wearing the khakis and purple polos of studious Whitman High academicians.

Wallace has his earbuds in, so he doesn't hear me at first. I shoulder check him. He takes one out and drapes it over his ear. "Huh?"

I repeat the question.

He shrugs. Pops his earbud back in and digs his hands deeper into his coat pockets.

"Cool," I say, and we continue walking in silence. We pass

a few kids we know along the way, but Wallace doesn't stop for any of them, so I offer nods of recognition.

I know something's weighing on him, but I've learned when Wallace gets like this, it's best to give him space. Otherwise, he's likely to snap for any little thing. Maybe the reality of that whole eviction action is finally hitting him, since the end of the month's less than three weeks away.

We arrive at the park and find five-on-five games running full on both courts, with like a couple dozen people on the sidelines waiting for next. A few people are watching, and a couple homeless dudes are checking the garbage cans for bottles. Wallace heads straight for one of the empty picnic tables on the far side of the courts, and sits down on the table with his feet on the bench.

I wander over to the sideline and ask this junior I know called Chops — either because he's got these real bushy sideburns, or because he's kind of shaped like a pork chop with his barrel chest and skinny legs — who's got next. Chops says his crew does, and then someone else tells me that their squad's after that. I ask if they need a point and a center, but both dudes tell me they're good. My guess is we'd have to wait at least an hour to see some action, so I join Wallace over at the picnic table. For some reason, he's picked the one that's busted and marked up with graffiti instead of the one people inexplicably keep clean, so I find the spot that seems least likely to give me tetanus.

The game running on the court in front of us is nothing to

write home about. The same dudes as usual trying to relive their glory days for an hour or so. It's not long before someone throws a hard elbow and the game stops so everyone can run their mouth about whether or not it's a foul. Things settle down eventually, and the game resumes. Wallace and I watch in silence.

"I forgot how good Bunny is," I say after a while.

Wallace takes out his earbuds. "Huh?"

"Bunny," I say. "I forgot how nice he is."

Wallace spits. "Man, fuck Bunny." And even though he's expressed similar sentiments before, his words feel laced with a new level of malice. Maybe he's mad I went to the game last night. I wonder if he's afraid I'll start hanging with Bunny again and leave him behind.

But that's not going to happen. I only went because my mom laid that guilt trip on me.

"You ever end up getting into his Facebook?" I ask.

But Wallace doesn't answer. He spits into the dirt again and sticks his earbuds back in.

And then I hear something beneath us. Almost like a tiny baby crying. I hop off the table and peer underneath.

"What's up?" Wallace asks.

The thing can't be more than a few weeks old. It's about the size of a softball. Skinny and shivering. Gray fur all matted. It keeps mewling over and over. "It's a kitten."

Wallace hops off the bench, stuffs his earbuds into his pockets, and crouches down next to me. "Damn."

He reaches underneath the bench. The kitten backs away and bares its teeth, which are so tiny they're like pointed grains of rice.

"Careful," I say. "It might have rabies. Actually, I don't know if cats get rabies. Do they?"

Wallace doesn't answer. He shakes his coat off and slips his hoodie off over his head. Using the sweatshirt, he scoops up the kitten. Though it looked like it was going to put up a fight, it lets Wallace lift it up. He even wraps the hoodie all the way around until only its face is peeking through, and then he holds the bundle to his chest.

Big-ass Wallace snuggling this kitten like it's his baby is such a funny sight I want to snap a picture with my phone. But he's all in protective mode, so I'd rather not have him tear my arms off my torso.

"Let's get her home," he says, shedding his sullenness for concern. "Poor thing's probably starving."

We leave the courts behind, walk back to Wallace's car, and drive to his apartment. All the while, I'm thinking about how funny it is that people can act so hard and then turn around and give you a glimpse that there's more to them. I know some people around our way have it rough and have to toughen up to survive, but my theory is they're putting up the same front as Wallace. I wish we could all agree it's dumb and drop the act. Then everyone could go around doing stuff like saving stray kittens instead.

Now, we don't go to Wallace's apartment very often.

There's not much to it. It's a nice neighborhood that's been getting nicer the more the city develops the university and the hospital, but he lives on the third floor of this house that somebody bought and split up into apartments. His apartment number's 202¾. No joke. Wallace sleeps on the old couch in the living room because the only bedroom belongs to his grandma.

So I kind of expect it to smell like old person when we walk in. And it does. I try not to wrinkle my nose or show that I notice. I keep my coat on because it's chilly in here, like at Bunny's when their heat's broken.

I sit down on the threadbare couch — a.k.a. Wallace's bed — and wait as he takes the kitten to the small kitchen just off the living room. He opens a cabinet with his free hand and pulls out a bowl that he fills with water. Then he sets it down on the countertop along with the bundled-up kitten.

The kitten crawls out of the sweatshirt and approaches the water like it's a trap. She sniffs with this little pink nose, and then decides to go for it. She lowers her head and begins lapping it up with this tongue the size of a pinky fingernail. When she finishes, she looks up at Wallace and starts mewling again.

"Not too much, little kitty," he says in this real soft voice.

As if it understands him, the kitten stops making noise and starts exploring the countertop. Its legs are all unsteady as it pounces around and goes right up to the edge like it's trying to decide if it should hop down.

"Gerald?" his grandma's voice calls from her room like a croak. "That you, boy?"

It's always kind of weird for me to hear my cousin called by his real name. Long as I remember, we've all called him Wallace because he looks kind of like Rasheed Wallace.

"Yes, ma'am," Wallace/Gerald calls back, eyes still on the cat.

"You pick up my pills?" she asks.

Wallace pulls a paper bag from the pharmacy out of his jacket pocket and then waves it in the air so she can hear it. "Got 'em right here, G. Stopped before school."

His grandma doesn't reply. I imagine she has fallen asleep or died.

"What are you going to do with the cat?" I ask, once I figure their conversation's not going anywhere else.

"Keep it. I'm gonna call it Bunny."

I let out a small laugh. "Why Bunny?"

Wallace grins. "It's a pussy, ain't it?"

And I can't argue with that.

21
BUNNY

It's Thursday, and I'm back at Whitman High staring into the trophy case that lines the wall outside the main gym. Coach Baum ended practice a little early as a reward for us winning our state group, and since Keyona plays point for Whitman's girls' team, I swung by to catch the end of their game. Unfortunately, it didn't go so well, and that's it for their season. At least she's got track to look forward to. That's her main sport.

But saddest thing to me isn't the loss so much as that it was their group championship and there was hardly anyone watching it. A handful of parents, a few friends, and siblings. No cheerleaders or band like for the boys' games. Place was so quiet you could hear every dribble, every sneaker squeak, every girl calling for the ball or the switch on a screen.

But they played their hearts out, and I respect that. Sweating for the sake of the game. And both teams were grinding —it just wasn't Keyona's that came out on top. That's how it goes sometimes.

I haven't been able to make it to any of her other games

this season because they're usually over before I make my way back to the city after my own practices, so this is my first time inside Whitman High in a minute. And even though it's kind of weird, it feels nice. Like slipping on an old shirt. Being back and sitting in those stands with mostly people of color feels right in a way I haven't felt at St. Sebastian's.

I let my eyes slide over the familiar line of basketball trophies behind the smudged glass as I wait. On the left are the oldest, dustiest ones, with the newer ones to the right. Team photos propped up against the sparkling bases track the racial history of the city: all white from the first half of the century, a trickle of color in the middle, and then nearly all Black or Puerto Rican or Dominican in the newer photos. All connected across time and race by nothing but a game.

The trophy farthest on the right is from our conference championship last season. I'm in the middle of the back row, looking a thousand years younger than I feel these days. Wallace stands directly to my right. Nasir, almost always the smallest on any team we've ever been on, is on a knee at the far left of the front row. I laugh a little, remembering how much he hated it when photographers would direct us to line up by height.

But the longer I look at that photo and trophy, the more I'm feeling like I called the wrong play in the middle of a close game. I miss all of this real bad, and maybe deciding to transfer to St. Sebastian's wasn't the right move. There's something about feeling like you belong, feeling like you're home, that nothing can replace. But when I made the decision over the summer, I kept thinking about what it'd be like on the other side. To have better facilities. More gear. More challenging academics. More scouts watching.

More.

Of course, things always look different from the other side. St. Sebastian's simply doesn't feel like *this*.

"It's not too late to help us put some more in there," someone says from over my shoulder.

I tense up, but relax as soon as I turn around to find Coach J smiling wide.

We shake hands, then he says, "I'm just playing. But, man, I still can't believe that season you had last year. Not even Moore put up those kinds of numbers his freshman year."

"Thanks, Coach," I say, my eyes drifting over to one of the tallest trophies in the case. It's from ninety-eight, the last time Whitman brought home a state title. Coach Campbell was only an assistant then, and Coach J was the team's starting two-guard. But Clark Moore, their starting power forward, was the star of the show. Led the team in about every stat and, after a year at Duke, went on to play a few years for the Clippers before heading overseas.

"You ask me," he says, "I think you're three or four times the player he ever was."

I wish people wouldn't say things like that. I know they mean well, but it makes me feel like if I don't play how everyone expects, I've let them all down.

"Nah," I say. "Maybe half on a good day."

"You're too modest, Bunny Thompson," Coach J says,

laughing. "Congrats on the group championship, by the way. Saw your line, and looks like you just keep getting better and better. But we all knew you would. You've got a great future ahead of you. The Unstoppable Bunny Thompson. You see, you're going places. I know you had to do what's best for you, but I'm glad I'll be able to say I knew you when."

Again, I don't think he's trying to lay the guilt trip, but all those feelings I was having—about how maybe it was a mistake transferring to St. Sebastian's—they feel like they're expanding. Like they're filling my chest and making it hard to breathe.

Thankfully, Keyona comes out of the gym right then, bag slung over her shoulder and hair still up in that tight ponytail she wears to keep it out of her face while playing. I can tell by her face she's disappointed her season's over. She hugs me without saying anything, then greets Coach J.

"We'll chat later, Bunny," Coach J says. "I'll leave you kids be. Good luck on Sunday with St. Agnes. I know you know what to do, but keep an eye on number twenty-one. Dude's got a nice J. Keyona, great game tonight. You win some, you lose some. You'll get 'em next year. I know you will."

"Thanks, Coach J," she says, still holding on to me.

"See ya, Coach," I say.

Coach J winks at Keyona. "Take care of our boy."

"I will," she says.

After Coach J leaves, I squeeze her tighter. We sway back and forth for a bit like we're slow dancing and kiss briefly a couple of times.

"Really, Key," I say, "you played hard tonight. You fought hard."

"Thanks," she says, her cheek pressing into my chest, making some of those bad feelings I had earlier melt away.

"Coach J is right, there's always next season."

"True."

"And track," I say.

"And track," she says. "Besides, we can't all be Bunny Thompson." She smirks.

I laugh. "I hear that guy's a chump."

She pulls away from the hug. "Hey, watch what you say about my man."

"*Your* man? Oh, so it's okay for *you* to claim *me?*"

She socks me in the shoulder, and I act like it hurts real bad. We laugh a little and then start walking side by side, my arm around her shoulder and her arm laced around my waist. We're moving real slow, and the rest of her team files past us on their way out the building. I try to ignore the side-eye some of them throw my way, which makes me feel like when that egg hit my window.

I shake it off as we leave the trophy case behind, walk past the empty classrooms, and push through the main doors. As they click shut, we stop on the top step. It's warmer out than I expected. The sky is clear, and there's even a couple of stars up there.

We haven't said anything this whole walk, because I know Keyona's like me in that she likes to have some silence for a bit after a loss. I don't know what she thinks about in that space, but I always get stuck on what I should have done differently. The shot I shouldn't have taken. The bad pass I made. The misstep I took on defense. But once we're outside, Keyona slides her arm from around my waist and takes my hand in hers.

Keyona. The girl who wouldn't let me go. I may not know if I made the right decision about transferring and all, but I know this is right, that this feels like that moment after the shot drops. What the hell was I thinking, trying to break up with her?

"What are you up to now?" I ask.

"Shower. Homework. Bed."

"Maybe I can come over, and we do some homework together?" I suggest.

"I wish. But it's a school night. You know how my parents are about that."

I sigh. "Thought I'd ask."

She sneaks me a quick kiss. Makes me smile like someone pressed a button. "If you're that bored, maybe you could try hanging with Nas again," she says.

My smile fails. "Don't know about that." We start down the steps toward where her car's parked on the street. The other team's bus is already gone. There are a few cars out front with their hazards flashing, probably waiting for their kids.

After a few steps, she says, "You know, he went to your game the other night."

I nod. "I thought I saw him. He say anything to you about it?"

"Only that he went."

I nod again as we reach the street and head right along the sidewalk.

"You haven't talked since then?"

I shake my head.

"Hmm. Maybe he's coming around. But you all are going to have to talk eventually if you want to be cool again."

I scratch the back of my head. Run my coat zipper up and down its track with my free hand. "I don't want to stir up anything that might cause more noise."

Keyona shakes her head. "Things won't magically get better. You need to have it out eventually, Bunny. You. Need. To. Talk. To. Each. Other." Those last few words she punctuates with kisses to make sure I'm listening.

Once we reach her car, she turns me so my back's against the passenger door, and then she leans into me. Goes up on her tiptoes and presses her lips to mine. We start making out and my heart starts thumping like it's about to jump out of my chest. I start feeling warm all over as our lips continue to trace each other and my hands slide down her back, and I can't even believe I tried to break it off with her.

Some passing car beeps its horn, and then another car honks at us, and then another, like it's become a thing everyone's doing. We start laughing even as we're still kissing.

22
NASIR

t's Friday night and I'm with Wallace, headed to a party for some reason. We've been driving around for approximately a decade looking for a parking spot, but the cars are packed tight along every curb in a five-block radius. I've already suggested we head back—especially since we've wasted so much time that my curfew's only about an hour away—but Wallace straight ignored me. He's in one of his moods. His jaw's set, grinding a cigarette between his teeth as he guides the car down the street in a slow roll.

"There," I say, pointing up ahead at a break between two vehicles. Wallace pulls up. We both groan when we spot the fire hydrant.

Wallace slams his fists on the steering wheel. "Goddammit, motherfucking, bitch-ass motherfucker," he mutters around the cigarette. And that's a lot of cursing, even for him. "Man, how many goddamned fires they having up in here that they need these jawns, like, every three feet?"

I stay quiet.

We drive up a couple more blocks and then start to circle

back around for about the thousandth time. And I know it's Friday night and I'm a teenager, so I'm supposed to be all excited about going out. But honestly, it's never really been my thing. My ideal Friday night is a few uninterrupted hours of video games. Anyway, the black hole of happiness that is my cousin isn't helping.

"Maybe it's a sign," I say, "that we should go home."

Wallace exhales a thick cloud of smoke out the cracked window, spits, and then holds up his middle finger. "Here's a sign for you, cuz. What's it mean?"

I'm thinking about how I need my own car when I spot someone pulling out half a block down. My head whips back as Wallace guns it, then my body lunges forward against the seat belt a couple seconds later when he slams on the brakes.

But the other car doesn't pull away completely. Just sits there, half in, half out. Wallace lays on his horn, forgetting that it hasn't worked since that one time someone cut him off and he held it down until it ran out of noise. Rolling down his window all the way, he leans his head out and shouts, "Yo, hurry the fuck up, man!" through cupped hands.

But the car still doesn't budge.

"Probably plugging an address into their GPS or something," I say, hoping to calm my cousin down.

Wallace starts breathing hard through his nostrils, eyes fixed ahead on the back of that car like he didn't even hear me. His hand goes to the door handle—but he doesn't pull it. My guess is he's deciding whether or not he should step out, yank the driver from behind the wheel, and beat him sense-less. I wouldn't put it past him tonight, with the mood he's in.

But a moment later, he moves his hand to his cigarette and takes one long drag like it's holding him together before flicking the butt out onto the street. He turns the music back up until I can feel the bass rattling all the loose pieces in his car and in my body, and then he leans back.

When the other car finally drives away, Wallace pulls the world's quickest parallel parking job, tapping the bumpers of the cars in front of and behind us. I glance around for wit-nesses, but Wallace isn't sweating it. He kills the engine and steps out without a word, slamming the door behind him and leaving me in the lonely quiet.

To be honest, I spend some time wondering if I should chill there on my phone while Wallace gets this funk out of his system. But I can't shake this feeling like I'm the only thing standing between him and trouble. After a few moments, I get out and spot Wallace ahead, turning the corner at the end of the block. I'm not about to run for no reason. Even if I lose him, I'm betting it won't be hard to find the party by the noise alone.

Sure enough, I start to feel the steady thumping of bass before I hear it. I pass a few clumps of people in the streets coming from the same direction, stumbling and laughing. All loudness and liquor.

I follow the pounding bass to a stoop crammed with people. They're spilling out the doorway, down the steps, and into the street. I don't recognize anyone. Most look like they're college age, and most have a drink in one hand and a cigarette or blunt in the other. Some don't. But everyone's chatting it up and nodding their head in time with the bass beat.

I take a deep breath like I'm about to plunge into a churning ocean, and then head inside. Some lineman-looking dude stops me at the doorway and says there's a ten-dollar entrance fee. Wallace didn't tell me about that, but luckily I have some cash on me. I hand over a ten, and then he lets me slide past him into a small living room packed with bodies, the furniture pushed to the walls. The light is low, and the hot air is thick with the scent of smoke, alcohol, a mixture of perfumes and cologne, and BO. The Sixers game is playing on mute on a huge flat screen but nobody's watching. Everyone's swaying with the beat of a Kid Cudi track, which is blasting from a couple of standup speakers set up in the corner of the living room. Some people are rapping along, drinks raised into the air, while others are in their own world grinding on each other. I move to the wall and make my way around as I scan the crowd for Wallace. Eventually, I catch a glimpse of his lopsided fade heading into the kitchen. I call his name, but the music drowns it out. I push through the crush of dancing bodies, doing my best to catch up with him.

The kitchen's as packed as the living room and nearly as loud, except instead of dancing, most of the people in here are trying to make conversation by shouting directly into each other's ears. No sign of Wallace, though. Someone I don't know gives me a fist bump, points at the fridge, and says something I can't hear. I ask him if he knows Wallace, but I don't think he can hear me either, because he smiles and nods and hands me a cup before walking away. There's some red liquid inside. I sniff it, and even though it looks like juice, it's definitely got alcohol. I'm not trying to go home drunk, but I hold on to it so maybe I'll appear more like I belong than I feel.

I stand there for a while scanning the room. I start feeling claustrophobic, so I make my way to the back door and slip outside to catch some fresh air. The backyard's long and narrow, without any grass, and surrounded by row houses looming over the fence.

It's quieter, cooler, less crowded out here. A few small groups of people stand around smoking and chatting. It doesn't take me long to spot Wallace at the far end of the backyard near the gate that leads to the alleyway. Except he's not drinking or smoking or dancing. He's arguing with some dude. More accurately, he looks like he's pleading, gesturing wildly with his hands. The other dude stands there as impassive as a mountain, muscular arms folded over a barrel chest, looking like his patience is running real thin. I hang back.

Eventually, the dude must be tired of Wallace, because he starts to walk away toward the gate. Wallace grabs his shoulder like he's trying to stop him, and then the guy turns around and swings. His fist cracks into the side of Wallace's jaw, and Wallace drops to the ground like a sack of bricks. A few people standing around call out, "Daaamn!" and "Yoooo!" but nobody moves to help—not even me. Before Wallace can recover, the big dude disappears through the gate and into the alley.

I put my drink down and walk over to where Wallace is pushing himself off the ground. I reach for his arm to help him up, but he brushes my hand away.

"You okay?" I ask.

Rubbing his jaw, he gets back to his feet and spits blood. "Fucking golden, cuz."

"What was up with that, Wallace?" I ask.

Wallace straightens his hat and brushes the dirt off his jeans. People around are watching us and snickering. Someone's holding up a phone, probably recording in hopes Wallace will do something funny that he can post online.

"Wallace," I repeat, "why'd that dude hit you?"

"Lost a bet," he says quietly, touching his fingers to his lips and then looking at the blood shining on them under the street lamp. "And couldn't pay up."

I open my mouth to ask another question, but he cuts me off.

"You ready to roll?" he asks, and walks away before I can answer.

23

BUNNY

When I come through the door after practice on Saturday, I find my entire family on the sofa in the living room watching *WALL-E*. My dad's got his arm around my mom. Justine and Ashley are gazing at the screen like they're hypnotized. Jess is sitting on the floor with her back against the foot of the sofa and her computer on her lap.

Everyone together like this is a rare enough sight these days, and I'm just about to throw my stuff down and join them when I notice Nasir sitting at our kitchen table staring at his phone.

Except for the twins, everyone looks up at me. Jess stops typing. I pull down my headphones as Nasir slips his phone into his pocket.

I turn to my parents about to ask, *What the hell is this?* but my mom shoots me a look that makes me keep my mouth shut.

"Look who stopped by," my dad says.

Nas gets out of his seat and comes over to me. He stands there for a moment while everyone pretends like they're not watching us. Then he asks, "Hey, man, can we talk?"

Seeing him in our house after all these months is throwing me off, and I'm trying to process why he's even here. It seemed clear when I tried to catch him at his place the other night that he didn't want anything to do with me. Then again, he did go to my last game, so maybe Keyona's right about him coming around.

"Yeah, okay," I say.

Nasir follows me upstairs to my room. I didn't expect company, so I've got clothes here and there, and an unmade bed. At least the sun is shining through the blinds, making things look kind of nice. I drop my gym bag onto the floor, slip my headphones off my neck, and set them on my bookshelf. When I turn back around, Nas is still standing in the doorway, looking around my room like he's not sure if he should step all the way inside.

And then I find myself looking around, too, trying to imagine what he's seeing. Most everything is the same as the last time he was here. Besides the Nike team gear St. S gives us for free lying around on my floor, the only new stuff I can think of is a few things I tacked onto the wall above my bed, a St. Sebastian's team photo next to our Whitman shot from last season, a ticket stub from the first movie I went to with Keyona next to the photo strip we got from the photo booth there.

"Your squad ready for tomorrow?" he finally asks, hands in the pocket of his hoodie and eyes still everywhere but on me.

"Yeah," I say. "Think so."

He nods. Wanders over to my desk. Leans forward to get a better look at that photo strip of me and Keyona. I almost apologize about getting with her, but then I stop myself after I remember all Keyona said when I tried to break up with her about how nobody could claim her.

Eventually, Nasir speaks again. "Bunny Thompson, State Champion . . . has a nice ring to it. Yeah?"

I sit down on the edge of my bed. I lean forward, rest my elbows on my knees, and start cracking my knuckles. "Might be a bit early to say that. Besides, a win tomorrow only makes us the non-public state champs. Still need to win three more to take the state for real."

"I think you got it, B," he says. "But I wish it would have been with us."

I'm not sure what to say to that, because it gets me feeling both proud and guilty, so instead I say, "Thanks for dropping by the game the other night."

Nasir pulls out my desk chair and sits down. Then he reaches over and picks up this little standup figure I've got of Kevin Durant next to my desk lamp. "My mom made me," he says, turning little Durant over in his hands.

"Oh," I say, like hearing that doesn't hurt.

Downstairs, I hear footsteps move across the house. Cabinets opening and shutting. Pots and pans clanging together. Faraway laughter.

"There was supposed to be, like, a big blizzard or something this weekend," I say. "But it looks like they were wrong."

"Yeah," he says, and leaves it at that.

Nasir's not saying anything else. And this feels wrong. Not wrong as in bad, but wrong as in not how it used to be. Just to do something, I unzip my gym bag and throw my practice clothes into my laundry hamper. Then I grab my phone and plug it into my charger. Finally, I pull out the new sneakers St. S gave everyone for the playoffs. Soon as I do, though, Nasir looks over and raises his eyebrows.

"Damn," he says.

I stuff them back into my bag and zip it up. "Nike hooks us up."

"That legal?" he asks.

"Yeah," I say. "I guess they think it will promote their brand if the team's good enough, and they hope that if one of the players makes it and becomes an all-star, they'll keep wearing that same brand."

"Seems sketchy," he says, as if accusing me of something. I shrug.

And now I'm wondering if his mom made him come over like how she apparently made him come to my game. He definitely isn't acting as though he wants to be here, and if he's going to keep on like this, part of me would rather he go on home.

But another part of me is glad he's here, even if he is acting salty. I remember what Keyona said about how me and Nas will have to talk about these last few months to be cool again. I know she's right.

"How's Wallace?" I ask after a couple more moments of awkward silence.

He shrugs. "Going through some stuff right now."

I wait for him to tell me more, but he doesn't.

"Too cool for Pokémon?" he asks instead.

"Huh?" I say, caught off-guard by the question.

He puts the little Durant standup down and points at the corner of my desk, where I've got a shoebox filled with college brochures. That's the *maybe* pile. It takes a moment, but then it hits me—he's talking about the Pokémon figurines that I used to keep there. The ones he got me for my eleventh birthday. Guess that's one difference in my room I forgot.

"Nah, just put them away," I say. "Had to make space."

He lets out a sarcastic laugh. "Yeah, of course you did."

"Why you say it like that?"

"You know why."

"So we're going there?"

"Guess so."

I take a deep breath. Measure my words before I say them. "I didn't push you out of my life, man. You stopped speaking to me."

He shakes his head. Starts bouncing his leg up and down like he does when he's getting upset. "You decided to transfer without even telling me, Bunny. How was I supposed to take that?"

"You could have been happy for me."

"Why?"

"I had a chance to go to a better school."

"Better?" He lets out a bitter laugh and stands up. "Yeah, I get it. You think you're too good for us."

"I didn't say that, Nas. You know why I had to do it—I don't have a dad with the GI Bill waiting to pay my way through college like you do."

He pushes the chair in hard enough that it bangs against the edge of my desk. "Man, those are excuses. I know exactly why you did it, but you won't even acknowledge it."

"Oh, really? Why don't you go ahead and tell me why, then?"

He laughs again. "You're looking out for yourself so hard you forget that everyone else exists. So it's nothing to you to leave us behind."

And before I can ask him how wanting to help my family is selfish, he's out. I hear him stomp down the steps and then I hear the front door swing open and slam shut. I know if I looked out the window, I'd see him crossing the street back to his place, but I don't.

"Bunny?" my mom calls up the steps. "Everything okay?"

"Yeah," I say. "Nas had to go."

Before she can ask me any more about it, I duck into the bathroom and turn on the shower. As it heats up, I stare at my reflection in the mirror and wonder if Nas was right.

24
NASIR

D amn," I say to Wallace, glancing at the scoreboard one more time as we shuffle out of the gym in the crush of the crowd.

64–30, St. Sebastian's.

I shake my head and can't help smiling, even though things still aren't right between Bunny and me. "A thirty-four-point win in the state tournament," I say. "That's nasty."

Wallace isn't feeling it, even though he was the one who wanted to come here. He got all grumpy soon as St. S took the lead about thirty seconds into the first quarter, groaning and cursing every time Bunny hit a shot.

"Am I supposed to be impressed?" he asks. "Just beat a bunch of weak-ass rich kids. We'll see how he does against the public schools this week."

He's in a bad enough mood that I don't mention the fact that the non-public champion's taken the Tournament of Champions eight out of the last ten years. Instead, I think about how this wasn't even one team versus another. It was Bunny running a skills clinic. Any fool could see there was a world of difference between him and everyone else on the court tonight. I mean, even in the way he does something as simple as dribble or pass. Hard. Fast. Controlled.

That was it: control.

Bunny controlled the ball, and he controlled the game. He was like an expert surgeon taking the scalpel with a steady hand and slicing with laser precision. No wasted movements. No emotion. No mistakes. Just control. No doubt in my mind that if they hadn't changed the rules, he could head straight to the NBA out of high school.

As if echoing my thoughts, I hear some balding white guy in front of us tell the already bald man next to him, "Damn, that kid can play."

"I'll give you that," Baldy says. "But he doesn't belong here."

"Don't tell me you're still upset about Clay?" Balding asks.

Baldy scoffs. "It's my boy's senior year, for Christ's sake, and Coach Baum has him riding the pine."

I turn to Wallace to see if he's hearing any of this, but he's scanning the crowd as if he's looking for someone.

"But we're winning," Balding says. "Can't argue with that. Barbara told me that alumni donations for this quarter are quadruple what they were for all of last year. You think that's a coincidence? Imagine what happens if he takes us all the way. Plus, we have him for two more years."

Have him? That's some foul word choice right there.

Baldy shakes his head. "The school's not what it used to be, that's all I'm saying."

Even though Bunny and I got into it last night, I'm feeling

mighty protective of him right now. When the crowd inches forward, I step on the heel of Baldy's loafers, which probably cost a couple hundred dollars.

"Hey!" he says, pulling his foot away and casting a condescending gaze at me.

"Oops," I say, hands up but a smirk on my face. "My bad."

He makes a sound of disgust and then turns around and says to Baldy in a low voice, "See what I mean?"

I'm about to step on the back of the dude's shoe again when Wallace says, "Yo, I've got some business to attend to. Wait for me."

Before I can protest, he slips away. I glance around, spot Bunny's mom and dad holding hands with the twins as they chat up some other parent. I know Bunny must be happy about his dad being here, since he's usually working. I'm not trying to have another awkward-ass conversation with the entire Thompson family like I did the other night, though, so I move to rejoin the exodus to wait for Wallace outside.

But a girl's voice behind me calls my name a couple times. I turn to spot Keyona standing outside the flow of humanity. Soon as our eyes meet, I know she wants to talk, so I make my way over like I'm swimming to shore.

"Are you sticking around to say hi to Bunny?" she asks when I reach her.

"Wasn't planning on it," I answer.

"Oh. How are you getting home?"

"Wallace," I say, glancing in his direction. He's chatting with some group of white kids over by the bleachers.

Right then, the door to the home locker room on the other side of the gym bursts open and players start coming out in their street clothes. Bunny's, like, the sixth or seventh guy out, and you can feel the energy in the place shift soon as people notice. A fair number start to make their way over to him. A few pull out their phones to snap pictures. There's even a couple kids holding permanent markers and that issue of *ESPN* magazine that he was in. It's a blond cheerleader that reaches him first, though, and she practically jumps into his arms. I peek over at Keyona to spot a flash of dismay on her face before she regains her composure. After the cheerleader withdraws her tentacles from his body, he's swallowed by a crowd of admirers slapping him on the back and congratulating him on the win.

Bunny makes eye contact with us and shrugs like he's some benevolent king obligated to fulfill unpleasant duties. I'm hoping to dip before he comes over here, but when I look over to Wallace, he's still deep in conversation with those random kids.

"So," Keyona says. "Heard you went to Bunny's yesterday."

I nod. Figured he'd tell her all about that.

"And your mom made you?"

"She made me go to the game," I say. "Not his house."

"So why'd you go to his house?"

I shrug.

A reporter and her cameraman cut through the crowd. They train the camera on Bunny, and then kick on a small spotlight on his face, washing out his dark skin. The reporter then slides in next to him and holds up a mic.

"Well, I'm glad you did," Keyona says. "Even if you guys got into it." She gestures with her chin at the crowd. "All of this is getting a little crazy for him, and it's only going to get crazier come June fifteenth."

"Yeah, I know."

"He needs a friend again. A *real* friend, Nas."

"Looks to me like he's got plenty."

"It's not the same," she says.

Bunny says something into the mic that I can't hear. Everyone around him laughs, especially the blond cheerleader that had given him that big hug. But Bunny himself isn't smiling.

"He's got you," I say. It hurts my heart to acknowledge that out loud, but letting this crush go feels kind of nice. Like releasing a balloon and watching it float up into the atmosphere.

"I can't be everything to him," she says.

I know she's right. And it's not like I don't want to squash this beef between Bunny and me. Not only because my patience with my moody cousin is wearing thin, but because I want my friend back. Only there's something in me that can't admit that out loud. Something that feels like he hurt me so I need to make him hurt back. Never mind that I know that logic doesn't lead to a good place.

A few moments later, Bunny manages to escape from

his fan club and starts walking toward us. I move to go, but Keyona puts her hand on my forearm. "Stay," she says.

I sigh and do as she says. Bunny reaches us a few moments later. He gives me dap that turns out real awkward again—this time because he goes in with the closed fist and I go in with the open hand—and then he wraps his arms around Keyona.

"Great game," she says, kissing him on the lips, like, two feet away from my face.

I nod toward the departing reporter. "Can't wait to catch the highlights on ESPN."

Bunny looks down. "Just local news, man."

"So Washington High on Tuesday. You ready? You know the public schools go harder than those cushy private schools on your side of the bracket."

"Yeah, I think so."

"They have that guard headed to Georgetown, right? With that nice shot?"

Bunny nods. "Miles Beasley. I played summer ball with him."

"You have a plan for stopping him?" I ask.

"Of course he does, Nas," Keyona says. "But if he told you, he'd have to kill you."

It's a corny joke, but we all laugh, because we're looking for an excuse to. Except something happens and our laughter turns real, and for a moment, things start feeling right.

But before it feels too right, someone grips my arm again.

This time it's Wallace. "Time to roll, cuz," he says. "We've got to get back to Whitman—this place is making my skin lighter by the second."

"You're already light-skinned," I remind him.

"Exactly."

Bunny laughs, and Wallace's eyes dart to him like he just noticed Bunny's standing there.

"What's good, Wallace?" Bunny says, and holds out his fist for a bump.

Wallace looks at it for a moment and then turns to me. "I'll be in Nisha." Then he walks away.

"What's up with him?" Keyona asks after he's out of earshot.

"He's going through some personal stuff."

"You said that yesterday," Bunny says. "Anything we can do?"

I shake my head because I don't even know what I can do. Then I stand there for a moment, considering whether I should go after Wallace or ask Bunny and Keyona if I can catch a ride back to Whitman with them. In the end, my pity for my cousin wins out. I say a quick goodbye to Bunny and Keyona and then hustle through the crowd and out of the school because I wouldn't put it past him to abandon me here. Thankfully, his car's still sitting in the lot. I pull open the door and slide into the passenger seat.

"About time," he says, and turns the key in the ignition.

It clicks and clicks, but it doesn't start.

"Shit," Wallace says. He tries again a few times to the same effect. "Like I need this fucking shit right now."

He pulls the lever to pop the hood and then steps out of the car, leaving his door open. "Throw me the tire iron," he says. "It's probably the starter."

I look around my feet. "Where?"

"Glove box, I think," he says, then pulls the hood up all the way, propping it open with the little rod that swings out.

I open the glove compartment and immediately spot a bit of metal peeking out from underneath some papers. I push them aside and then—

I freeze.

My heart skips a beat, because it's not a tire iron.

It's a gun.

Part of me wants to pull it out to see if it's real. Could be one of those airsoft guns. But are those made of metal? Even though my dad was in the military, my parents never let me have any type of toy gun—yet even I know this isn't a toy.

I don't touch it. I'm not about to put my prints on a weapon. I cover it back up with the papers I had moved aside and then click the glove compartment closed. Forget the tire iron.

"It's not in there," I say, my voice as shaky as my hands. I sit on them.

"Sure?"

"Yeah."

He goes around the rear of the car and pops the trunk.

"Fuck. You're right. Here it is." He walks back to the front and starts hitting some part of the car's engine or something over and over again with the tire iron. The clanging of metal striking metal rings out across the parking lot. After some time, the tapping stops. Wallace tosses the tire iron into the back seat and slides back in behind the wheel. He turns the key, and this time the engine turns.

"Guess Nisha just needed some sense knocked into her."

"Not cool," I say.

"I was joking, man. Chill."

I consider pressing him on this, but right now there's something else we need to talk about. "What's going on, Wallace?"

"What do you mean, what's going on?" He looks me up and down. "Why are you sitting on your hands? You that desperate for some action?"

"I'm not playing, man."

He glances at the glove compartment and then back to me. I see him work it out, and then he smirks. He throws the car in gear and pulls out into the street. "You found my piece, huh?"

I'm quiet for a moment, trying to work out the right way to handle this. I decide to be direct: "Why do you have a gun, Wallace?"

"Why's anybody ever got a gun? For protection, Nas."

"Why do you need protection?"

He doesn't answer right away. Instead, he opens the center console with one hand while steering with the other and digs out a pack of smokes. He taps the bottom of the pack against the steering wheel four times, pulls a cigarette out, and sticks it in his mouth. He doesn't light it yet. "You really want to know?"

I'm not sure I do, but I nod.

He drops the pack back into the console and pulls out a lighter. He cracks the window, which lets in a rush of cold air, and then lights the cigarette. "I've made a few bad bets."

"On the Sixers?"

He shakes his head.

I think for a moment, and it hits me. "High school ball?"

He nods.

Then I remember the other day when he wanted to go to Bunny's game. The rear door in Justin's bodega that he disappeared through. That dude clocking him in the backyard at that party. "You've been betting against St. S, haven't you? With a bunch of different people. Not just a few."

"Man, with all the hype he's got around him, the odds are unbelievable. All it would take is for Bunny to have one bad night — only one — and I'd walk away with enough to help G make rent for at least a few more months."

I shake my head. "And then what?"

He turns left at the next light. "And then I'd figure out something else."

"But Bunny hasn't had a bad night," I say. "So you've been losing all these bets?"

He takes another drag. "Yup."

I clench my jaw. I don't know what to say, because I'm so

floored by Wallace's stupidity. He and his grandma are about to get evicted, and here he is plunging himself deeper into debt. And I'm guessing if these guys are the kind of gamblers betting on goddamn high school basketball games, they're probably not the most forgiving types.

Wallace flicks his cigarette out the window even though he lit it not too long ago. "Look, a couple of weeks ago, when I first told you about me and G's situation, you said you wanted to help. You remember that?"

"Yeah," I say. "I do."

He steers the car onto the highway and then shifts to a higher gear. As we speed up, the wind rushing through the cracked window gets loud enough that he finally rolls it up. Then it's quiet in that way when there's a lot of noise and then suddenly there isn't.

"You really mean that?" he asks. "Or were you saying it to say it, like how everyone else always does?"

"Of course I really want to help, Wallace."

"Then help me win one of these bets."

"How am I supposed to do that?" I ask.

"Make it so Bunny's not a factor."

My eyes flick to the glove compartment, and my stomach drops.

Wallace glances at me and notices the look on my face. He bursts out in laughter. "Nah, man. I'm not talking about shooting him. What do you think I am?"

I exhale. "Damn, Wallace. Did you have to phrase it that way?"

"Sorry, cuz. I didn't grow up in a bookstore. What I meant was, I want to catch him on some recruiting violation so he can't play anymore."

"What do you know about recruiting violations?"

"Man, I read the NJSIAA and the NCAA rulebooks online. With all those regulations, there's no way St. S got him to up and transfer out of Whitman all of a sudden without doing something shady."

I scratch the back of my head. "I don't know. That could get real serious. Might get him banned from ever playing in the NCAA. Then what?"

"Nah," he says. "We won't get him on anything that deep. I promise. Just something that might end up with him sitting a game or two so I can turn things in my favor." Wallace waits for an answer, and when I don't give it, he goes on. "I found an article where something like this happened. School got caught paying off a credit card bill for their star player's mom. Guess they found some text where the mom was bragging to her friend about how her kid was so good that his new school hooked them up like that."

"Damn. What happened to him?" I ask, part of me wondering if Wallace is fabricating this story on the spot.

"Had to sit for the rest of the season. That's it. The state was mostly mad at the school for taking advantage of the kid."

"So what'd they do to the school?"

"Nothing," he says, laughing. "Just issued a strongly worded statement."

I turn it over in my mind. The season's almost over anyway, so if they punish Bunny, I guess it wouldn't be that big a deal. Not like he's a senior. "So what do you expect me to do?"

"Be my inside man," he says. "Find something I can leak."

"But we're not tight like that anymore."

"So get tight again."

I shake my head in disbelief. I knew he was desperate, but I can't believe this. Anger starts to rise up in me right alongside fear of what might happen to my cousin if he keeps making stupid bets and St. S goes all the way. I want to reach over and smack him. "This is a whole new level of dumb, Wallace."

I expect him to throw some insult back at me, but instead he gets real quiet. The tires hum on the roadway. The wind rushes past the windows. Finally he says, "What the fuck am I supposed to do, Nas? Let them push G out of the place she's lived in for the last twenty-seven years? Be happy about living in my car or sleeping on the streets?"

I almost let this slide, but Keyona's voice is still in my head. "You could have gotten a job. I tried to help you find one."

"Doing what—flipping burgers? That's not about to pay any real bills, man, and you know that."

"Stop making excuses, Wallace. Own this. Accept some responsibility for once."

I look to him for a response, but he's gazing at the road ahead.

"If it came down to it," I say, "my parents would let you stay with us. I know they would."

"That's real nice you believe that, but I don't. They hate me. Same as everyone else who knows me. I'm a straight fuckup, and they're afraid I'm turning you into one, too. I see it in their eyes every time I'm at your place—tell me I'm wrong."

I don't say anything, because he's not.

In fact, neither of us says anything for the next few miles. When we exit off the highway back into Whitman, I'm still roiling with anger that Wallace was dumb enough to get himself into this mess and because of what I'm about to say next—especially since Bunny and I were starting to smooth things over. At the end of the day, though, he'll be all right. He's got the world looking out for him. I'm the only one in Wallace's corner.

"I'll find something you can use," I say, gazing out my window and watching the city lights slide past.

25

BUNNY

I t's Monday, the day before the first round of the Tournament of Champions, and practice is about over. Each squad's at a hoop, taking turns at the line. I'm with Eric, Drew, and the other starters. Each time someone sinks a free throw, the rest of us call out our group total, clap once, and get the ball back to the shooter. He stays on the line until he misses, and we stay on the court until we drop a hundred combined.

Eric's up now, and he's made a bunch in a row, so we're almost done. He hits one more, and the five of us call out, "Ninety-four," then clap. Drew grabs the rebound and bounces it lazily back to Eric, and he lines up his next shot.

Nobody talks or plays around during this routine. It's kind of relaxing, like we're meditating. The repetition, the count, the simple goal. When you're on the line, that's how it is. Time stops, and it's all on you. You take a deep breath, go through the same motions as always, and hope it goes in.

Eric sinks another one.

"Ninety-five."

Clap.

Tonight, though, there's an extra quiet beneath the normal quiet. Nerves, I guess. This is the first year in a few St. Sebastian's has made it this far, so most of them are new to the playoff pressure. Plus, most of the guys are seniors, so this is their last shot. Nobody says it, but I bet all of them are thinking about how this could be their final practice.

"Ninety-six."

Clap.

But my own thoughts aren't on the game. Instead, Nas's words keep bouncing around my brain.

You're looking out for yourself so hard you forget that everyone else exists. So it's nothing to you to just leave us behind.

I tell myself over and over again that he's wrong. I'm doing this for my family. So my mom doesn't have to work herself to death. So my sisters can be whatever they want and not have to worry about student loans hanging over their heads forever. So my dad's bookstore doesn't close its doors.

"Ninety-seven."

Clap.

Nas will be all right. He's smart enough. He'll get into a decent college and won't have to worry about tuition, thanks to Uncle Sam. When we were kids, he always used to talk about wanting to become a doctor, and I don't know if that's still what he's all about, but it's not hard visualizing him in one of those white coats with a stethoscope draped around his neck.

I know Keyona will be all right, too. She's at the top of our class and right on track to become a scientist like she's always wanted. Wants to cure cancer, since it took her mom when Keyona was little.

Eric's next shot clangs against the front of the rim. We rotate, and it's my turn on the line. Drew grabs the rebound and rolls the ball my way.

I pick it up, spin it in my hands as I set my feet at the line.

Nasir was right that things weren't too bad for me at Whitman. I was pulling decent enough grades, and our squad had potential.

But after last season, all these people started putting the idea of transferring in my ear, the idea that I could do better. Mostly they'd catch me before or after an AAU game, when I was by myself. Usually they'd hint at what I'd get if I played for them, but some of them straight up said it. Gear. Exposure. Scholarships.

One of them, from a school up north, implied that they had a house ready for my family to move into.

I dribble hard once and put up the shot. It slips through the net with a sweet *swoosh*.

"Ninety-eight."

Clap.

Rebound.

I ignored all that noise—at least until Coach Baum came up and spoke to me while I was in DC for nationals. Maybe it's because he wasn't trying to do anything extra, anything that seemed too wrong. He kept it simple and honest. Said I wouldn't pay a dime because the school would hook me up between a need-based grant and a sponsor willing to cover the rest—which he assured me was legal—but that he wasn't going to offer me the world like everyone else probably was, just the chance to be part of one of the nation's best high school basketball programs and access to the world-class academics the school was known for. Plus, unlike most of the other schools, I could get to St. S by public transportation and wouldn't need to move out of Whitman.

"Ninety-nine."

Clap.

Rebound.

Throughout that week, I kept thinking about it. St. S regularly sends players to Kentucky, Duke, UNC, UCLA, and powerhouses like that. Even some to colleges with weaker programs but amazing academics like Harvard or Stanford. So the more I thought about it, the more it felt like when you hear the train rumbling through the tunnel but you're just starting down the steps. You've either got to run and catch it, or let the doors close on you and watch it pull away from the platform. I caught that train—told Coach Baum before I left DC that I was down.

I spin the ball in my hands, set my feet again.

Was it the right call? I don't know.

I dribble once and shoot. Everyone's hands are getting ready to clap since I rarely miss from the line, but the ball circles the rim and pops out. There's a moment of hesitation and then everyone rotates, Drew taking my place at the line.

I don't think Whitman High is as bad as people usually assume it is. When I was there, I liked most of my teachers, and most of them always made sure we learned about Black folks in whatever subject we studied—something St. S only does in February. But every year the newspapers would put out some article about the low test scores, and those people talking to me about transferring made it clear that the best colleges wouldn't be impressed by decent grades at a school with that reputation.

But there's not a single teacher at St. S with my skin color. They all look surprised when I say something thoughtful in a class discussion or quote a line from a reading assignment in English without looking at the page. And they say "your parents" to everyone else but "your mom" to me.

Problem is, even if I wanted to switch back, I don't think the students at Whitman High would welcome me with open arms.

Then again, who knows? Nasir texted this morning, apologizing for what he said the other night, and asked if I wanted to meet at Word Up after dinner. I've been looking forward to that all day long.

And then I get an idea. I glance at Coach.

Drew sinks number one hundred, and we shoot around until the other groups finish and Coach Baum calls us in. We huddle up, arms draped around each other's shoulders. Coach looks us in the eye one by one and gives a short speech about how this week's outcome is going to depend on how well we work together.

"Together," he repeats.

The team heads to the locker room, but I hang back.

"Coach," I say, "can we talk?"

26

NASIR

When I walk into Word Up, Billie Holiday's playing over the speakers and the store is as warm and as book-scented as always. Bunny's sitting at one of the café tables reading, Mr. Thompson's behind the register, and an old woman is on one of the couches tapping away at her smartphone. Besides these three souls, the place is dead. I don't even see Zaire's cat.

I say hello to Mr. Thompson as I walk over to Bunny. He marks his page, sets his book face-down, and stands up. We shake like a couple of oldheads, and then he gestures to the seat on the other side of the small table. "Have a seat, man."

"What are you reading?" I ask.

He flips it over, and I check out the cover. *The Book of Light* by Lucille Clifton. I nod like I think it's a great choice, even though I've never heard of it before.

I start having second thoughts about all this, and I'm a moment away from making an excuse and ducking out when that old woman on the couch suddenly lets out a string of curse words. Bunny and I turn to look and she's pulling that universal face everyone makes when they've lost a game.

Then Bunny and I turn back to each other and get a case of the church giggles—you know, when you're laughing at something that's not that funny and you can't stop. It's a few moments before we catch our breath, and I spot Mr. Thompson smiling out of the corner of my eye. If he knew why I was really here, though, he'd be kicking me out.

"You want to go up to the roof?" Bunny asks.

"Sure," I say.

So we get up and go out the back door, leaving behind the warmth and Billie Holiday's beautifully unsteady voice for the cold and the quiet. We start climbing the fire escape, and it's not long before Bunny stops ahead of me and points at the window to the second-floor apartment where Zaire lives above the store. We start laughing all over again, because dude's lying on his couch in his boxers watching TV in the dark with his old cat chilling on his stomach. I push Bunny to keep him moving before Zaire hears us snickering out here.

When we get up to the roof, two things hit me right away: the view and the wind. Shivering, I zip my coat all the way, pull up my hood, and bury my hands in my pockets. Then I wander over the flat surface to the edge that faces west and take it all in. It's been a minute since I've come by the store, but it's been even longer since we came up here. The stars are almost all washed out by the light pollution, but the Ben Franklin Bridge is lit up blue over the Delaware River, and Philly's glimmering orange and white on the other side. But all of that's the same as I remember. It's the area right around the store here in downtown Whitman that I barely recognize, with the new development reminding me about Wallace's situation and why I'm here.

Bunny stands next to me, overlooking the city, silent. After a bit, he says, "Borders are kind of weird, huh?"

I shrug. "I guess."

He goes on. "We're in Jersey right here in Whitman, but if we cross the river, we're suddenly in Pennsylvania."

"And?"

"And that's strange to me. Whitman feels more like Philly than it does like any of the other towns around us. But it's not. Almost like someone drew the lines wrong."

I think about this for a couple beats. "You high?"

He lets out a small laugh and shakes his head. "Just something I find myself thinking about lately, is all. Sorry."

"Look," I say. "I wanted to meet up to tell you I'm sorry. About the other night. I was out of line."

"You already apologized."

"I wanted to do it in person," I say. "Seems like it means more." Though I don't really mean it at all.

He takes a deep breath. "Appreciate that, Nas. But maybe you were right about some stuff."

"Like what?" I ask, hating him for acting so cool about this.

"Like how I don't belong there."

I nod. "So come back to Whitman."

He takes another deep breath. Looks down at his feet. "Maybe there's another solution."

"Like what?"

"Maybe"—he pauses, then raises his eyes to me— "maybe you could transfer to St. Sebastian's?"

I hold his gaze for a moment, and then I turn away and bust out, sending my laughter out over the rooftops.

"I'm serious, Nas," he says.

"Yeah," I say, no longer laughing. "And while I'm at it, I'll get my parents to buy me a Maserati, I'll put a down payment on a penthouse in one of those Philly high-rises, and then I'll book my flight to Europe for spring break. What do you think, Bunny: Paris or Venice?"

Bunny shakes his head. "Hear me out, man. I'm being real. It's not impossible."

"You sure about that?" I look away. "How are you even affording to go there? The bookstore doesn't look like it's do- ing so hot."

"A combination of a grant and a sponsor."

"What's a sponsor?" I ask.

"Some oldhead who helps me out by covering what my grant doesn't."

"Huh. That legal?"

He nods.

I make a mental note to do my own research later. "Well, unless they're about to throw any of that to a second-string point guard with a B-plus average, let's go ahead and file this idea under 'Impossible.'"

Bunny walks a little closer to the edge and peers down at the alleyway below. "If you could, would you?"

I clench my jaw and grind my teeth a little as I think about how to even begin to answer that question. "There's no point in even thinking about that," I finally say.

Then he says, "I talked to my coach. Told him how out of place I felt this year, and that I've been thinking about transferring back to Whitman."

"Have you?" I ask.

He shrugs again.

"What'd he say?"

"Got real nervous. Asked what they could do to make me feel more at home. So I asked him if he could—"

"Get me in," I finish.

Bunny looks at me. "Coach said he could make it happen, Nas."

"For real?"

"For real."

"Damn," I say, because I don't know what else to say. "Damn," I add a moment later, because the right words still fail to come to mind. I was mad Bunny left me behind, and now he's offering to take me with him—literally. I look out over the city in the direction of Wallace's place.

"You probably didn't expect this," he says.

"Understatement of the year."

"But you don't need to make a decision now." He runs a hand over the top of his head and exhales. "Think on it. Talk to your parents, and know the offer stands. Know it's possible."

"Cool," I say flatly. And I can tell by his face that he's

taken aback I'm not acting all happy and grateful about this news. Instead, I'm trying to hold in my anger at the fact that Bunny thinks he can wave his magic basketball wand and fix everything. But this doesn't make me forget about how he jumped at the chance to leave soon as he could. Who's to say he wouldn't abandon me again?

He looks away. "You should come by the school. Check it out before you make up your mind."

"Sure," I say. Even though I really don't want to, I need to find out something Wallace can use.

"Cool," he says, nodding. "How about tomorrow? It's a home game, so you can hang afterward, and I can show you around."

"Sure. Yeah. But, man, it's getting pretty damned cold up here," I say, turning away. "I'm headed back inside."

So I do, and Bunny follows me down.

27
BUNNY

fter Nas walks out and the door swings shut, my dad looks up from his computer screen behind the register. "What was that all about?"

I shrug. "Trying to figure things out."

"You two friends again?"

"We're getting there, I think." And I feel good when I say those words.

"Good," my dad says, and then laughs. "He used to be one of my best customers."

I wonder what was going on in Nasir's head up on that rooftop. I knew he wouldn't say yes to transferring right away. I mean, I didn't when Coach Baum first approached me. But still, Nasir didn't say a whole lot or ask many questions.

But I laugh at my dad's corny joke and slip the Clifton book back into its place on the shelf. I grab my bags and am about to head back home when my dad clears his throat. "Can I talk to you about something while I've got you, Bunny?"

By the tone of his voice, I know whatever it is must be serious.

"Sure," I say, then wander over and lean on the counter across from him. The counter's surface in front of the register's usually filled with little stacks of flyers advertising all kinds of upcoming events at the store. Poetry readings. Hip-hop shows. Community meetings. Stuff like that. But right now the space is clear.

I wait for him to speak, but instead he slips off his glasses and cleans the lenses with the hem of his shirt. He puts them back on, sits up on his stool, and crosses his arms over his chest.

"As I'm sure you know," he says, "business has been slow lately."

No, don't say it, I think, because I know exactly where this is going.

"Well, not just lately, but for the last couple of years."

No. Don't.

"We've been losing more than we've been making."

No.

He takes a deep breath and exhales slowly. Then he says it: "Someone's made an offer on our building. A generous offer."

"And?"

"And Zaire and I are going to sell."

My heart sinks into my stomach. I drop my bags and lean against the back of the couch near the counter. I feel like I got the wind knocked out of me. "Come on, Dad—you can't. Don't."

"I know you love the store, Bunny, but nobody loves it as much as I do. Not even Zaire, I think, and we started it together." He looks around. Billie Holiday's still playing softly. "So you need to trust me when I say it's really not feasible anymore. We've been running on fumes for a long time."

"Maybe you could—" I start to say, but he cuts me off.

"Zaire and I have thought through all the scenarios, Bunny. Trust me."

I shake my head. "The community needs this place."

"It used to," he says. "But not anymore. Things change."

Forget change. Switching schools this year was all the change I needed. "Who's buying it?"

"Some developer."

"They keeping it a bookstore?"

He looks at the shelves. "Once we sell, we don't have any say in what they do with it."

"What are you going to do?" I ask. "For work, I mean?"

He shakes his head. "Not sure. I'll find something, though. Don't worry about that. I'm not as young and beautiful as I used to be, but I think I'm a lot smarter now." He lets out a small laugh, and so do I. Not because it's that funny, but because both of us need it.

"Mom knows?"

"Of course," he answers. "She was heartbroken. After all, this is where we met . . . but she understands. This will help cover some bills for a while, and we'll be able to take care of most of Jess's student loans so they're not following her around the rest of her life."

He doesn't say anything about setting aside some to pay my future tuition because we both know what's expected of me.

"Zaire have to move?" I ask instead, thinking about him upstairs asleep in front of his TV with Damba on top of his stomach.

He nods. "He's got some money saved up. He'll be fine."

"Damn," I say.

"Yup."

Then we just stand there for a few moments. The album that he's got playing over the store's speakers ends, and silence fills all the empty spaces around us.

"Sorry to tell you this now," he says. "I wanted to wait until after the season, so you didn't have to stress about it. But it looks like the sale might be moving forward pretty soon, and I wanted to give you the heads-up."

"How soon?" I ask.

"The contract's getting drawn up now. Maybe a month or two."

"Damn," I say again, looking around the place.

"Yup," he says again.

"I'm sorry, Dad."

He laughs. "It's not your fault, Bunny."

"I feel like you told me someone's dying," I say. "Is that how you feel?"

"Feels like part of me is dying," he says. Then he claps me on the shoulder, changes his tone. "You eat yet?"

"Nah," I say. "Came straight here after practice to meet up with Nasir."

"What do you say I close early and we grab a bite at the Vietnamese place down the street?"

My dad never closes early, so I know this is really happening. "They still in business?" I ask, only half joking.

"For now."

We laugh. Again, not because it's funny, but because sometimes that's the only way not to cry.

28

NASIR

t's Tuesday night, and St. S just tore up Washington High, 72–51. The Washington players hang their heads and make a beeline for their locker room soon as the clock runs down. Their fans gather their things, faces looking like they ate something sour, while the St. Sebastian's crowd is all wide smiles and high-fives.

As the bleachers empty out, I look at Wallace sitting on the opposite side of the gym over in Washington's section, face buried in his hands. I came to the game with the Thompsons and sat with them, but I've been watching Wallace over there rooting for Bunny's opponents the entire time. I'm guessing he was stupid enough to bet against St. S again.

Of course, this means he's in even deeper trouble.

Since I know it will be a while before Bunny comes out to show me around the school, I make my way over to Wallace. He looks up when I start stomping up the bleachers.

"Oh, now you want to come over?" he asks.

"It was too packed in here, man."

"Yeah, okay. Well I saw you over there with Bunny's

family." He stands up and walks down to the court. "They adopt you yet?"

I follow after him. "That's not fair, man. You're the one who wanted me to get close to him again."

He stops near midcourt out of bounds and turns on me. "And how's that going, cuz?"

"It's only been a couple days."

"So you haven't found out anything yet?"

I don't want to tell him about Bunny asking me to transfer, and I'm not entirely sure why that is. But I feel the need to tell him something, so I check to make sure nobody's too close and lower my voice. "I thought I had him on this thing where some 'sponsor' is covering part of his tuition and school fees. But I looked it up, and apparently, it's legit."

"You try his email yet? His phone?"

"For what?" I ask.

"What do you think? Something shady, man."

I shake my head. "These people know the rules, Wallace. And they know how to get around them. There's stuff going on all the time according to Bunny, but he also said nobody puts anything in writing."

"So you haven't checked?"

I hesitate. "No."

"If you don't want to do it, at least find out his password. Or get me his phone, laptop, whatever. I'll look myself." Then he turns away. "Just do it quick. There's only two games left."

"I'll try."

"Yeah, okay. I'm out now. You need a ride?"

I shake my head, look away. "I'm going to hang with Bunny for a bit."

"Good idea." He puts a hand on my shoulder, and his tone softens. "I know this isn't easy for you, Nas, and I know I can be a dickhead some of the time—okay, a lot of the time—but I appreciate you trying to help out me and G. Nobody else is." He chops the air with his other hand to emphasize his point. "Nobody. It means a lot is all I'm trying to say."

I know he's only trying to strengthen my resolve, but it still feels nice to hear him acknowledge that. "It's cool, Wallace. You'd do the same for me."

"You're a good cousin," he says. "A good friend."

I don't say anything to that.

We say goodbye and go our separate ways. A moment later, the players start coming out of the locker room. Like last time, Bunny gets mobbed by a group of adoring fans and local media. I sit in one of the chairs set up on the visitors' side and gaze at the league, group, and state championship banners for all the different sports that hang on the gym walls, everything from football to water polo. I get sick of looking at them pretty quickly and pull out my phone as I continue waiting.

Eventually, Bunny frees himself from his subjects and makes his way over.

"You ready for the grand tour?" he asks.

I put my phone away, stand, and stretch a bit. "I guess. Just let me say thanks to your mom for driving me."

I do, and then Bunny leads me to a door on the opposite

side of the gym that opens onto one of the hallways. Each classroom we pass makes me angrier and angrier at St. Sebastian's. I mean, damn. The outside is this hundred-year-old stone building, but the inside is completely renovated. Everything is so neat and clean and new. Perfect corners. Unmarred walls. Flat-screen TVs mounted everywhere. Floors look like they're waxed every day. And even though it's night right now, I can imagine how during the day the natural light probably pours through the tall windows that line the hallways and classrooms.

If this school were a kid, it'd be one of those kids so spoiled you want to punch him in the face to toughen him up a little bit.

"We're almost there," Bunny says, a few steps ahead of me.

"Where?" I ask. But he doesn't answer.

We walk past a door that says POOL 1. The next door says POOL 2.

Sweet Jesus.

We turn a corner. Neither of us says anything for a while, but then Bunny finally speaks, not bothering to turn around.

"Sorry about Keyona. I know you had a thing for her."

"Ain't no thang, chicken wing," I say, trying to turn it into a joke. But Bunny doesn't laugh.

"It's not like I went after her or anything," he says, still walking ahead of me. "I was pretty miserable here right from the jump. All the guys were mad at me for stealing this kid Clay's starting spot. Real popular senior. And back home, nobody wanted anything to do with me anymore." He pauses, maybe to make me feel guilty, and then adds, "Keyona was one of the only ones who still treated me like nothing changed."

"Sounds like a strong foundation for a relationship," I say, all sarcastic. Because, what? I'm supposed to feel sad for Bunny Thompson, Rising Star?

He leads us through the cafeteria, which looks like the food court at the rich mall, and then through a set of double doors. The lights come up automatically.

And damn.

This library.

Like everything else, it's all open spaces, high ceilings, and windows. The circulation desk sits in the middle of the room like a command center, surrounded by shelves and shelves of neatly arranged books. There are couches, tables, study carrels, plants, computers, and an aquarium.

There's also a spiral staircase leading to a second floor.

"What's up there?" I ask. "God?"

Bunny laughs more than I think he's going to, and I end up laughing because he is, and for a moment it's almost like it used to be, but only for a moment, and then I go back to thinking about how unfair it is that some kids get all of this.

"Nah," he says. "Study rooms."

I stroll away from Bunny and start perusing the shelves. Most every book at Whitman's library looks like it's been there for at least a century, pages all dog-eared and bindings barely held together with layers of yellowing tape. Each one decorated with at least one penis drawing somewhere within its pages.

Bunny comes up beside me, smiling like some little kid showing you something he made. "So what do you think?"

"It's no Word Up," I say. I notice Bunny's face change, like I said something wrong. I'm not sure what it is, so I add, "But it's all right," just to say something. I start walking my fingers across a row of books in the fiction section, ticking off the names of all the "classic" writers. But I don't come across any Black writers until I notice they're segregated over in the African American Literature section. I wander over there and slide out *Invisible Man* by Ralph Ellison. I've always wanted to read this one, but I haven't gotten around to it. I crack it open, and the spine creaks. It has that fresh paper and ink smell, like I'm the first person in its pages.

"You can take it with you," Bunny says.

"Yeah, right," I say.

"For real." Bunny turns on a machine behind the desk and pulls his student ID from his wallet. He scans the book with this barcode reader once the machine's powered up, and then he scans his card. "There you go."

"Umm . . . okay. Thanks, I guess. But wouldn't you rather me buy it from the store?"

He turns away without answering and wanders over to the aquarium humming and bubbling in the corner. I join him. It must be a saltwater tank because it looks like a chunk scooped from the Great Barrier Reef. There's coral that looks like rock and coral that looks like brain and coral that looks like a hundred waving fingers of orange velvet. Red, yellow, blue, striped, dotted, transparent fish dart through the water, chasing one another or nothing at all.

"Nice, huh?" Bunny says, waking me from the water's trance.

"Real nice," I agree. "How much is tuition here, anyway? A million or two?"

"It's like thirty," he says, avoiding eye contact.

My eyes widen. "Thirty *thousand?*"

He nods.

"A *year?*"

He nods again.

"Damn," I say, shaking my head in disbelief that you can fill a whole school with kids whose parents have that much money. No wonder it looks like a college campus. I clear my throat. "I bet they hook you up with all kinds of stuff since you're their star player, right?"

He laughs. "Nah, it's not like that."

"You sure?"

"Just the basketball gear. But the school doesn't even pay for that. Nike does."

"So let me get this straight: Nike *gives* shoes to rich kids?"

"In a way," he says. "Remember like we talked about before? It's a business arrangement. An investment, I guess."

I know Bunny's showing me this so I'll seriously consider the opportunity to transfer here, but I can't stop thinking about Wallace. Nobody's offering him any grants. No sponsor's volunteering to pay his tuition. Nike's not hooking him up with gear. It seems backward that so many people want to help those who need it least and ignore those who need it most and then find a way to justify that in their own minds. "I bet."

Bunny leans against one of the bookshelves and slips his hands into his pockets.

I cross my arms over my chest. "So what's it like to actually go here?"

"It's all right." He smooths a hand over the top of his head. "The classes are a lot harder, but it's chill for the most part."

"So what's wrong with it?" I ask, because I can tell he's holding back.

He thinks for a moment like he's either searching for the right words or deciding whether or not he's going to share them with me. "It's weird."

I glance around this nice-ass library. "What's weird?"

"Fitting in," Bunny says.

"From what I see, all the rooms have high ceilings, so it seems to me you'd fit fine."

"Ha. Ha. You know what I mean."

I shrug. "Everyone on the team and in the stands back there seems to love you. You're like their king. I don't see what's so bad about being instantly popular."

He shakes his head. "I'm not a real person to them. I'm not their friend. I'm this kid who's helping their basketball team win. Most days I don't feel like anything more than their mascot."

Bunny walks over to a different section of the library that has a few leather sofas. He drops into one, and so I do the same. He puts his big feet up on the table and stares at his sneakers.

"What about that tall kid?" I ask. "The center? I've noticed you talking to him a few times. Isn't he your friend?"

"I talk to him—and a few other people—but I don't know if I'd call them friends. It's hard. Like, the other day, I was talking to our point, Eric. He's saying how his parents are trying to decide between buying a vacation home that costs a million dollars in Cape Cod or one that costs one-point-three million in Miami. Asked which one I'd buy if I was them."

"You serious?"

"Yeah, man. And it's tough as hell hearing that kind of noise so much. Kids complaining about which European country they have to go to over the summer, or the fact their parents bought them a car but not the one they really wanted. Makes me want to reach over and slap some sense into them sometimes."

We laugh.

He goes on. "Going here's like when you buy new shoes but they're the wrong size. Like, at first it's kind of uncomfortable, and you convince yourself you just need to break them in. But after a while your toes start to hurt, then your whole foot. Pretty soon things ache so bad down there it's all you can think of, but you're trying not to show it because you want to seem like you appreciate those new shoes."

"For real?"

Bunny leans forward, resting his elbows on his knees. "People see me — a Black player from the city — and they automatically got all these stereotypes they want to lay on me before I even open my mouth. Anything I do, anything I say, gets measured against that first. It's like they've always got me under a microscope."

"Yeah, I feel you," I say.

"Nah, you don't," he says. And it surprises me. Bunny's not usually the type to straight up challenge someone like that. Maybe it's because it catches me off-guard that I don't say anything, and he continues. "You might know the feeling every now and then, but I know it almost every single day since transferring here, Nas. Even something as simple as *how* I talk. Never mind *what* I say. If I speak too 'Black,'" — he puts air quotes around the word — "then they're going to put me in some box in their minds, and I'm going to have to fight even harder to work my way out. If I change it up too much and don't speak 'Black' enough, then I feel like I'm being fake."

"Why do you care so much about what they think?" I ask. "Why can't you just be you?"

He laughs. "See — the fact you have to ask that question means you don't really understand how it feels."

"I don't get why you're telling me all this," I say. "This is like the worst recruiting pitch in the history of the world. Seems to me you're making an argument against this place. Why don't you come back to Whitman High?"

He shakes his head. "I don't give up, Nas. If you know

anything about me, you should already know that. It's the main reason I'm as good as I am at basketball." He looks around. "This is a great school, and it's the truth that going here will help get me into the best colleges in the country. And I want the best. I'm not giving up that future just because I feel like I don't belong. Nah, I'm going to carve out a place for myself before I'm through."

Damn. Here I was trying to find out something that might end Bunny's season, and now he's got me feeling sympathetic. I push out of the seat and wander back over to the aquarium. I tap on the glass, trying to get this big red fish's attention.

"Don't do that," Bunny says, still over on the sofa. "It shocks them or something."

I stop tapping the glass. The big fish drifts behind a chunk of coral. "I still don't get why you want me to go here."

"So you can have the best, too."

"Right," I say. "And that's the only reason?"

He gets up and stands next to me so we're both gazing at the water. "You're my crossover."

"What's that supposed to mean?"

"When I've got a tough defender guarding me, I can almost always use my crossover to shake him."

"Right," I say, not feeling too pleased about being compared to what amounts to a tool. "So you think having me here to be miserable alongside you will make it easier?"

He answers my question with a question. "Remember Gabe? And what happened to him?"

I think back on the memorial in Virgilio Square. So much

has happened between Bunny and me, and me and Wallace, since then that I haven't thought about it much lately, which gets me feeling guilty. "Of course."

"Okay, now imagine going to a school every day with hundreds of kids who don't."

"Oh," I say. Then a moment later, "But if you tell someone about him, then they might understand you better."

He shakes his head. "Maybe. But they already think people getting shot is the only thing there is to Whitman, and talking about it will only make them think that even more. Difference between you and them is, yeah, you know about that, but you also know the other side of Whitman."

I nod, thinking about the sledding hill, the community gardens, the block parties and cookouts, Whitman High's purple and gold, Bunny's dad's bookstore, the roof, our friends, families. But I don't know what to say. I gaze at that aquarium like the right words are going to bubble out of the filter.

"But you know what the worst part of all this is?" Bunny asks.

"What?"

"When people from back home treat me like I've forgotten all that. Like I'm the worst kind of person for wanting to put myself in a better position to help my family."

"You mean people like me," I say, staring at that fish that won't look at me and holding myself back from tapping on the glass again.

Bunny doesn't say anything.

"Why not get Keyona to transfer instead?" I ask. "She's been better to you than I have."

"Because it's not the same," Bunny says. "You're like my brother."

I can't even say how much that means to me, so I don't.

"Besides," he adds, "if she started going here and then we broke up, that'd be awkward as hell."

We laugh.

I know I should be prodding for more information about how St. S recruited him exactly, or what kind of gear they're hooking him up with specifically. Maybe try to catch him on video admitting to St. S offering to hook me up to get him to stay. But it's not in me right now. I mean, I still want to help Wallace, but now I kind of want to help Bunny, too.

The thing is, I don't know how to help one without hurting the other.

Bunny and I walk outside to snow. It's nothing heavy, nothing that's going to stick. But it's still the first snow of the season, which is kind of weird, since it's nearly spring. We head toward his sister's car, not saying anything else. We watch the flakes fall, thin and light and melting soon as they hit any surface.

I guess that's the thing. You never know when winter's really over. It can be all sunlight and sprouting grass one day, and then cold and ice the next. Tonight, I can see my breath. The air is cooler and smells like winter clothes held close to the nose. Clouds blot out the stars and the moon. The world is still.

Once we reach the car, Bunny breaks the silence. "So . . . you want to go blazer shopping this weekend?"

I force a smile and look away. "Need some more time to think on it."

"But you're thinking about it?"

"Yeah," I say. "I am."

And this time I mean it.

29
BUNNY

t's Wednesday after practice. Jess needed the car today, so
I'm walking to the bus stop, the temperature still dropping.
I've got my phone pressed to my ear, my angry girlfriend
at the other end of the line.

"Why would you do that?" Keyona says in a tone that
makes me wonder what I said wrong. All I did was tell her
about what was going on with Nasir. Thought she'd be excited about how I found a solution that could fix our friendship while also helping me feel a bit more at home at St. S.
To be honest, I'm not in the mood to fight. My muscles are
tired and sore, and the thing about my dad selling the store is
weighing on me.

"You know why," I say, not without my own touch of attitude. "I don't get why you're mad about it?"

"Because it's stupid, Bunny," she says right away.

"Why's it stupid?" I ask.

"Shall I count the ways?" she says. "One: you could get
in trouble with the state. Maybe even the NCAA. I know you
know you can lose your amateur status doing something like

this. I know you've been good so far with sticking to the rules, so why break them now? What if this gets out?"

I shrug, even though she can't see me. "It's not going to. It's not written down anywhere. And Coach said so long as Nas goes through the application process like everyone else, they can make it look legit. Nobody would be able to prove that they let him in for me. The only other person who would know that would be Nas, and why would he ever say anything?"

"You don't think it's weird he started coming around again soon as playoffs rolled around?"

"What's that supposed to mean?"

"It means you never know with people," she says.

"I know Nas," I say.

"The more success you have, Bunny, the more people are going try to get something out of you. I'm just saying that you should keep that in mind."

None of this makes sense to me, and I feel like my head's about to explode. "Let me see if I understand this. You're the one that's been going on and on about how we needed to squash that beef between us, and now that we did, you're mad at me for it, and you're calling him fake?"

"Oh, everything's cool now, is it?"

"Yeah," I say, getting loud. "It is."

"He ever apologize?" she asks.

I switch the phone to my other ear. "Of course."

"Really? He apologized for not speaking to you for more than half a year? Because if he did, you must have forgotten to tell me about it."

I don't answer right away, because she's got a point. He apologized for the argument we got into when he dropped by my house, but he never said sorry for turning his back on me. But because we're in the middle of a fight, my pride prevents me from straight up admitting she's right. Instead I say, "I'm the one who did him wrong. I transferred. I left him behind. Not the other way around."

"All you did was switch schools, Bunny. You didn't cut him out of your life. You were the one texting him and knocking on his door. He was the one who was refusing to answer."

I don't want to talk about Nasir anymore, so I ask, "What's the other reason I'm dumb?"

"Huh?"

"You said that was number one."

"Oh," she says. Then she hesitates, like she's trying to decide whether to keep going. When she speaks again, her voice is soft and low. "Why didn't you ask your coach to get me in?"

It's the same question Nasir asked. But it was easier to give him an answer because I knew he'd understand. I don't know if Keyona will. "I don't know," I end up saying like some fool.

"Oh," she says, that single syllable sinking on the line between us like a rock in water.

"I'm sorry," I say. "But maybe—"

"I have to go," she interrupts. "Bye."

"Wait, Keyona," I say, but the only response I get is the beep letting me know she ended the call.

30

NASIR

t's Wednesday night. I'm with Wallace in his sad, little-old-person-smelling, soon-to-be-evicted-from apartment watching *Sesame Street*. I can't say why, exactly. He texted me saying that he was feeling down and needed to hang with someone, so I said okay even though I have homework to do. He came by a few minutes later, picked me up, and drove us over to his place, me spending the entire ride trying not to think about that glove compartment. Now we're sitting here on the raggedy couch where he sleeps, Wallace nodding his head like he's really learning a lot about the letter *F* from Grover right now.

Bunny the kitten appears and starts prowling and purring around my legs, looking a lot healthier after about a week with Wallace. She eventually hops onto the couch and settles into his lap, and he strokes her head.

After a while, Wallace breaks the silence. "Don't suppose you found anything yet." He keeps his eyes on the puppets.

I should have known that was what he wanted to talk about. His eviction's coming up, and what with the semifinals tomorrow night and then the championship on Sunday, he's running out of time.

"Nah," I say. "Sorry."

"You even trying, cuz?" he asks. "I know you've been spending a lot of time with him these last few days. You must have found out something."

"Of course I am, Wallace. But there's nothing."

"So you hacked his phone? His laptop?"

I don't say anything.

He sighs. Looks down at the kitten. "Sorry, little buddy, guess both of us are going to be back on the streets soon."

I see this for what it is—but it still makes me feel bad. Should I tell him about the offer? I looked it up, and that could definitely get Bunny and St. Sebastian's in trouble with the NJSIAA if I had proof. I'm almost about to mention it when I think of another way.

"I'll try to get you his phone," I say. I know he's not going to find anything on it, but maybe this will at least make Wallace feel like I'm doing what I can for him. As for his financial problems, I'll ask my parents again if they can lend him and his grandma some money to start renting somewhere else.

Wallace grins. "I appreciate that, cuz. Think you can get it tonight?"

I check the time on my phone. It's almost nine. "It's late, man. Maybe tomorrow."

"Bunny's not going to bed early like G does," he says. "He'll still be awake. I can drive you over there now."

On the TV, Grover's using his weird, garbled voice to run through words that begin with *F.*

Fantastic.

Fancy.

Funny.

I sigh. "Fine."

Wallace scratches Bunny the kitten behind her ears, and she closes her eyes and tilts her head up like it's the best thing in the world.

I stand up to go, but Wallace keeps watching *Sesame Street.* "I want to see how this turns out," he says.

Grover tells us he's about to reveal his favorite *F* word. Wallace goes ahead and guesses exactly what you'd think Wallace would guess. He's wrong.

"Friendship," Grover says in this awestruck whisper.

Grover's friend Kermit comes on, and they start talking about friendship. I don't hear much of what they say, though, because Wallace starts laying down a theory about Cookie Monster being a metaphor for a crackhead even though he's not even in the scene. To be honest, it makes some kind of sense. But I'm not really in the mood.

"Can we get this over with?" I ask. "You're the one who wanted to do it right now."

"Yeah, all right." Wallace says. He clicks off the TV, sets down the cat, and gets up.

As we walk out, Bunny the kitten's meowing like she's sad that we're leaving. It's the last sound I hear before we shut the door behind us, and it gets me thinking about all the stray cats still out in the streets that nobody bothered to pick up.

Famished.

Fearful.

Friendless.

Fucked.

31
BUNNY

After showering, I head downstairs to catch a few minutes of *ESPN News* before bed. Except Jess is set up on the couch, typing away at her laptop with her books spread out around her, watching some cooking competition show.

"Mind if I change the channel?" I ask, picking up the remote from the coffee table.

She keeps typing. "Oh, Nasir decided he didn't want to hang? I thought you guys were cool again."

"Huh?"

"What do you mean, 'huh'?" she asks.

"What are you talking about with Nasir?"

She finally stops typing and cocks her head. "Are you messing with me, Bunny?"

This is, like, the most confusing conversation of all time. "I have no idea what you're talking about, Jess."

"Nasir stopped by while you were in the shower. He said he'd wait, so I let him up to your room. You didn't see him?"

I shake my head.

"Huh," she says. "Guess he must have changed his mind and slipped out while I was working on my paper."

"Weird."

"Yeah. Anyway, you still want to watch something? Give me, like, ten more minutes. I want to see who gets eliminated."

"Nah, that's all right," I say. I head back upstairs to my room, wondering why Nasir would have up and left without saying anything to me. I wasn't in the shower long. Come to think of it, why'd he drop by to begin with, instead of texting about whatever he needed?

I wonder if he made a decision about transferring to St. S and wanted to tell me the news in person. I pick up my gym bag and start digging through for my phone so I can text him to see what's up, but I can't find it. I search every pocket, like, five times. I dump everything out. I go through each item in the bag one by one.

Still no phone.

I search every spot in my room where it might be — on my dresser, in the pockets of the clothes I was wearing today, on the floor — then every spot there's no way it would be — under my bed, at the bottom of my sock drawer, in the twins' bedroom. I go downstairs and ask Jess if she's seen it around.

"Did you leave it at school again?" she asks.

"Maybe," I say. It wouldn't be the first time I put it down inside my locker while I was changing after practice and accidentally left it there.

She mutes the TV, and I have her call my cell a few times while I walk around listening hard. But nothing. Maybe she's right. Guess I'll have to check the locker room in the morning.

"Can you text Mom and Dad and let them know I lost my phone?" I ask Jess. "Don't want them to worry, in case they text me and I don't answer."

"Sure, but you better hope it turns up," Jess says. "You know they can't afford to buy you another one right now."

"Yeah, I know. Pretty sure it's at school."

"Done." She puts her phone down and unmutes the TV. Then she returns to working on her paper.

I thank her and go back upstairs to peek out my window at Nasir's house, wondering if I should pop over to see what he wanted. His window is lit up, but it looks cold out, and I'm still all warm from the shower. I try to catch him online instead. I don't have any emails or missed chats from Nasir, but the green dot next to his name in my chat list tells me he's online. I go ahead and message him asking what he needed.

There's nothing for a few seconds, then it shows the little dot-dot-dot that means he's typing, so I wait. But after a few minutes, there's still no reply. I'm thinking about how it must be a pretty long message when the green dot next to his name disappears.

32

NASIR

After swiping Bunny's phone and handing it over to Wallace, I'm trying to get this geometry homework finished. I'm usually decent at math, but all the numbers and symbols and shapes on the page melt into meaningless scribbles.

I slam the book shut and roll onto my back. There's this sinking feeling in my stomach. Like when you're going up the stairs in the dark and you reach the top but your foot reaches for one more step. There's that moment where you think you're about to eat it, and that's how I'm feeling. Except it isn't going away.

I close my eyes and press the heels of my hands against my eyelids as I ask myself for the thousandth time if I just made a giant mistake. I'm pretty sure Wallace won't find anything—but what if he does?

I knew that by choosing to help Wallace, I might hurt Bunny.

I knew that.

But so what? Bunny will be all right. Like Wallace said,

worst that happens is this ends his season. That's far from the end of the world. Bunny will still get two more years to win a state championship. It's not nearly as bad as Wallace's potential homelessness. And who knows? Maybe getting in trouble would make Bunny decide to return to Whitman High, and I wouldn't have to make a decision about his offer.

I think about picking up my phone or opening my laptop to respond to the message he sent me a couple of hours ago, but I don't want to lie to him. Instead, I go to the window, I pull aside the curtain just enough to see out but not to be seen. The block's quiet. Nothing but empty sidewalks and parked cars sitting under streetlights that wash everything in that sickly orange light. Across the street, the Thompsons' windows are dark.

"Still awake, I see," says my dad's voice, making me jump. I turn around to find him standing in the doorway.

"Yup." I wander over to my desk chair and sit down.

He glances at my desk. "Schoolwork?"

I consider telling him about everything going on. The stuff between me and Bunny. Wallace's plan and my part in it. The opportunity to go to St. S. Instead, I shrug.

"Bunny?"

I shrug again. "Kind of."

He comes inside and takes a seat on my bed. "Want to talk about it?"

"Why'd you move back here?" I ask, my eyes on my hands.

"To Whitman?"

"Yeah. After you got out of the air force, why'd you move back to the city?"

My dad leans back on his hands. "It's my home. I had a job waiting for me here. Family. Friends."

"But you had some money, right? Not like Mom has family here, and you could've taught anywhere. Why didn't you move somewhere else, somewhere nicer?"

"Like where? The suburbs?" He chuckles.

"I guess."

"I went all over the world with the air force. You know what I learned, Nasir?"

"What?" I ask.

"A place is only as good as the people you've got around you."

This sounds like a lie adults tell kids to make them feel better. I imagine pictures I've seen on the Internet of waterfalls in Bali, canals in Venice, turquoise lagoons in Palawan. "Really?"

He nods. "I've got history here. That counts for a lot in this world."

"What about Mom? She left her home. Her friends. Her history."

"Sometimes people leave," he says.

"Why?"

"To find something better, I suppose. Make some new history."

My mind goes to *The Grapes of Wrath,* which I picked up after finishing *Of Mice and Men.* The Joad family left home for something better. Only they never found it. Like how Bunny's been struggling to find his place at St. S. Say I transferred to help him out, would I find anything better?

Of course, then there's people like Wallace who get left behind, who get forced out, who don't have a choice and don't have anywhere better to go.

"But just because you leave some place doesn't mean you have to forget it," my dad adds.

"How do you know?" I ask.

"How do you know what?" my dad asks.

"When it's better to leave?"

My dad shrugs. "You just do."

And that sounds like another lie adults tell kids.

33
BUNNY

'm in history class Thursday morning thinking about tonight's game when the classroom phone starts ringing.

My teacher stops lecturing to answer it. As she's listening to the person on the other end, her eyes slide to me.

"Bunny," she says, "you're wanted in the headmaster's office."

I ignore everyone *ooh*ing like I'm in trouble and head out into the hallway. Soon as I'm out there, though, my heart starts thumping in my chest like I'm on the line at the end of the fourth quarter in a tied game. The headmaster is a sports fan and likes to call me down to chat about our games sometimes, so maybe he wants to wish me luck.

Hopefully.

I straighten my tie and make sure my shirt's tucked in all the way around. I step inside the main office, and the secretary flashes me that secretary smile.

"Go on in," he says.

I nod and make my way into the headmaster's office.

Headmaster Stevens grins like he's having trouble on the toilet. That's pretty much his default face. "Good morning, Benedict. Come on in."

He steps aside, and I see we're not alone. Coach Baum and my sponsor, Dr. Dietrich, are sitting in front of his desk. I'm kind of thrown seeing Dr. Dietrich here, since I usually only see him at games.

"Have a seat, Benedict," Headmaster Stevens says, and then everyone take turns shaking my hand. He tugs at his vest before taking his own chair. "So how are you doing? Classes going well?"

"Yes, sir," I say, still trying to work out what this could be about.

"Good, good. That was an outstanding performance the other night," the headmaster says. "Outstanding. What were your stats?"

Coach Baum answers for me. "Thirty-one points. Sixteen rebounds. Two assists." Except he says it like he's regretful for some reason.

Dr. Dietrich strokes his thick beard. I notice a crumb caught in it near the corner of his mouth. "We're proud to support you, Benedict," he says, echoing Coach's strange tone. "To give you this opportunity."

"Thanks," I say. But everyone throwing around my full name makes me nervous as hell.

There's a lull in the conversation. I know they didn't all gather here in the middle of the day to congratulate me on a game that happened two days ago. A sense of dread grows in the pit of my stomach like I'm on a roller coaster clinking toward the top of a big drop.

Headmaster Stevens clears his throat. "Do you like it here at St. Sebastian's, Benedict?"

There it is again. I try to ignore it. "Yes, sir."

"Good," he says. "We enjoy having you here. You add a lot to the school, and not only with basketball."

"Thank you, sir?" I say—like a question, because I have no idea where this is going.

Headmaster Stevens sighs. He leans back and crosses his arms over his chest. "So I'll be straight with you: why are you trying to sabotage this?"

I sit up and scrunch my face in confusion. I look to Coach, but he won't meet my eyes. I turn back to the headmaster. "Sir, I don't understand?"

He holds my gaze for a few moments and then says, "I received a call from the director of the New Jersey State Interscholastic Athletic Association this morning. She told me that late last night somebody forwarded her an email—written by you—in which you claim that St. Sebastian's promised to pay you—beyond any grants or scholarships—in exchange for transferring."

"That's a lie," I say immediately, because I know I've never ever written an email like that. Who even sends emails anymore? My hand goes to my pocket for my phone to check my Sent folder and prove it to them, but then I remember I don't have it. It wasn't in my gym locker this morning like I thought I would be.

"She forwarded me the email herself, Benedict." He turns his computer screen around so I can see it.

I lean forward. Sure enough, the address in the original Sent line is mine. I scan the short paragraph that I supposedly wrote. It pretty much says exactly what the headmaster just said it did. "I lost my phone. Someone must have found it and sent that." I shake my head, lean back, and laugh. "Someone's messing with me."

Nobody else laughs.

"Who forwarded it?" I ask.

Headmaster Stevens says, "There's no way to know. The sender used a proxy service to access another site that allows people to send email anonymously."

I point at the time stamp on the forwarded email, which shows it was sent late last night. "I didn't write that email, sir. Like I said—I lost my phone. Or someone stole it."

"Sure, sure. I believe you, Benedict—we all believe you —but even so . . ." He looks to Coach.

"What?" I ask.

"The state needs to do its due diligence."

I sit up straighter and turn to Coach. "They're going to investigate?"

Coach runs a hand through his hair as he nods. He clears his throat. "And until they make a judgment . . . you have to sit."

My stomach drops, and I feel real lightheaded all of a sudden. "We've got a game tonight."

Coach grimaces. "I know, Bunny. And I hate like hell that

you won't be able to play, but there's no way around this. It's a direct order from the state. If we put you in even for a second, the game'll be a forfeit."

"Even if we know that email's fake?"

He nods.

My heart's racing, my armpits feel all warm, and a cold sweat's forming on my forehead. I wipe it away. What the hell's going on?

Coach Baum says, "You have to understand, Bunny, when people see a talent like you—someone destined for greatness—they want to do everything in their power to bring you down. Heck, I don't know why, but they do. It's human nature. They don't know you, but they hate you for no reason other than that they'll never be able to touch your God-given talents."

"I worked hard to get good," I say, starting to feel numb all over.

"I know that," Coach Baum says. "But people don't want to believe that they're unsuccessful because they're lazy. So they have to believe it's luck."

But I know all this. I've been dealing with people hating on me for no real reason since I first stepped onto the court.

Coach Baum continues. "Normally the state doesn't pay close attention to recruiting. They know we bend some of the rules. Heck, everyone in the country does. It's always been understood that we're simply trying to give players like you the best shot in life we can. So the state's always looked the other way."

Players like you. I know what that's code for. I also know this whole arrangement isn't as altruistic as he's trying to make it sound.

"But not this time," Headmaster Stevens says. "They're coming after us."

"Why?" I ask.

"The press," Dr. Dietrich says, speaking for the first time in a while. "The bastard forwarded your email to the newspaper, as well. And the timing couldn't be worse. Expect to see an article on their site before you get out of school today."

"It wasn't my email," I say.

Coach Baum says, "I'm sure you heard about that sophomore in Texas who was really twenty-two years old?"

"Yeah," I say. "But I'm not twenty-two."

"That's not the issue," Dr. Dietrich says. "The problem is that the paper's running a whole series right now, investigating—as they put it—the 'seedy underbelly of high school sports.'" He points out the window. "So it will make the NJSIAA look bad if this goes unexamined."

My chest tightens. "How long will all this take? Any chance they'll finish it before tonight?"

Headmaster Stevens says, "Given that we're in the midst of playoffs—and the pressure our lawyer's already putting on them to resolve this—the director said they'd rush it." He sighs. "But she warned me that the earliest they'd have any answers for us would be tomorrow. And since the weekend's coming up, Monday looks more likely."

"But the championship is Sunday," I say.

The headmaster glances at Coach, then back to me. "If no decision is made by then, then you'll have to sit the championship—assuming we win tonight." He clears his throat. "Do you have any idea who might have done this, Bunny? If we find the person and they confess, that might clear up all of this before it goes too much further."

I've been thinking about this while he's been talking. If someone found it in the locker room, then that means it might even be one of my teammates. "Clay, maybe."

Headmaster Stevens and Coach Baum exchange a look, and then the headmaster asks, "Why would Clay do such a thing?"

"I don't know. I took his starting spot."

The two exchange another look. "Any other possibilities?" Headmaster Stevens says.

It seems pretty obvious to me, but then it clicks.

I was in the shower when Nasir dropped by. Then I couldn't find my phone when I went to text him. He must have taken it, which means he must have sent the email. But why?

I lean back, close my eyes, and put my hands over my face. I can't believe this is happening, and I can tell from everyone else's silence there's more bad news coming. Sure enough, Headmaster Stevens opens his mouth again a few moments later. "Anyway, the state championship might be the least of our concerns, Benedict."

"What do you mean?"

He takes a deep breath. "If they charge us with violating

the recruiting regulations, we'll have to forfeit every game you've played in this season. There's even a chance we could be suspended from competition next year. And . . . you could lose your amateur status."

"Which means, you won't be able to play in the NCAA," Coach clarifies, even though I don't need him to.

"But there's nothing to find," I say. "The email's fake."

"An investigation could turn up something else."

"Something else?" I ask. "What do you mean?"

Nobody answers, and nobody looks me in the eye.

"You mean like what I asked you to do for Nasir? Or is there something else?"

It feels like an eternity before Headmaster Stevens speaks again. "Our lawyer will sort this out, Benedict. In the meantime, do not talk to anyone—your friends, your teammates, your girlfriend, not even your family—about any of our arrangements. Any. Of course, this applies to electronic communications, as well. Email. Text. Facebook. Snapchat. Whatever you kids are using nowadays. None of it. Never say St. Sebastian's is paying for this or Dr. Dietrich covered that. Do not discuss any promises that may or may not have been made to you or your family last summer or since then. Understood?"

I lean forward, rest my elbows on my knees, and hang my head. I always suspected that not everything going on here has been aboveboard. I don't know exactly what we're doing wrong besides the thing with Nasir, but I know that if there was nothing else the investigation could possibly uncover, he would have said that straight up.

"Also," he says, "refrain from accepting any gifts. For example, if a store tries to offer you a free shirt, or if a restaurant wants to pay for your meal, if someone offers you free tickets to anything—decline. Do not accept anything. Do you understand?"

I nod, like the fool I am. I used St. Sebastian's, and they used me. But it's my future that's slipping away. Not theirs.

Headmaster Stevens continues. "If anyone in the press contacts you, direct them to me."

I nod. But I'm barely listening anymore. The room feels like it's spinning. I want to throw up.

"Good." The headmaster forces a smile. Straightens his tie and tugs at his vest. "Listen, you're a good player, a good student, and a good kid, Benedict. You deserve to be here. Don't let anyone make you think otherwise."

I loosen my own tie and unbutton my shirt collar so I can breathe.

Headmaster Stevens asks, "You did file a police report, yes? About your phone?"

"Not yet," I say. "I thought I left it here at school."

"Did you tell anyone last night when you noticed you didn't have it?"

"My sister," I say immediately. "And she sent a text to my parents."

He writes something on a sticky note. "Excellent. That

should help." The headmaster passes me the square of neon yellow paper. "Have them take a screenshot of the message and send it to me at that number."

"Yes, sir."

"Everything will be okay," Dr. Dietrich says. "The director is an old friend of mine. We went to Princeton undergrad together. Good woman. Used to call her Shots because—"

"Don't worry, Benedict," Headmaster Stevens says, interrupting Dr. Dietrich. "We won't let them delay this until Monday. We'll fight as hard as we can to get you on the court Sunday."

I know this is supposed to make me feel better, but it doesn't. First, not to be cocky, but I'm not too confident St. S will make it past tonight without me. Second, I'm still trying to figure out why the hell Nasir would do me like this.

"If nothing else," Coach Baum says, "you've got plenty of time to bring home the hardware. And if worse comes to worst, there are other routes into the NBA besides the NCAA —you could always play in Europe for a year after graduation."

I don't lift my head. "Can I go back to class?"

"One more thing," Headmaster Stevens says. "About your special request—for your friend . . . Naseem?"

"Nasir," I say.

"Right. Anyway, until this all gets sorted out, let's hold off making any promises to Najid about his possible place at St. Sebastian's next year."

I let out a sarcastic laugh. "Yeah, no problem, sir."

With that, they tell me not to worry about a dozen more times and that they'll let me know as soon as they hear anything. Then I head back to class, my mind replaying that conversation like I'm listening to the worst track in the world stuck on repeat.

34
NASIR

I pull the trigger the moment the Nazi zombie shambles out of the darkness and into my crosshairs. Head shot. Blood, brain matter, and skull fragments spray the wall. Its headless body slumps to the ground.

I reload and then peer into the gun's scope, scanning the dark hallway in the flickering light. There's nothing except shadows, but I can hear them approaching. The tortured moaning. The dragging limbs.

When one finally rounds the corner, its yellow eyes two points of light in the darkness—*BANG*—I take it down with a single shot. As it collapses, another appears behind it. I fire again—but this time I miss. Three more stumble into view.

Taking aim at the zombie out front, I pull the trigger. Nothing happens. I check my ammo.

Damn—empty.

I switch to my knife. The nearest zombie lunges at me. I slash at it. I take some damage, but it falls. I can't even take a breath before the next one's on me, and the next one, and the next.

My screen goes red. I fall back. Stare at the ceiling. My consciousness fades as the pack of Third Reich zombies feasts on my innards.

Damn.

Almost made it to the next level.

Before I can mourn too much, my phone buzzes. I shut off the console and move over to my desk, where it lies in a wedge of afternoon sunlight spilling between the window and my blinds.

It's a text from Keyona.

We need to talk, it says.

My stomach lurches a bit, because I know what it's about. I tap Ignore and turn my phone face-down.

The article's right in front of me, still pulled up on my computer screen. THE SINS OF ST. SEBASTIAN the headline reads, with a shot of Bunny driving through the lane underneath it. Still in shock, I reread it for the hundredth time since it posted about half an hour ago. The article doesn't identify the person who leaked the message, but it's not hard for me to connect the dots. Wallace couldn't find anything incriminating, so he got creative and sent a fake email to himself from Bunny's account, claiming St. Sebastian's is paying him to play, and then he forwarded it to the director of the NJSIAA and to the paper's sportswriter. But the worst part of all of this is the section that talks about the possible consequences. Wallace assured me that Bunny would have to sit the rest of the season and that would be it, but it seems like shit could get a lot more serious than that.

This all better be worth it tonight.

My phone starts buzzing again. This time Keyona's calling. I tap Ignore, and a moment later, she texts, **Why'd you do this to Bunny?**

So I guess they pieced it together. Except it wasn't me — I just gave the phone to Wallace, and he did what he did.

I don't reply, but that doesn't stop Keyona. Her text bubbles start piling up, carrying on a one-sided conversation.

Please, talk to Bunny. He's confused and hurt.

He thought you were friends again.

I know you're reading this.

You show up. Bunny's phone disappears. That story breaks.

Coincidence?

Yeah, right.

Don't be a coward — own up to what you've done.

Nasir???

NASIR????

She tries calling again, but I hit Ignore again.

Answer the fucking phone.

ANSWER IT.

I hope you know how much this hurts him.

This might ruin his future.

Your FRIEND'S future.

Fine, don't say anything.

My phone grows quiet. I close the browser window with the article about Bunny and shut off the screen. The sliver of sunlight on my desk shrinks as the sun sets.

And then one more text comes through from Keyona: Make it right, Nasir.

But I don't know how I could, or if I even want to. Wallace was in a tight spot, and I was trying to help him out. Yeah, it sucks for Bunny right now, but the email's fake. The state will probably figure that out quickly enough. Who knows, he might even get to play tonight. But if he doesn't, St. S will lose, Wallace will make the money he needs, and the world will move on.

What's done is done. I know my shot at going to St. S flew out the window along with our friendship, but I never wanted that anyway.

So Keyona's wrong. There's nothing to make right—most everything is as it should be.

The only thing that's not right?

Nazi zombies.

I power my console back on and go kill some more.

35
BUNNY

'm sitting in a seat by myself in the back of the bus as we ride to the game. I've got my hood up and I'm gazing out the window, watching the sun set over suburbia. Usually I listen to music on these rides. Nothing too hard. Mostly that old stuff my dad plays at Word Up, since it's so relaxing.

I don't have my phone, though, so tonight it's just the sounds of the bus in my ears. The rumble of the engine and the suspension groaning when we drive over bumps. The semi trucks flying past us on the highway. My teammates chatting up the cheerleaders, who split the ride with us.

It always bothers me when the other guys talk on the bus like this, and it's getting on my nerves more than usual tonight since I can't drown it out. They're laughing and carrying on like they're on a field trip to Six Flags, not like we're headed to the state semifinals. They should be running through plays in their mind and trying to get mentally prepped.

After all, they have to do this without me.

All day I was waiting to be called down to the office again, waiting for some good news. But as the school day wound down, so did my hope. When the team met up at the front of the school before getting on the bus, Coach put a hand on my shoulder, sighed, and said a single word: "Sunday."

Too bad we're not going to make it to Sunday. Not without me. I'm not trying to be arrogant or anything, but the numbers don't lie. On average, I score about a third of the team's points each game. Sometimes half.

That's why I'm not feeling too optimistic about Sunday.

Or about the future in general.

I'm pissed at Nasir for backstabbing me. Keyona and I still haven't worked things out. And my dad's selling the bookstore.

Not to mention a lot of the D-I schools will probably lose interest in me. Even if the state doesn't find anything, the rumors that have already started going around won't ever go away. The way the NCAA has been cracking down lately, coaches are trying to stay far from any potential scandals.

For some reason, my thoughts shift to when Nasir and I went camping in the Adirondacks with his dad the summer before seventh grade. I had never been real camping before. It wasn't something my dad did. And, damn, was I miserable out there. Bored. Covered in mosquitoes. Afraid I'd be eaten by bears or snakes or wolves.

Anyway, the campsite we were planning on staying at was taken, so we had to hike farther along the trail and set up in the dark. And it rained our first night, the moisture soaking through the tent and leaving the three of us cold and damp.

I was the first one up the next morning because I don't think I even slept. I unzipped the tent and stepped into the sunrise. The light spilled through the trees like gold threads. And I remember heading through the forest to take a leak and coming up on this ridge. A valley stretched out at my feet.

I'd never seen a view like that before, so clear and crisp in every direction. I thought I could even spot our car parked along a road in the distance.

It's kind of stupid, I know, but I remember thinking that our lives must be something like that. Like when we're alive, we're stuck down in that forest, lost in the trees, lost in the dark. But when we die, we find ourselves up on a ridge, looking out over every moment we lived. Everything would make so much sense. Point A. Point B. The path we took. The path we should have taken.

Whenever I've thought of the future, I've tried to imagine it like that. State championship. College scholarship. NBA. I'd be able to save the bookstore, send my parents to Hawaii or something, pay off Jess's student loans, help the twins go to any college they want.

But now I can't see things from that ridge anymore. I'm down in the valley, deep in the trees. Lost and alone in the dark.

Someone slides into the seat with me, interrupting my thoughts. I turn to find Brooke. She smells like some citrusy shampoo, and I can tell by her bare legs sticking out from underneath her winter coat that she's wearing her cheerleading outfit.

"How are you holding up?" she asks, making a sympathetic face.

"I've been better," I say.

She brushes a strand of yellow hair out of her eyes and behind her ear. "This is bullshit."

"You're telling me."

Brooke sits there quiet for a few moments and then says, "So there's a party after the game. At Stacy's. I know you don't normally come to these things, but you should come."

"Thanks, but I'm not really in the mood."

"It would be good for you. If we win, it will be a celebration. If we lose, you can drown your sorrows in cheap beer."

"I don't think so," I say. "I don't even drink. Besides, we've got school tomorrow."

"It'll be fun," she says. "Eric and Drew are going. Drew's even bringing his boyfriend, and he never does that. Nobody will force you to drink, and you can always leave early."

"Thanks, but—"

"Come on, Bunny. You've been going to school with us for, like, six months, and you almost never hang out. Don't you get lonely?"

"No," I lie. "I have friends back in Whitman." A second lie. "And a girlfriend." Maybe a third lie—she's still mad at me.

She shoulder checks me playfully. "Come on . . ."

"I'll make a deal with you," I say. "I'll go if we win."

Her face lights up. "Really?"

"Yup," I say. "We can even have a drink together," I add, since there's no way we're walking away with the W tonight.

She gives me a little hug in the seat, her hair brushing against my face. "I can't wait!" Then she slides out of the seat and returns to the front of the bus with the other cheer-leaders.

I move to slide my headphones back on, forgetting they're not around my neck.

36

NASIR

take a break from killing zombies to find that it's just past seven o'clock. That means the St. S game is under way.

I thought Wallace would try to get me to go with him, but he wasn't in school, and I haven't heard from him all day.

When I return to my room, I check my phone to make sure. There's nothing except a couple more harsh texts from Keyona from over an hour ago. I clear them from my notifications and reread the barrage she sent me earlier. One sticks in my head: Make it right.

37
BUNNY

There are about two minutes left on the clock in the fourth quarter, and Oak Hill just threw the ball out of bounds.

Somehow, we're not getting destroyed. In fact, we're only trailing by five.

I'm at the end of the bench like a chump, though, still wearing my khakis, blazer, and tie. Sweating more than my teammates.

It's not right. I don't have a leg or arm or hand in a cast preventing me from playing. I'm not even in foul trouble. Nah, I'm fine. Perfectly healthy.

Perfectly powerless.

Yet the team's doing all right without me.

Of course, a big reason for that is because Oak Hill's all-American point guard, Luis Garcia, has the flu. He was trying to play through it, but he looked like death. Slow to react and wasting time-outs so he could run to the sideline to vomit. They finally sat him at the half and put in their second-string guy, who's so nervous he's been dribbling around like a squirrel looking for a lost nut.

So with each team's best player effectively a nonfactor, the whole game's been back and forth, like watching Ping-Pong. And it's killing me knowing that if I were in, this wouldn't even be close, especially with Garcia sick. The whole crowd is probably thinking the same.

Anyway, the ref hands the ball to Clay, who's playing power forward in my place, and blows the whistle. Clay's defender jumps up and down, waving his hands and legs all around to try and block the pass. Clay's scanning for an open man but can't find one. Even from the opposite side of the court I can see the panic on his face.

The ref's about to blow that whistle for a five-second violation when Clay lobs it deep. Drew snatches it out of the sky, hands it off to Eric, sets the pick, rolls, gets the ball back, and puts it in for two.

The crowd goes nuts.

Now we're only down by three.

Oak Hill inbounds and we run a full-court press. They break it, get deep in the paint, and answer with two of their own, quieting our fans.

Just like that, Oak Hill's lead is back to five. Except now there's only a minute thirty-seven left.

I lean forward, ready to rip off my school uniform like Superman and sub in for Clay. I try to catch Coach Baum's eye, hoping he'll ask me to, but I know that I don't even exist to him right now.

The game resumes. Clay inbounds to Eric, and Eric

pushes it up court. Number thirteen on Oak Hill, their two-guard, slides over to double-team Eric. Eric panics. Picks up his dribble. He starts pivoting like mad, trying to get clear from the tangle of arms and legs. He sneaks a pass through to the wing and our shooting guard, Hunter, forces a flat-looking three that I'm sure is going to brick hard—but it finds its way to the bottom of the net.

The gym explodes and our bench rises, throwing our arms around each other's shoulders.

The lead's cut to two. A minute twenty left. An eternity in this game.

People start clapping and stomping in rhythm, running that old *DE-FENSE* chant.

My heart's beating three times as fast as normal. My adrenaline's flowing, but it's got nowhere to go. God, I want to be on that court with the ball in my hands at the top of the key. I want to break ankles with my crossover, drive to the lane, and throw it down so hard the backboard shatters.

Instead, I loosen my tie. Shift my weight from one foot to the other. Cup my hands around my mouth and shout, "DE-FENSE," in time with the crowd.

We're still running a press, and this time we do it right. Force their point right up to the sideline. But he bounces it off Eric's leg, and the ball rolls out of bounds, so they get to reset at half-court.

Oak Hill inbounds right away. Their second-string point dribbles back and forth just past midcourt to waste the clock.

The crowd's shouting for Eric to foul and force him to the line, but that'd be dumb, since there are still a few possessions left in this game. We've got to let them burn some seconds and then force the turnover or a bad shot.

Finally, the point fires a bounce pass to their small forward, who bricks an open ten-footer. Drew snatches the rebound, outlets to Eric on the wing, who zooms past our bench like a jet. Even though it's two-on-one, Eric pushes it to the hoop, faking right and taking it to the left to put up a floater —that gets swatted out of the air.

But the ball wasn't the only thing the Oak Hill kid gets a piece of. He knocks Eric down hard onto the floor, which brings the whistle.

Shooting foul.

Drew helps Eric back to his feet, and then Eric limps to the line.

He could tie it up here.

Except he doesn't. His first one's short, kissing the front of the rim. But he sinks the second one, so now we're only down by one with fifty-two seconds on the clock.

Oak Hill calls a time-out.

Our guys jog over and huddle around Coach Baum, panting hard. The bench players—and myself—we gather around the outside of their circle, peering over their shoulders to feel like we're part of the action. It kills me not to be in the center of that circle. I can't hear what Coach is saying with the crowd so loud, and I can't even see the defensive setup he's drawing on his little whiteboard. He keeps pointing to his head for some reason.

Eventually, the buzzer wails, signaling the end of the time-out. My teammates hustle back into position. I slink back to my spot on the sideline and wrap my arms back over my fellow bench riders' shoulders, my hands still itching for the ball.

I glance over at my family in the visitors' section of the bleachers. Even though they knew I wouldn't see a second of play, they all came. My dad even closed Word Up early again.

The whistle blows.

The Oak Hill forward takes a couple seconds and then rifles a pass up court, but it's deflected and everyone starts diving for the ball. Nobody gets a grip on it, and it rolls out of bounds.

The ref gives it to Oak Hill.

"Bullshit!" one of my teammates calls. Coach Baum shoots him a look, and the kid shuts right up. But Coach can't shut the crowd up from yelling the same thing.

Oak Hill inbounds again and then holds it for a few seconds. Eric glances at Coach Baum to see if he wants him to foul yet, but Coach shakes his head.

The Oak Hill kid finally puts the ball on the floor, but only for a couple of dribbles before gunning a pass to the two-guard on the wing, who sends it right back. For some reason, Clay drifts up from the block and lunges for the interception. Not only does he come up empty, but he bumps into Eric, knocking him over. The Oak Hill kid blows past them into the lane. The rest of our D collapses on him, which is exactly what he wants, and he whips it back to the shooting guard who's wide open just outside the arc.

But his shot ricochets off the back of the rim and pops into the air. The ball hangs forever before dropping into a tangle of outstretched hands. A few guys wrap their arms around it and fall to the ground. Whistles pierce the air. Jump ball.

Since this is high school, they don't actually jump for it— possession alternates. Our crowd erupts when the ref's arm flies out to signal that it's ours.

Clay inbounds, launching an overhead pass across court that finds its way to Eric, who holds it. After a few seconds, Eric drives and then kicks it out to the wing, who dumps it to Clay. Clay pivots and banks it off the glass for two to put us up by one.

Oak Hill inbounds to their point right away, and he pushes it up along the left sideline. While we're still getting back on D, the squirrelly point guard lowers his head. I can tell before his foot hits the ground that the kid's decided to force it, to be the hero. He's got time, and he's got open teammates on both sides of the court, but sure enough, he doesn't even glance their way as he drives. He gets stuck in the paint, picks up his dribble, pump-fakes a pass to the top of the key, and then Euro-steps to lay it up from the left.

But the shot bounces off the backboard and right into Drew's open hands. He clears some space using his elbows and hands it off to Eric. Oak Hill's coaches are shouting for them to foul. It takes a few seconds, but they finally get a hack in on Eric. He takes the line. Ref signals to indicate that it's a one-and-one situation. If he sinks the first one, he'll get another. If he misses, it's live.

Ref bounces him the rock. Eric takes a deep breath, dribbles it three times to his side, spins it in his hands, and then puts it up.

He drains it, and we're up by two.

The ref gives it back. Eric repeats the same three-dribble routine as before and puts it up, but shot's too far right and glances off the rim. Oak Hill snags the rebound, but we press them hard, careful not to foul.

No time-outs left and only a few seconds remaining, Oak Hill's point breaks our press with that squirrelly speed. A few steps ahead of everyone else, he pulls up at the three-point arc and takes the wide-open shot. I watch with dread as the ball rolls off his fingertips and sails spinning through the air as the game clock drops to zero.

38

NASIR

Whenever Wallace comes up to my room, he usually flies up the steps two at a time and bursts through my door like the police. But tonight, he's trudging up slowly like a death row inmate marching to the electric chair.

I know exactly why. I saw the score online: 55–53, St. Sebastian's. Somehow they pulled it off *without* Bunny.

It seems like forever before Wallace appears at the top of the stairs, and when he does, he walks past me with his hood up and head down, wordless and reeking of smoke. He plops down on my mattress without pulling off his hood.

"Were you there?" I ask.

He doesn't answer. Just drops his face into his hands.

"How bad is it?" I ask, knowing he must have had a lot riding on it since he knew before anyone else that Bunny would be sitting.

"You can't even imagine, cuz."

"How much do you owe?"

He shakes his head and moans like a dying cow, hands still covering his face.

"It'll be okay," I say.

He looks up at me, eyes bloodshot, and lets out a bitter laugh. "You think everything's gonna be fucking okay, Nas?"

I don't answer, and he drops his head back into his hands. Except now he's clenching and unclenching his fists over and over again.

My eyes drift past Wallace, to one of the two photos tacked on my wall. It's a shot of Bunny and me when we were nine, arms draped around each other's necks. We had just won this two-on-two tournament we used to play in every spring. I remember that after the last game this chubby little kid wiped his booger on my hand when we went to shake.

Bunny was amazing even back then. People we didn't even know would come and watch our games, *ooh*ing and *ahh*ing every time he schooled someone.

Sketchy old dudes always hung around at those tournaments, handing Bunny business cards, saying they'd never seen anyone like him and they were personal trainers and they could work with him for free even though they didn't normally do that and blah blah blah. We'd see some of the same ones every time, acting like they were his dad or coach or something, talking about his "natural talent." Like they didn't have anything better to do with their time than watch kids ball. Of course, we all knew their game: Try to get in good with a rising star and ride his coattails to the top.

But Bunny didn't go for any of that. Even though a lot of kids our way did, maybe hoping they'd find some pride or popularity, maybe a new father figure, or maybe at least someone to throw a little cash their way when new sneakers came out.

Nah. Bunny didn't need any of that. He stayed out of trouble. Listened to his actual coaches. Went to skills clinics and camps. Studied plays on YouTube. Put in extra time on the court, the track, and the weight room whenever he could. I've never seen anyone so focused and determined in my life.

I don't think anybody knows this, but Bunny doesn't even know how to ride a bike. Dude spent so much time practicing and learning to ball, he never got around to it.

My eyes slide to the other photo on my wall. It's Wallace and me at his eighteenth birthday party. We're sitting on his couch with those little cone-shaped hats, and he's got his arm around my shoulder as we both flash peace signs at the camera.

I use the term "party" loosely. His grandma threw it for him, and it was only the three of us plus one of her church friends plus an Oreo ice cream cake.

I lean back in my chair, cross my arms over my stomach. I notice a loose thread on one of my sleeves, so I wrap it around my finger and yank it out to keep it from unraveling any farther.

"Tonight was a fluke," I say. "No way they'll win the next one without him."

Wallace doesn't say anything.

"And if they do, you can move to Russia. I hear they have pretty favorable extradition laws."

He looks up at me, lip curled into a sneer. "You think this a joke, Nas?"

"I know it's not, I just—"

"Naw, you don't know," he says, cutting off my apology as he rises like he's going to hit me. "You're safe here in your warm house. You've got a bed instead of a couch. A fridge full of food. A mom and a dad who give a fuck about you." He gestures beyond me to my desk lamp. "You've got a fucking desk, man. And a fucking desk lamp. And whatever the fuck that shit is." He points at my plastic organizer that has little trays for paperclips and thumbtacks and a pad of sticky notes. "Shit, cuz. We're living in the same city, but we're in two different worlds. You may as well be on the moon."

Wallace storms out of my room, stomps down the stairs, and bursts through the door and out into the night.

I sit there for a moment, not knowing what to do, what to think, twirling that plucked thread around my finger. My dad appears at my door after some time. He leans against the frame, arms folded over his chest. "Everything okay?"

I shrug. And even though Wallace just got loud with me, I'm thinking about how nobody's probably asking him that simple question right now.

"I know you mean well," my dad says, "but some people are too far gone."

I don't say anything to that. I don't even nod.

He pushes off the door frame and then starts to walk away. But then he stops and turns back. "Hey, you see Bunny's team won?"

When I answer, my words are flat as pancakes. "Yeah, Dad. I did."

He nods. "When he gets home, you should slide over and say congratulations. All this noise with the state can't be easy on him. I bet he could use a friend."

"Maybe," I say, wondering if my dad would still love me if he knew what I did to Bunny. If he knew who I really am.

"Whatever you think is best," he says, and then goes back downstairs.

Problem is, I don't have any idea about that.

39
BUNNY

I pull down my hood as I walk through the door behind Eric and Drew and into the noise. I feel everyone's eyes on me, probably since I don't ever show up at these things. But I told Brooke I'd come by if we won, and a deal's a deal. Even though it's a school night, my parents said it was cool so long as I don't drink and I'm home and in bed by eleven. Guess they thought it'd be good for me to escape from the stress of what's going on with the state for a few moments.

Stacy's house is huge, of course. I can tell even with lights low. The ceiling's, like, two or three stories high with a few skylights, and there are hallways and staircases going off the entry room in different directions. The place is packed with kids who look happy that we won and happy to be out of their school uniforms. And even though Kendrick Lamar's blasting from some unseen, high-end sound system, hardly anyone's dancing. Most are standing around with those red cups, talking. I recognize some kids from around the hallways, but I don't know most, since I keep to myself. A guy who falls in that second category steps in front of me. As Eric and Drew keep walking, the guy gives me a high-five.

"Wesley Snipes!" he shouts.

I look over my shoulder. "What?"

He notices my confusion. "Sorry—I know that's not your name. It's just that you look like Wesley Snipes, dude."

For the record, I don't look anything like Wesley Snipes.

He pushes a red cup into my hand. It looks like it's filled with foam. "Hey, you know I used to live in Whitman?"

"Oh. What neighborhood?"

"Well, not like Whitman proper. But right outside it." Then he names the next town over, the place where a lot of the white people who used to live in Whitman moved to during the sixties.

The kid keeps talking, but I walk away and make my way through the house to catch up with what seems like the only two people I know here.

In the dining room, people are crowded around a long table. Like a visitor on another planet, I stop to see what's going on. There are red cups arranged in a triangle at either end. Two guys are trying to toss a Ping-Pong ball into the cups on the opposite end. Beer pong, I guess. I don't go to a lot of parties, so I've never seen people play it except on TV and in movies. One of them eventually succeeds, everyone cheers, and the other kid plucks out the Ping-Pong ball and downs the drink in a single gulp.

A moment later, a girl with long brown hair walks up, squealing with delight. It's Stacy.

"Ohmygod! Bunny!" she says, and then comes in for a

hug. She's all short, so I have to bend down so she can get her arms around my neck.

After I pull out of the hug, she goes up on her tiptoes and starts looking around. "Brooke's here. I have to find her."

"Why?" I ask. "I'm probably not going to stay very—"

She disappears into the crowd before I finish my thought.

My instinct is to pull out my cell to kill some time and avoid having to talk to anyone. Even if I did have my phone, though, I'm not sure what I'd do with it. Keyona had wanted to talk after the game, but I told her I was tired and going to sleep early. No way I'm about to hit up Nasir anymore. That leaves social media. But I stopped using most of those apps a while ago, and I definitely wouldn't want to hear what people are saying about that article the paper posted online this afternoon.

So I keep watching the beer pong game. There are a few more close shots before one finally makes it into a cup again. More cheering erupts as more beer is chugged.

I look into my own cup. The foam has settled, and it looks like it's only about one-third full now.

A few moments later, Stacy reappears. "Found her." She grabs my wrist and begins dragging me through the crowd. We leave the game behind us and cut through the kitchen, where someone's doing a handstand on top of a keg while the other kids are chanting. I kind of want to see what this is all about, but Stacy's on a mission. I follow her through a maze of hallways until we come out to the bottom of a staircase. Stacy lets go of my wrist and then points up the stairs. "Go."

"Why? What's up there?" I ask, more because I feel the need to say something than because I don't know who's up there.

She then puts her hands on my back and starts pushing me to walk up the staircase.

"All right," I say, and start going up on my own.

"Have fun!" she calls up to me in a singsong voice before slipping away.

The staircase curves around a corner, where I find Brooke sitting on the steps just above the landing, drink in one hand and phone in the other. She's in a T-shirt and jeans, but looks better to me than she does in the cheerleading outfit. Maybe it's because she looks more normal, more comfortable. She smiles when she sees me, puts her phone away, and says something. Even though it's quieter up here, it's still hard to hear with the party just below.

I can't hear you, I mouth.

She leans forward, and I put my ear next to her mouth. "You came!" she says. I feel the warmth of her breath on the side of my face.

Then we reposition so I can speak into her ear. "I said I would."

Brooke holds up her cup, and I clink mine against it—as much as you can clink plastic. Then I sit down on the step next to her.

"Didn't think I'd see you tonight," she says.

"Why's that?"

It hasn't gotten any quieter, so we have to keep taking turns talking into each other's ear.

She takes a drink. "I don't know. Some people say you think you're better than the rest of us." I must pull some kind of face because she throws up her hands in mock surrender. "Chill, Bunny. I didn't say *I* think that."

"They're wrong."

She shrugs. Takes another drink. "Well, you don't hang out with anyone at St. Sebastian's—"

"I hang out with Eric and Drew," I say.

"Really?" Brooke says, brushing her blond hair back. "Not counting burritos the other week, this is the first time I've seen you with them outside of school or basketball." Her eyes go to my cup. "By the way, I remember you saying something about having a drink with me if we won?"

Maybe to prove I don't think I'm better than everyone here, or maybe because I'm still upset about everything in my life, I down my drink in one gulp like the kids playing beer pong downstairs. It tastes nasty as hell, but I force myself to swallow every last drop, making a face as I do so.

Brooke smiles and gives me a high-five. "How do you like it?"

I gaze into the bottom of my empty cup. "Tasted like ass."

"Oh, so you're familiar with the taste of ass?" She laughs.

I laugh. "You know what I mean."

"True." She frowns like an emoji. "This beer's pretty shitty.

I told Stacy to spring for the better stuff, but she said no one cares. You get used to it, I guess." She takes another drink.

Maybe she's right. I'm starting to feel a warm glow at the center of my stomach. It's kind of nice, and I get why people drink, because I'm already wondering if another one will make my stomach warmer.

"Refill?" Brooke asks as if reading my mind.

I nod, and she takes me by the hand and leads me back downstairs to the keg, where some random kid fills my cup and then hands it to me while bowing as if I were royalty. Brooke laughs as I thank him. The kid refills Brooke's, then all three of us clink our cups together and drink. Before I know it, I've emptied mine. Brooke starts chatting with the kid as he refills my cup again. I drink it as I wait, and sure enough, as I stand there my stomach does get warmer and glowier, and I know that's not a word as soon as I think it, but I don't even care. I say it aloud: "Glowier."

A few people look at me, but I don't care about that either. In fact, there's a lot I suddenly find myself not caring about right now. Keyona. Nasir. The bookstore. The NJSIAA. My future.

As I get one more refill, Brooke leans into my ear and says, "Be careful, rookie," then she pulls me away from the keg and back through the crowd. I've got this floaty, drifting feeling, like I'm a boat.

"I'm a boat," I say.

"What?" she says.

"Nothing," I say.

We climb the steps, and I'm about to sit down at the same spot where we were before when Brooke leans in and says, "It's too loud to talk here! Let's go upstairs!"

I nod, because why not? And then I take another drink.

She smiles, turns around, and leads me all the way upstairs. To be honest, I try not to look at her butt, but it's right there and it's looking real nice in those jeans.

Before long, we reach the top. She leads me down a hallway and into a dark room, then closes the door behind us. The sounds of the party are distant and muffled.

Brooke flips the light switch. "That's better," she says, no longer having to shout.

It takes a moment for my eyes to adjust to the light and for my ears to stop ringing, but when they do I check things out. There's a dresser on one wall, a patterned chair with an ottoman in the corner, and a bed with a nightstand in the other corner. All clean and modern looking like it's right out of an IKEA catalogue. There's some abstract art on the wall, but no photos or anything personal anywhere.

Also, I think I can see Brooke's bra through her T-shirt.

"One of the guest rooms," Brooke explains.

I take a drink, imagining what it must be like to live in a house with *multiple* guest rooms. What it might be like to see Brooke's bra not through a T-shirt.

Brooke climbs onto the bed and positions herself so she's lying on her stomach, propped up by her elbows at the edge of the mattress so she can still hold her cup.

I consider lying down next to her but decide to sit in the chair instead. I lean back, put my feet up on the ottoman, and take another drink.

"There's so much I don't know about you, Bunny Thompson."

I nod. Drink. Enjoy the feeling of my stress slipping away with each sip, like fallen leaves floating downstream.

"How's dance going?" I ask.

She laughs again. "I can't believe you remembered." She looks into her cup, takes a drink. "It's going well. You really should come to our spring recital in April."

"Sure," I say, because anything seems possible right now. "Remind me when it gets closer."

We fall quiet, but it isn't even awkward. It "is what it is," as my dad likes to say. We're sitting there. I'm bobbing my head to the muffled bass beat I can feel thumping through the floor. Every now and then, one of us takes another sip. And it's all cool, all very cool, so cool I don't know why I don't do this more often.

Brooke asks me something, but I miss it. I move out of the chair and onto the bed next to her. "Huh?"

She laughs. Leans over and sets her drink on the nightstand. "I said, who are you?"

"Who am I? Um. Bunny, I think."

She laughs again. "I mean, like, who are you *really?* I know there must be more to you than basketball. But I don't know anything beyond that."

I shrug. "Not much else to know."

"Liar," she says, swinging around so she's sitting up on the edge of the bed just like I am, the sides of our legs touching.

"Well, if I told you everything, you wouldn't really understand." I lift my cup to my lips, but it's empty.

"Oh?" Brooke asks, brushing her blond hair behind her ear.

"Like, how much can you really know a person if your life is the complete opposite?"

"What do you mean?"

"All right. Here's one example." I gesture around the room. "Everyone at St. S is mad rich. I don't know what that's like. And I don't think I can, like how I don't think you all can get what it's like to grow up in the city. We can spend all day trading stories, but at the end of the day, most things you can't understand unless you experience it for yourself."

She doesn't answer right away, like she's choosing her words carefully. I watch her lips, which look nice and soft, as she says, "You're making a lot of assumptions about the kids at our school."

"Oh, yeah?"

Brooke crosses her legs and leans back on her hands. "Not all of them are rich. The school gives a lot of financial aid, you know. More than most Catholic schools. A lot of kids have grants or sponsors like you probably have."

"Yeah, the other students of color recruited for sports."

"No," she says. "Other kids, too . . . Kids like me."

I start to laugh, but she keeps a straight face. "For real?"

She nods. "Grants cover half my tuition." Before I can say

anything to that, she goes on. "And just because someone's white doesn't mean they don't have problems. If you talked to more of your classmates, like, really tried to get to know them, you might find a few whose problems aren't that different from yours."

"Right," I say, all sarcastic.

She draws away from me. "You don't have to be an asshole."

"Sorry," I say, without really meaning it. "I'm just telling you it how it is. I don't think your problems compare to mine."

"You don't even know what my problems are, Bunny."

"And you don't know mine. Not my real ones, anyway."

"So tell me about them."

Except I don't. We fall quiet, but this time it *is* awkward. I clear my throat. Stretch my legs a bit, consider leaving. I tilt my cup to my lips, forgetting that it's empty.

"I'm going back downstairs," I say, and start to stand up.

But Brooke puts her hand on my forearm, and we lock eyes. "Wait, Bunny. I think—"

I lean in to kiss her before my brain can register that's what I'm doing.

She pushes me away. "Whoa. I think you have the wrong idea."

"I—"

"You have a girlfriend, Bunny."

Right.

"You thought that since I asked you to come upstairs with me that I wanted to hook up?"

I think that is kind of what I was thinking, but I don't want to say it aloud. Of course, I don't need to, because my hesitation tells her enough.

"I asked you to come up here because I wanted to have a real conversation with you, to get to know you. You always look so lonely around school. I was trying to be nice."

"Oh," I say.

"Yeah. I'm going to go back downstairs." And then she's gone.

I sit there for a minute. It's a good thing she didn't actually let me kiss her. What the hell *was* I thinking?

I shake my head to try to clear it, and stand up. The world sways, so I steady myself against the wall and make my way downstairs. I find Drew and tell him I don't need a ride home because I'm walking, then I head outside.

The cold air stings but feels nice. I make my way down the long drive past the line of parked cars, leaving behind the noise and light. As I reach the bottom of the driveway, I turn toward the main road. There should be a bus stop somewhere over there. I could check if I had a phone, but I don't because my best friend stole it so he could betray me.

A gust of wind stirs the air, whipping around so it feels like it's coming from everywhere. I pull my hood up and pick up the pace. All of the houses around this way are like Stacy's. Enormous and set back in the trees at the end of long, winding, gated driveways. I wonder how many people inside of them are eating steak and lobster by the fireside right now as Jeeves stands by awaiting their next command.

I think back to the fall, when I first started at St. Sebastian's. The neighborhood right around the school is like this, too. I was walking to the bus stop one day when a couple of cops pulled up next to me in their cruiser, lights flashing. They got out, asked if I knew anything about a stolen car, and then frisked me. I didn't bother to point out that if I had stolen a car, I wouldn't be walking, and that the damn thing certainly wouldn't be stashed in my pocket. I stayed polite. Wasn't about to give them a reason to do anything else. Anyway, the police didn't find anything on me, and they went on their way.

But still, every time I walk through those neighborhoods, everything I felt in that moment returns. The shame. The anger. The powerlessness. And right now it's all magnified by how I'm waiting for some lawyers to decide my fate.

Seems like it keeps getting colder with every step I take. Any of that warm brightness the alcohol lent me is quickly slipping away, and the wind starts to sting more and more. I pull my sleeves over my hands and cross my arms over my chest, regretting that I left my coat in Drew's car.

I should have reached the main road by now. Maybe I took a wrong turn. I wonder if I should go back, but then again, what if it's just around the next bend, and I only need to keep going for another block or two?

I look up at the sky and find a few stars shining in the black. I study them for a few moments like I'm really about to navigate by the constellations.

40

NASIR

By Friday afternoon, I'm more worried about Wallace than ever. He wasn't in school again, and he hasn't been answering any of my texts. I even asked if he wanted to come over for dinner tonight, which is usually a sure way to get a response from him, but still nothing.

So instead of heading home, I catch the bus and get off downtown.

It's cloudy, cold, and windy as hell. The kind of wind that makes the traffic lights sway and sends empty garbage cans skittering across the street. I pull my hood up and keep my head down, only looking up every few blocks to check where I am.

I eventually arrive at Wallace's building and make my way up the narrow staircase to his apartment. I press the doorbell. Nobody answers, but I can hear Bunny the kitten on the other side, scratching at the door and meowing. I buzz it again and gaze at the peeling paint in the little entryway.

I'm about to leave when the door swings open. Wallace's grandma appears in one of those old lady nightgowns. She squints at me.

"Whatever you're selling, we don't want any," she says, and starts to close the door.

The kitten peeks out between her feet and meows. She sniffs the air a few times and then decides I'm not interesting enough and goes back inside.

"It's me — Nasir."

The two of us are unrelated, since she's Wallace's mom's mom. But I've seen her enough times in my life she shouldn't have difficulty placing me.

She squints even harder until her eyes are practically closed. Finally, there's a flash of recognition. "Ah. Sorry, dear. Eyesight's not what it used to be."

"Is Wallace around?" I peer over her shoulder at the couch, but it's empty. I also notice nothing's packed up, even though they're probably not long from eviction now.

"Who?" She scratches her head and squints at Bunny.

"Wallace?" I repeat.

The kitten reappears and makes a break for it, but Wallace's grandma shoves it back inside with a slippered foot. "Oh, you mean Gerald," she says. "I always forget you boys still call him by that ridiculous name."

"Right. So is Wallace — I mean, Gerald — home right now?"

"Nope. He's at the library."

"The library?"

"You know what a library is, don't you? That place filled with books they let people borrow," she says. I can't tell if she's being sarcastic or not.

"Yes, ma'am. I'll look for him at the library. Thank you, ma'am."

Much to my surprise, I do find Wallace at the library. He's sitting in the back corner of the computer lab, wearing headphones and staring at his screen in deep concentration. I notice he's got a fat lip, a cut across his temple, and a bruised cheek. After signing in at the front desk, I enter the lab and take a seat at the computer next to him.

"'Sup, Nas?" he says too loudly because his headphones are still on and he can't hear himself. A few people shoot annoyed looks over their shoulders.

Wallace doesn't seem to notice. He gives me dap, wincing as he does so. I glance down and see his knuckles are all cut up and bruised, too. He slips his hands into his hoodie pocket.

"What happened?" I ask.

"Nothing."

"Wallace. Come on, man. Be real with me."

"What the fuck do you think happened, cuz?"

The computers hum. The other library patrons click and clack away at their keyboards. I don't say anything, because I already know that someone probably came to collect on a bet from St. S's win last night and Wallace couldn't pay up.

"You need to go to the hospital?" I ask.

He laughs. "Nah, just a few scratches. Besides, no health insurance, remember?"

"Right." I search for a safer topic. "Your kitten's looking good, man. Real healthy."

"Makes me mad, thinking about someone abandoning some little thing like that," he says. "What's wrong with people?"

Well, I tried.

"I don't know," I say.

People glance at us again, trying to shut us up with their eyes. But whatever. I take a deep breath and lower my voice.

"Are you in danger, Wallace? Like, for real?"

"Always."

"I'm serious."

"So am I."

A big-haired white lady at a computer in the next row suddenly turns around and shushes us. Wallace gestures for her to wait a moment, digs into his pocket, and pulls out . . . his middle finger. The woman gets up and leaves in a huff. She returns a moment later with a mousy old guy who's got a mustache like from an eighties movie. The librarian, I'm guessing.

"Excuse me, gentlemen. I'm afraid I'm going to have to ask you to continue your conversation outside," he says.

"Why?" Wallace asks. "'Cause we're Black?"

"No. Because you're disrupting the library's other patrons."

I stand to leave, but Wallace remains seated. "Nah, fuck that, OG. I'm good." He slips his headphones back on, clicks Play on some music video he was apparently in the middle of watching when I came by.

The librarian sighs and then walks away. Through the

computer lab's windows, I watch him go up to a police officer hanging out by the doors chatting up some high school girl. For some reason, the police are always hanging around this place. I bet public libraries in the suburbs don't have their own force. And must be super exciting for them. *Law & Order: SBU — Special Books Unit.*

But whatever.

I put a hand on Wallace's shoulder. "Let's go, man. We need to talk some more anyway."

Wallace pushes my hand away.

A few moments later, the cop's looming over Wallace. He's a broad-chested dude with a crewcut. Pretty much how you'd imagine a cop to look. Everyone in the place has stopped what they're doing to watch this unfold.

Wallace finally looks up at the cop and then at me and then back at the cop. He slides his headphones off his head and offers them to the guy. "You heard this track yet? It's the new Beyoncé."

The cop does not laugh. "I understand you gentlemen have been asked to leave. Now, you can depart the easy way or" — he pauses and taps the cuffs on his utility belt — "the hard way."

I hold my breath, try to will Wallace not to do anything stupid.

"Sure thing, Officer," he says, grinning. "This has all been a terrible misunderstanding. My associate and me were about to go. Weren't we, Mr. Blake?"

"Yeah," I say, exhaling with relief.

Wallace powers down the computer, pushes his chair back, and stands. "It really is a great album," he says to the cop, winking. "Her best one yet."

We walk outside to find that it's snowing lightly again. Everything's covered in a thin layer of white. Wallace finds the cop's cruiser and uses his index finger to draw a penis in the snow that's accumulated on the windshield.

Then he continues around to the back of the building like I'm not even there, but I follow. He leans against the brick, takes out a cigarette, and lights up. In the overcast daylight, his face looks even rougher than it did back inside the library. He's squinting at something in the distance, and I'm watching the wind carry his smoke away.

I zip up my coat and pull on my gloves. Wallace only has a hoodie, but he doesn't look cold.

"Can I say something?" I ask.

"You've got a mouth, don't you?"

I take a deep breath. "This isn't working—this whole betting against Bunny thing. You have to see that."

Wallace takes a drag on his cigarette.

"Give it up, Wallace. We'll figure out something else."

He laughs, shaking his head.

"And fix what you did to Bunny. Make it right," I say, repeating the words from Keyona's text. Because if Wallace gives up this scheme, then there's no reason why Bunny shouldn't play on Sunday.

"I think you mean to say what *we* did, cuz."

I nod because it's true. If it wasn't for me, it wouldn't have gotten this serious.

Wallace is silent for a while, like he's actually considering it. Finally, he says, "It's too late."

"It's not," I say. "Just don't make any more bets. And send another anonymous email admitting that the first one was fake."

Wallace takes one more drag and then flicks the butt away. Then he pulls out Bunny's phone from his coat pocket and hands it to me. "Can I be straight with you?"

I slip the phone into my pocket. "Of course."

"Yeah, I've been making small wagers here and there. But soon as I had that phone in my hand and I knew what I could do, I took a slightly different route."

"What do you mean by that, Wallace?"

"Told my bookie I had a tip. That I knew for sure who wouldn't be winning on Sunday."

"You thought St. S wouldn't even go to the championship because of what you were going to do to Bunny."

"Right," he says.

"Only, they won without Bunny."

"Right," he says again, sadder this time. "Now I've made the wrong people mad."

I think for a moment, trying to take all this in. Then I ask, "Who?"

"You don't know them," he says. "They run all the books in Whitman. High school sports. NBA. NFL. Even the goddamn

Olympics and shit. You name it. If you're looking to place a bet in this city, they're the ones setting the odds, and at some point, your money's probably passing through their hands. Anyway, they ended up agreeing to pay me for the tip, and I told them how Bunny would be out of the picture."

"So what's the worst that can happen? They don't let you place any more bets?"

Wallace laughs and shakes his head. "Man, you remember Gabe?"

I nod.

"Word on the street is that the bullet he caught by accident was meant for someone who fucked with these guys."

I lean against the wall like the wind's been knocked out of me. Everyone knew that kind of stuff happened in Whitman, even if you didn't run in those circles. It was easy enough to ignore it, to stay out of that world—but that didn't mean it was going to stay out of yours.

"Damn," I say. "This is serious."

"No shit, cuz. That's what I've been telling you."

"Can't you go somewhere until this blows over?" Even saying it sounds ridiculous, though. Like I'm in some corny movie about gang violence.

He spits. "They're not the type to let something like this blow over."

"What if you gave them their money back?"

"Can't. I already gave it to the landlord so he'd let me and G stay a few more months. Wanted to do that right away because I knew if I didn't, I'd end up spending it all."

"There has to be something we can do."

"Pray that the state doesn't make a decision before Sunday. St. S got lucky last night, but no way they'll win the championship without Bunny."

Suddenly, I'm overwhelmingly sad for Wallace. It's a heavy feeling, like a basketball-size stone sitting in my stomach. Yeah, he fucked up. Bad. And the thing is, he's always been kind of a fool. Type of kid who packed his snowballs with rocks. Who blew off homework because he didn't understand it and didn't want to admit it. Who would hang out long past when we were done playing just to get invited to dinner.

But for some reason, it's still not easy for me to write him off. And that feeling wins out over wanting to push him to fix Bunny's situation.

"It's not right," I say, meaning all of it, meaning everything.

Wallace doesn't speak for a few beats. The snow gathers on his shoulder as he looks down and leans back against the wall like all the life's gone out of him.

"That's your problem," he says. "Somehow you got it in your head that the world even knows what *right* means."

41
BUNNY

As I wait for the bus Friday after practice, I can't shake this bad feeling that's following me. I drank way more than I should have last night, so I was slow and heavy all day. In practice, Coach Baum kept telling me to "look alive," and I think he suspected it was more than just my nervousness about what's going to happen with the state. It didn't help I had to run with second string again while Clay got to play my spot with the first team. Making a hundred free throws with the backups took about a million years.

I'm also thinking about how messed up everything feels right now. I can't believe I tried to kiss Brooke, and then I made a fool of myself wandering lost around Stacy's neighborhood until Drew found me and drove me all the way back home to Whitman.

The snow's really coming down now. Thick flakes are sticking to everything. Everyone at practice was saying they heard it's supposed to die down in the next few hours, but it doesn't seem like it. Thankfully, the bus pulls up with a squeal, I swipe my pass, and make my way down the aisle as the driver pulls away from the curb. There's only a couple other people on here, so I swing my gym bag and backpack off my shoulders and take a seat in the middle.

A few minutes into the ride, my phone starts buzzing with a call. I'm borrowing one of Jess's old phones, so I have no idea who's calling, since my numbers aren't programmed into it. I flip it open. "Hello?"

"Bunny?"

My heart starts thumping the moment I recognize Coach Baum's voice. There's only one reason he'd call me after we spent three hours together at practice.

"Yes, sir?"

"I just got off the phone with the state." He pauses.

"And?"

"And . . . you're starting on Sunday!"

I close my eyes, exhale, and start laughing. "Thank God."

"Don't thank God. Thank Dr. Dietrich's connections. To be honest, I really didn't think this was going to go our way."

"For real?"

"But no matter. It did. The NJSIAA's going to release an official statement in the morning. So rest up tonight, and bring your A-game to practice tomorrow. I've been reviewing Fairview's tapes, and I've got some new offensive sets to get you all ready."

"Yes, Coach. I will. For sure. Thank you. Thank you."

"And, Bunny?"

"Yes, Coach?"

"No parties again until after we win."

"Yes, Coach."

I flip the phone closed. Cheesing like a madman, I do a little dance right there in my seat. I catch the bus driver looking at me like I'm crazy in the long rearview mirror that runs over her head, but I don't even care.

42

NASIR

S aturday morning I wake up to a text from Keyona that only contains a link. I'm kind of afraid of where it's going to take me, but I click on it anyway.

A PDF opens. It's a press release from the director of the NJSIAA. I sit up and read it through. Then I reread it to be sure I understand it correctly.

Sure enough: Bunny's off the hook.

It says that they found neither Benedict Thompson nor St. Sebastian's to be in violation of any of the NJSIAA regulations, and that it appeared the email in question had been sent from his stolen phone—though, they couldn't determine the responsible party due to steps taken by the sender to maintain anonymity. It concludes by saying that Bunny could immediately resume participation in NJSIAA-sanctioned events.

I put my phone down.

Damn.

As I think about how Bunny's off the hook, I catch myself smiling. I'm genuinely happy for him, genuinely happy that what I did isn't going to ruin his life.

But then I remember Wallace, and my smile sinks like the *Titanic.*

I consider talking to my parents about everything, but it doesn't take me long to decide that's stupid as hell. They'd definitely want to call the police, and then I would end up in trouble for stealing Bunny's phone, and Wallace would end up in trouble for the email, for all his under-the-table wagers, and for snitching.

Damn.

Why does one person's win always mean another person's loss?

Maybe it doesn't have to. Maybe it's time for me to do right by both my friends, not just one.

I check the time and find it's about eight. I know Bunny will definitely have practice today, but I don't know when. I throw back my covers and climb out of bed. Put on some clothes and rush downstairs, past my parents cooking breakfast, and across the street to Bunny's house. I knock a few times before his dad answers.

"Nasir!" he says. "Good to see you. Hear the news?"

I'm kind of surprised he actually does seem happy to see me. I guess Bunny never told him about my part in this mess. "Yeah, I did. It's great, Mr. Thompson. Bunny still around?"

"Sure is. Still sleeping, but it's about time for him to get up." He opens the door all the way and steps aside. "You can go ahead and save me the trouble of trying to wake him. You know how he sleeps like a rock."

I step inside, wave to the twins watching cartoons in front

of the TV and to Ms. Thompson frying bacon in the kitchen, then I head upstairs.

Sure enough, when I enter Bunny's room, he's out cold. I almost laugh aloud, though, because he's wrapped in his comforter like a six-foot-five burrito, his head and his feet sticking out either end. I sit down on the edge of the bed and give what I think is his shoulder a little shake.

"Bunny," I say. "Get up, man."

He stirs but doesn't wake, so I shake him a little harder. Gradually, he opens his eyes. Looks at me. Blinks a few times. "Nas?" he asks, voice groggy.

"Yeah, man. It's me. Can we talk?"

He slides one arm out of the burrito and rubs his eyes. Then he slides the other one out and pushes himself into a sitting position. He runs a hand over the top of his head. "Get out," he says.

"Bunny, please, I—"

"Man, you can't do me like that and then walk in here like we're still cool." He nods toward the door, eyes still bleary. "Get out."

"At least let me apologize."

He glares at me, weighing my words. He doesn't tell me to leave again, so I take that as a sign that he's willing to hear me out.

"I swiped your phone." I pull it out of my pocket and set it on his desk.

He looks at it. "Yeah, I solved that mystery."

"And I'm sorry for that, Bunny. For real, man. I am. But I didn't send that email."

"Right. Then who did?"

"Wallace."

"Wallace?" Bunny asks, pulling a face. "Is that fool really still hating on me for transferring to St. S?"

"Nah," I say. "It's more than that."

And then I tell him everything. About the landlord raising Wallace and his grandma's rent. About how he started betting against Bunny, hoping to cover the difference. About how he approached me for help when he got real desperate, and about how I gave it to him because somebody needed to. And finally, about the mess he's locked himself into.

Then I say, "I need you to lose tomorrow."

Bunny draws his knees to his chest and sits there staring into space for a while. Without looking at me, he says, "I appreciate you being honest with me about everything, Nas. But are you really pulling me into this, asking me to throw the game?"

"I hate that I am," I say. "But I am."

"Even if I agree to do this, if I get caught, you know how much trouble I could get in?"

"I do. But it's the only way, man. If St. S loses, those dudes Wallace made the arrangement with will get what they want and will probably let Wallace off the hook."

He doesn't respond.

"I know it's asking a lot," I say, "but you can keep it close.

Nobody will know. And now that you're in the clear, there's always next season." He doesn't seem convinced, so I press on. "It's just a game, Bunny. How's that more important than Wallace's life?"

He shakes his head. "What'd Wallace ever do for me, Nas? Name one thing."

"Nothing," I say. "I know he's done nothing but cause you trouble. Like I said, I know I'm asking for a lot."

"Then why should I lose on purpose for someone who's never done anything for me?"

"I don't know," I say.

"It's real messed up that you're putting this on me, Nas. I mean, I appreciate you owning up to what you did, and I can maybe forgive you, since nothing came of it besides me sitting one game. But Wallace is your cousin, not mine, and you know basketball's more than only a game to me." He shakes his head. "Wallace made some stupid choices. He has to deal with the consequences now."

I look down. "Then don't do it for him. Lose the game for me, Bunny."

He laughs. "For you?"

His laughter makes me angry. "Man, you up and transferred without even saying anything to me about it. Not a single word."

"It was my decision," he says.

"That doesn't mean you needed to make it alone. Why didn't you even ask what I thought about it? We were supposed to be best friends."

Bunny looks away, shaking his head. "It's my life."

"And isn't anyone else part of it?" I ask, my voice rising. "I had to find out from Chops, man. From freaking Chops—down at the courts. Forget you transferring, forget you asking for my opinion—you know how much it hurt that my friend didn't even care enough to tell me before announcing it to the world?"

Bunny draws in a deep breath and lets it out slowly. "I thought you'd tell me to stay at Whitman."

I stand up. "Honestly, I don't know what I would have told you. But it would have meant something to me—it would have meant that I meant something to you—if I could have had the chance to tell you anything at all. Instead, it was one more example of how you care about basketball, about your future, about winning, more than you care about anything else."

"It's not like that."

"It's not?" I ask. "Then lose Sunday."

"Nasir, it's the state championship."

"Bunny, it's a game."

Bunny looks up at me. "A real friend wouldn't ask me to do something like this, Nasir."

"I'm sorry," I say. "But I wouldn't be asking if I thought there was any other way to save Wallace."

43
BUNNY

I spend most of the day thinking on what Nasir said. Practice doesn't go as well as I hoped it would because I'm so distracted, and when I get home I'm acting so off that everyone in my family keeps asking me what's wrong. Makes sense. I should be back to my old self, given that I'll be playing in the state championship tomorrow. It still gets on my nerves, though, so instead of sticking around, I head over to Keyona's.

She only lives a few blocks away, but it's snowing like crazy. I'm wondering if they might even delay tomorrow's game. Part of me thinks that would be good, since it would give me more time to figure everything out, and part of me thinks that would be terrible, since it would force me to sit with this decision even longer.

"Is basketball the only thing I care about?" I ask Keyona as soon as she opens the door.

"What?" she asks as she lets me in. "You walk through this blizzard just for that?"

"Kind of," I say, and step inside.

Her house is warm and smells like baking cookies. Her

family's Great Dane trots up to greet me. I scratch him behind the ears for a bit as Keyona's stepmom wanders over, hugs me, and makes small talk about the whole eligibility situation and the game tomorrow. Keyona's little brother keeps on playing a video game in the living room. Keyona pulls me away, and her stepmom calls up a reminder to keep the door open.

Her room's messy as always. Bed unmade, clothes all over the place, a few empty glasses on the nightstand. She pushes some stuff aside to make space for us on her bed, and then sits down on it with her back pressed against the wall.

I wander over to look at the pictures of us she printed out and tacked on her bulletin board. Even though we've been texting a bit about the whole stolen phone thing, we've never resolved anything between us.

"You okay?" she asks. "Nervous about the game?"

"In a way."

"It's all right, Bunny. You got this."

"What do you think about the question I asked you?"

"You mean if basketball's the only thing you care about?"

I nod.

"Let me guess. You tried to work things out with Nasir?"

I nod again.

"I don't think it is," she answers without hesitation, which makes me feel better. But she's not done. "It's just that when you're really into something, you get hyperfocused on that thing, and everything else becomes an afterthought."

"What do you mean?"

"What did Nasir tell you?" Keyona asks.

"That he was mad—no, hurt—that I never talked to him about my decision to change schools."

"And what did I tell you the last time we talked? Like, real talked. Not texted."

I think for a moment, mentally replaying the conversation we had on the phone as I walked to the bus stop a few days ago. "That you were mad I didn't ask you to transfer to St. S instead of Nasir."

"I wasn't mad, Bunny," she says. "I was hurt, like Nasir. Not so much because you didn't ask me to transfer to your school, but because just like with him, you didn't even come to me about it. You were so focused on fixing things between the two of you that you didn't consider asking me what I thought about all of it."

I sit down at her desk because it's a heavy thing to ask someone about your faults and have them actually lay them out there. "Oh."

"You've got to learn to ask for help."

It would make perfect sense to bring up the whole Wallace situation right now, but I don't want to drag her into that mess like Nasir did to me. It's for her own good. So I nod and let the moment slide past.

"And, yeah," she says, drawing her legs to her chest, "there are times when I get jealous of the game like it's another girl." She meets my eyes and smiles. "Then again, there are times you focus on me so hard that it makes everything better for a while."

I look away. Do I tell her about Brooke? It's not like anything actually happened. If I'd ended up kissing her, it'd be another matter altogether.

I consider everything she's told me and decide that if I'm not going to tell her the truth about everything with Wallace, then I should at least come clean about that.

I take a deep breath. "I've got something to tell you, Key," I say, and the smile drops off her face. And then I do. I tell her about that night, and she listens without saying a thing.

When I finish, she stares past me for a long time, jaw clenched, rocking back and forth a little. "Please leave," she says, the anger barely contained.

"Key, I'm sorry, I—"

"I'm glad you told me, Bunny. I appreciate the truth, I really do. But what did you expect?" She's still not looking at me, and her words are coming out quicker and louder. "That I'd listen to this story about how you were stressed so you got drunk and tried to hook up with some random girl—who, thankfully, had enough sense to reject you—and then be cool with it?"

"It won't happen again," I say.

"How am I supposed to believe you?" she asks. "I never thought you'd let it happen once."

"I'm just trying to be straight with you," I say. "Would you rather I hid it?"

"Of course not," she says. "I'm glad you told me. If I would have found out about this another way, I'd probably be pushing you out the window right now instead of having words with you. But that doesn't mean I have to be cool with it."

I look at my palms. "Are we over?"

"I don't know, Bunny," she says. "I've got to think about it. But right now, I need you to leave."

I sigh as I stand up. "You still coming to the game tomorrow? I want you there."

"I know you do," she says. "I need to figure out if I want to be there."

"Okay," I say. "I get it." Then I leave, since that's what she wants.

44

NASIR

F or the first time since last year, Bunny's staying over. He showed up on my doorstep after dinner, said he had thought about it, and claimed that he couldn't care less about Wallace but that our friendship was more important to him than basketball.

Then he held out a ticket to the game and asked if I wanted to watch him lose.

So now we're doing just like we used to. Video games. Nerf wars. Dunk contest on the little hoop on the back of my bedroom door. We stay up late, since the game's not until the early evening. We get yelled at by my dad for being too loud. We even bust out my old Pokémon cards and get in a few rounds playing with half-remembered rules. We talk about the future and how amazing it's going to be.

It's like we're little kids again. I think with a true friend, you always kind of feel like a little kid. You don't have to pretend to be cool or tough. You don't have to worry about feeling embarrassed or ashamed. You act how you want to act, and I think that deep down everyone wants to be that immature, that fearless.

Man, I missed the hell out of this.

45

BUNNY

'm lying there in the darkness on Nasir's bed while he's in a sleeping bag on the floor. I can tell by his even breathing that he's fast asleep, but I'm wide awake like a kid on Christmas Eve. I can't stop thinking about the game tomorrow.

Actually, later today, because it's nearly three a.m.

Fairview's got two guys to worry about. Their center's this towering kid from somewhere in eastern Europe who has nice range. He's headed to Duke. And their point is this short Black kid who just moved up from the South and who everyone swears is the second coming of Allen Iverson. He's a sophomore, like me.

Eric and Drew will have their hands full. As power forward, I'm going to have to help out. Double the center down low. Protect the lane when the point drives. But I can't be in two places at once.

Everyone else on that squad's solid, but nothing to worry about. One of those two gets into foul trouble or something, and it'll be a completely different game.

Of course, we've got to lose in the end. But that doesn't

mean I can't do some damage and keep it close along the way.

"Nas," I whisper. "You awake?"

He doesn't respond.

I slip the pillow out from under my head, whack him with it, and then drop back down like I'm still sleeping.

Nasir pops up, head swiveling back and forth. "What? Huh?"

"What?" I say, rolling onto my side.

I can see him rub his eyes by the pale light from the street lamps that leak through his curtains. "Did you just hit me?" he asks, his voice still thick with sleep.

"Nah, you must be dreaming, man," I say, laughing.

"Oh." He lies back down.

A car alarm starts going off in the distance. A minute or so passes before it stops.

"Nas?" I say.

"Yeah?"

"Thanks for letting me stay over."

"No problem. Just like old times, right?"

I sigh. "Like this year never happened."

The room falls quiet. I roll onto my back, stretch my hands behind my head, and look up at the ceiling. I wonder if it's still snowing.

The heat kicks on, the vent blowing warm air up the side of the bed.

"Nas?" I say.

"Yeah?"

"Did I make a mistake? By transferring, I mean."

Nasir's quiet for a few moments. Long enough that I start to wonder if he fell back to sleep. But then he speaks. "Honestly, I don't know, man." He sighs. "At first, I thought so. Thought you were making the biggest mistake of your life."

I prop myself up on an elbow. "What changed?"

He sighs. "Guess I realized I was getting it twisted. Making it all about me."

"I'm sorry," I say. "I should've talked to you when I first started thinking about transferring. Got your thoughts on it instead of just up and deciding."

It feels good to say it aloud. I've wanted to for a while, but I couldn't. I guess it's easier speaking in the dark where it's like nothing exists except your words.

"Thanks, Bunny," he says. "That means a lot. And I'm sorry I stopped talking to you. That wasn't right."

"Maybe a little wrong, a little right."

"Maybe it doesn't even matter," Nasir says.

"What do you mean?"

His sleeping bag rustles as he turns toward me. "When you asked me to transfer to St. Sebastian's, it got me thinking a lot about everything in a new way. Seeing things how you probably saw them when you were figuring out whether you should do it or not. Seeing how it's not so easy."

I nod, even though he can't see me. He goes on.

"When you're going one place, that always means you're leaving another. Your back's always facing some way."

I put my hands behind my head and stare up at the ceiling in the dark. "I'm not sure it's that simple. I feel like there can be room to care about more than one thing, more than one place."

"Maybe," Nasir says. "Or maybe not."

"Even though I'm at St. Sebastian's, I still care about everyone in Whitman," I say.

"For now. But what about after you go off to college? After you make it into the NBA? You'll forget about us."

"I won't."

"Why not?" Nasir asks.

"Because Whitman's my home," I answer. It's that simple.

Neither of us says anything again for a while. I'm thinking about what that means, and how it'll feel a little less like home once Word Up officially closes. Then I realize that I haven't told Nasir about that yet. So I do.

"You serious?" he asks, sounding more awake than he has during the conversation up until now.

"Yup," I say.

"Maybe we can hold a fundraiser or something? Set up one of those websites where people can donate and make a video about the store or something to promote it."

"Dad and Zaire already signed the paperwork," I say.

"Damn."

"Yup."

"So when's it officially closing?" he asks.

"End of April," I answer.

"What are the new owners turning it into?"

"No idea yet," I say.

"I'm going to miss that place."

"Me too," I say.

"Maybe after you make your millions, you can reopen it. Call it Word Up 2."

"Word Still Up."

"Word Up Again."

"You Thought Word Was Down, But Now Word Way Up."

We laugh.

"That'd be cool," I say. "But I'll need someone to run it while I'm on the road. You down?"

I hear Nasir shift in his sleeping bag. "Of course, man," he says, even though we both know if I really did buy the store back my dad would run it again. "So long as I can live upstairs like Zaire."

We laugh. And even though we're laughing, that sounds to me like the best possible future. "What about becoming a doctor?" I ask, coming back to reality. "That still the plan?"

"Maybe. I don't know," Nasir says. "I know I want to help people, but I'm not sure if that's the way I want to do it. Maybe I'll be a teacher like my dad, or something. Or serve. I don't know. I have this feeling that things can be better, but they're not going to get that way unless we make it that way. It's like doing good just for myself or my family doesn't mean a whole lot in the grand scheme of things."

"That's easy for you to say. It's only you and your parents, and y'all are doing okay. But for some people, just being able to help their family means everything."

"True," he says.

Our conversation falls into a lull. Somewhere nearby a dog starts barking and then stops. I consider Nasir's words. Like if you think about it long enough, you might decide to chill in your room for the rest of your life, wondering.

Finally, I break the silence. "By the way, now that I'm in the clear with the state, I think that St. S offer still stands. You think about it any more?"

"Yeah."

"And?"

Nasir's quiet for a moment, and then he swings his pillow and hits me right in the face. Laughing, I yank it from his grip, stand up on the bed, and whack him with it several times while he curls into the fetal position on the floor. We're both laughing so hard that I eventually run out of energy, drop the pillow, and fall back onto the bed. It takes us a couple minutes to stop and catch our breath. When I finally do, I suddenly feel real tired. Or maybe *peaceful* is the right word. Yeah, peaceful.

Everything feels softer, glowier.

Everything feels right, even though it isn't.

I listen to a siren wailing far away as I slip into sleep like the moon sliding over the horizon.

46
NASIR

I wake to the sunlight in my eyes and the sound of a snow-plow scraping along the street below my window.

It's almost eleven according to my phone. "Bunny — wake up," I say. But the bed's empty and made. Guess he took off.

I stretch, sit up, and peek outside. The sun's shining for the first time in days and reflecting off the snow so everything's bright and blinding. The cars and sidewalks are covered in several inches. And even though the street's just been plowed, it looks icy.

According to the ticket Bunny gave me, the game's at five. He said I could catch a ride with his family, since it's, like, an hour and a half away, so I make a mental note to check with them about what time they're planning to leave.

For now, I throw back the curtains to let in even more light, and climb into bed.

47
BUNNY

I'm sitting at a window in the back of the bus, watching the snow-covered world slip past. Like usual, most of the team is chatting or flirting with the cheerleaders, who we're splitting the bus with again. Except this time we're riding in one of those nice coach buses. There's some extra energy in the air today since it's the biggest game most of these guys will ever play in their life. But I've got my headphones up with some Nat King Cole on low, trying to clear my mind of the fact that everyone's counting on me and I have to let all of them down for Wallace's sake.

The St. Sebastian's locker room's nice, but this a whole new level. Red carpet. Black leather couch. Open lockers made of wood like what the pros have, our fresh-pressed jerseys already on hangers inside of them. On the wall, the red Rutgers R and three words: ATTITUDE, COMMITMENT, ACCOUNTABILITY.

In the leftmost locker I see my jersey. Number twenty-three. Not for LeBron, but for Jordan. He was my dad's favorite player back in the day, so he became mine too.

While my teammates play around and fight over a spot

on the couch, I slip out of my street clothes and into my uniform. I pull on my warmups, lace up my sneakers, and slip my headphones back over my ears. I sneak out to the court early, Cole crooning in my ears.

I'm the first to walk into the arena. My heart starts racing soon as I step onto the waxed hardwood, which gleams under the lights. The empty seats tower in the darkness above and all around. Everything feels holy, like I'm in church.

Granted, the Rutgers Athletic Center's not nearly as big as the Sixers' stadium. But it's big enough to make me feel like I'm dreaming, to make me feel like maybe this is the beginning of everything.

I search the shadows for the section where my family and Nasir will be sitting. Maybe Keyona. I count the rows and seats until I find their exact spots, committing it to memory.

Satisfied, I make my way to the rack on the sideline and pick up one of the balls. The leather feels soft and smooth, expensive. Like it's fresh out of the box. I bounce it hard a couple times with both hands to test the floor, and the sound thunders through the vast space like a heartbeat. Then I dribble out to the top of the key and stare at the rim.

We might be taking the L tonight, but I promise myself that if Nas takes the spot at St. S, I'll bring us back here next year. Because as amazing as all this is, I can't help but imagine how much more amazing it'll be to snatch a rebound and then spin to find Nasir waiting on the wing, hands out, calling for the outlet pass.

48

NASIR

t's about fifteen minutes to tip-off, and this place is packed
and buzzing. According to the lady who takes our tickets,
all eight thousand seats are sold out.

And a big reason for that?

My boy, Bunny Thompson.

He's on the front of the game program. His name crack-
les in the air. Someone even made a big cardboard cutout
of his face. Everybody wants to see what he'll do tonight,
so when he makes it big they can brag that they knew him
when he was starting out—as if he hasn't been playing and
training for years.

I kind of wish I were wearing a shirt that said BUNNY'S BEST
FRIEND, or something like that but way less corny. Maybe at
halftime I can hijack the loudspeaker and make an announcement or something to let people know.

But then again, there's a feeling in the pit of my stomach I can't ignore, reminding me that maybe I don't deserve
that claim. After all, I was the reason he almost didn't play
tonight, and now I'm the one asking him to drop the biggest
game of his life so far. I keep telling myself it's for the right

reason, though. Nobody's cheering on Wallace or making cardboard cutouts of his face. No way he could even have gotten tickets for this. He's probably alone somewhere, refreshing the state's basketball site and waiting for the game to start, hoping for a St. Sebastian's loss. At least I'll be able to give him that.

Before we head to our seats, the Thompson family makes a stop to use the bathrooms and grab some food, so I go on ahead. I show my ticket to the usher standing at the top of our section's steps and then look around at the nearly full arena. The crowd's humming, and music blasts from the speakers. Down on the court, balls arc through the air and clang off the rim as the teams shoot around. Fairview's in green jerseys with white lettering, and St. Sebastian's in white with red lettering. I spot Bunny easily enough just as he sinks a long three. I smile and find row H.

As I scoot past some people toward my seat near the middle, I'm surprised to find Keyona with Anna, the friend she was with the other night. Last night Bunny told me about what went down and how he wasn't even sure if they were still together, but here she is, hands buried in the front pocket of her St. Sebastian's hoodie. Anna's in her ear, probably pointing out the most attractive players, but I can tell by Keyona's eyes that she's analyzing their skills, not their looks.

I sneak a glance at the seat number on my ticket and of course, it's the one right next to her. So I make my way over, sit down, and say, "What's up?"

Anna gives me some side-eye. Keyona doesn't even react.

I look down at my sneakers. Retie the laces. Join the girls in watching the teams. I let my eyes wander over to Fairview and spot their two all-stars chatting on the baseline, apart from the rest of their team. A true point and a solid big man are a deadly combo. Practically unstoppable because they can burn you from the outside or down low. But then again, St. Sebastian's has Bunny, a one-man wrecking crew.

I watch him below. He backs down one of his teammates, and then pivots and puts up a fadeaway. It kisses the glass perfectly, finding the bottom of the net.

The Thompsons arrive a moment later. They scoot past me with their food and drinks to their seats on the other side of Anna and Keyona, greeting them like family. And suddenly Keyona's all smiles and softness like she flipped a switch.

As the warmup clock winds down, both teams head back to their benches. The lights dim. The announcer introduces the starting five on each squad, his voice booming across the arena. The two stars from Fairview—a point guard named Santos and a center named Yurevich—get some decent noise, but the place absolutely explodes when Bunny's name echoes through the speakers, which makes pride and shame surge in my chest.

Instead of quieting down so the announcer can introduce St. Sebastian's center, everyone keeps on cheering. It's a rising wall of noise, building like a wave that won't stop crashing. The announcer tries to go on anyway, but you can't hear a thing he says into his mic. Eventually, the crowd falls silent as some kids' choir sings the national anthem, and then the starters take their positions around center court and a tense nervousness settles over the building.

My own nervousness is different from everyone else's, though, because unfortunately I already know how this is going to play out.

The ref steps to the circle with the ball and bounces it with both hands a few times. He says something to the teams as the centers crouch low. The ref blows the whistle as he tosses the ball into the air between them.

Game on.

49
BUNNY

Yurevich tips the ball to Santos, who lays it in before any of us knows what's happening.

Damn. That kid's fast as hell.

I inbound to Eric but hang back. Santos's pressure's too much, and he gives it right back to me. I push it downcourt, easily handling my man.

I split a double team, drive into the lane, and kick it out to Eric back at the top of the key. He takes the open shot, but it banks left and drops right into Yurevich's hands. He outlets to Santos, who takes off on the fast break, leaving Eric in his dust.

Just like that, we're down 0–4.

I know I'm supposed to lose tonight, but I'm not going down like that.

This time, when Eric crosses midcourt, I make a beeline for the basket. Eric fires it to Ethan, our off guard, who immediately hits me cutting into the lane, and I take it around Yurevich for two.

"Slow him down," I tell Eric as I hustle back on D.

I know we can't keep up this pace. Santos is too fast. This

run-and-gun style is his kind of game, not ours. If I'm going to keep this close, we're going to need to control each possession.

But Santos blows past Eric and passes to the wing, who reverses back to Santos. He dumps it to Yurevich on the block, so I slide over to double him with Drew. Trapped, he sends it back out to Santos, who gives it to their shooting guard, who drains a long three like it's nothing.

I answer at the other end with a midrange jumper. Fairview hits another three. When Yurevich slides over to double me, I find Drew on the block for an easy two. Fairview scores on a give-and-go. Eric bricks a shot. Yurevich hits a nasty hook. Ethan forces a three and air-balls it straight out of bounds. Santos breaks Eric's ankles with a crossover and then launches a floater straight over me that drops right in. I get called for a three-second violation under the rim.

Damn.

6–16, Fairview.

Fairview brings it up court, swings the ball around the perimeter, and dumps it to Yurevich in the paint—at least they try to. I intercept the pass and push it up court before Fairview's D can recover. I've got my man beat on the first step and shake Santos at midcourt with a spin move. Straight to the hoop and throw it down hard—first dunk of the game. The crowd explodes.

But there's a whistle.

I look at the ref: he motions traveling.

People start booing. No way I walked. But I don't say

anything—I don't need a tech. I shake my head in disbelief, get back to my man, and let Coach Baum spit a few choice words.

Fairview brings it down and scores on a baseline jumper. I answer with two in the paint. With only a few seconds left in the quarter, Santos misses a reverse lay-up. I grab the board and fire it to Eric, who pulls up at the arc and buries a quick three right before the end of the quarter to make it 11–20, Fairview.

We head to our bench and gather around Coach Baum, heads spinning. He stares at each of us in turn as we wipe the sweat from our foreheads, chug some water, and wait.

Finally, he speaks.

"Slow it down."

That's all he says. He doesn't take out his little board and draw up sets. He doesn't even tell us how.

"Slow it down," he repeats. Then he takes a deep breath and indicates for all of us to do the same.

We all do, and we all exhale when he does.

"Slow it—" he starts.

"Down," we finish.

The whistle blows. Since Fairview won the tip, it's ours to start the second quarter. But, of course, they run a press. Eric brings it down and dribbles right into a trap. Santos tears it out of his hands, and it's two more for them.

I answer with a midrange jumper. Yurevich misses from the corner. Eric bricks from the arc. Santos threads through the lane for a lay-up, but the ball circles the rim and falls out.

I grab the board, bring it up court myself, hit Drew on the block, and he banks it in for two. Fairview's two-guard responds with a three. I miss from the baseline. Santos drains a long two. I brick from up top, grab my own rebound, and kick it back out to Eric, who bricks from downtown. Santos scores on a give-and-go.

I glance at the scoreboard: 15–29, with just under five left.

So much for slowing it down.

I don't waste a second inbounding to Eric, but Santos forces him right into another trap. Eric passes back to me, but someone gets a hand on the ball. Santos comes up with it and races to the hoop. I move between him and the rim.

He fakes right and then crosses over left, but he can't shake me. Head down, he keeps driving. He ducks under my arm for the finger roll, but I swat it straight out of bounds.

The crowd gets loud. A rush of adrenaline courses through my body.

But there's another whistle: foul on the shot.

I throw my hands out. "I didn't touch him!"

"Careful, Twenty-Three," is all he says over his shoulder as he meets Santos at the line.

Once again, I shake my head. Santos buries both.

Soon as the ball's back in my hands, I'm ready to make them pay. I inbound to Eric and follow behind as he takes it up. Soon as he sees the trap coming, he gives it back to me, and then I'm gone. Shake my man with a crossover and then take it straight to the hoop. Yurevich steps in the way, but I've got too much momentum to stop or kick it out. I leap through him and slam it hard with both hands, swinging on the rim for a second before dropping back down to earth.

But the good feeling's ruined by the sound of a whistle —the ref signals an offensive charge on me.

This time, I can't hold back. I step to the ref. "You blind? He was moving!"

His face gets red. "This is your warning, Twenty-Three. Calm down." He walks away.

"Bullshit!" I shout at him.

Another whistle: tech.

The crowd starts booing, and it feels good to know they're on my side. What doesn't feel so good, though, is Coach subbing Clay in for me since a tech counts as a personal foul, which puts me at three. Still the first half, and already I'm in danger of fouling out, so I can't blame him. Head down, I make my way to the bench. Coach makes me sit next to him. I really don't want to. I know what he's going to say, and I don't want to hear it.

"What are you trying to prove?" he asks, his eyes on the action as play resumes.

Someone hands me a cup of water. I down it, then grab a towel and wipe my face. I'm breathing hard, trying to control my anger, but it doesn't seem like I'm going to even have to try to throw this game. "Nothing."

"You could've fooled me."

I shrug. "I want to win." It feels like a lie, knowing what's on the line with Wallace. But it's technically true. I do *want* to win.

"We all do. But you're not going to do it from here, are you?"

I don't answer. I watch as Santos steals the ball from Eric and scores on a fast break for what feels like the millionth time tonight.

"You've got to settle down. Play smart," Coach Baum tells me. "I know you're full of energy since you rode the bench the other night, but there's still plenty of game left. But if you get two more fouls, you're done."

I nod. Glance at the clock. Three and a half minutes left.

"Can I go back in now?" I ask.

Coach shakes his head. "At the half."

I exhale. Lean back. Down some water, crush the paper cup, and toss it over my shoulder. Yurevich backs Drew down and spins inside for two off the glass.

Now it's *The Santos and Yurevich Show*. They drop bucket after bucket, while we're getting so many bricks we could build a house. And I'm sitting there, powerless again.

The only good thing is that Santos gets called for reaching in on back-to-back possessions, so Fairview's coach subs him out. He notices me watching him return to his bench, so he smirks, points at the scoreboard, then brushes his shoulder off.

19–37, Fairview.

As the final seconds in the half run down, I start heading to the locker room before the rest of the team. The buzzer blares at my back.

50
NASIR

All around the arena people stand, stretch, and make for the bathrooms or concession stands. I shift in my seat and look up at the scoreboard. St. S is down bigtime.

Even Bunny can't seem to handle Santos and Yurevich on his own. Whenever he moved up to help with Santos, he left Yurevich open down low. Whenever he slid over to help with Yurevich, he left Santos open up top. Maybe I can work on my game this summer so that can be Bunny and me next year.

"You want anything, Nasir?" Ms. Thompson asks as she slides out of the row with Mr. Thompson and the little kids in tow.

"Nah, I'm good," I say. "But thanks." I poke Justine and Ash as they go by. They giggle and try to slap my hands away. Anna asks Keyona if she wants to go to the bathroom, and they both leave.

Jess stays behind, though, pulling out her phone. I watch the cheerleaders perform their halftime routine. They're nice to look at. The blond one Bunny tried to make out with is especially cute.

I stretch my arms over my head. Roll my neck. Lean back. "So," I say to Jess. "What's new on the Internet?"

"I'm reading," she says, without taking her eyes off the screen.

"What are you reading?"

"A book."

"What kind of book?" I ask, ignoring her sarcasm.

"The kind with words."

I shrug. "I prefer the kind with pictures."

"Cool." She swipes the screen. The cheerleaders gyrate. I yawn.

"Seriously, though," I say, "what are you reading? Something social worker-y?"

She puts her finger on a word to mark her place and looks up like she's seeing me for the first time. "Social worker-y?"

"Yeah. Anyway, why do you want to be a social worker? I heard they don't make much money."

"They don't," she says. "But I want to help people."

"I feel you," I say, thinking about what Bunny and I were talking about last night. "Me too."

"Really?"

"Yeah."

"So what do you want to study, then? When you get to college."

I shrug. "No idea. I like reading. Maybe I'll be an English teacher or something. Come back and work at Whitman High."

She nods, slides her phone back into her pocket. "Right on."

And I feel my face getting warm, remembering how I used to crush on her hard back in the day. She's three years older than Bunny and me, so she never hung out with us. But she was always around. Beautiful and far away, like an angel.

But suddenly, she seems much closer.

I clear my throat. "So you think St. S is going to win?" It's a stupid question, since I already know the answer, but it seems like something that makes sense to say.

She shrugs, props her arm up on the armrest, chin in hand.

I laugh. "Don't you have faith in your brother?"

"I do. But he needs to start passing more. Nobody can do everything alone."

"Not even Bunny?"

"Not even Bunny."

We settle into a comfortable silence and watch the cheerleaders wrap up their routine.

The stadium refills. The rest of the Thompsons return, along with Keyona and Anna. I poke Justine and Ash again as they slide past me on their way to their seats.

The teams jog back onto the court to wild applause. I try to catch Bunny's eye, but he's got that look on his face. Focused. Determined. The only thing that exists for him right now is the next sixteen minutes.

51
BUNNY

airview's press is so loose it's insulting. We break it, and I post up. Coach really stressed the slow-it-down business, so I pretend like I'm fighting for position while the guards just keep tossing it back and forth like they're playing monkey in the middle.

After a couple more passes, Santos gets annoyed and lunges for the interception. But he's a second too late, and Eric glides to the hoop. The defense collapses into the lane, so he whips it behind the back to me, and I drop an easy two off the glass to make it 21–37.

Back on defense, I'm covering Yurevich now, and the dude can't shake me. So Santos launches a long three. It looks right on — perfect arc, slow backspin — but it hits the heel of the rim and pops straight up. Everyone leaps, but I rise above them all and snatch it out of the air, clear the area by swinging my elbows, and then hand it off to Eric.

We run down about twenty seconds just passing it along the perimeter, barely putting it on the floor at all. Santos sags back, too nervous to try for the steal again. Eventually, Eric gets a good look and fires a jumper. It bricks, and I fight my instinct to try for the put-back and tip it to the top of the key. Frustration getting the best of him, Santos swipes for a steal and gets called for reaching in.

I clap. Finally a good call.

We inbound and reset our offense. With the defense sitting back, Eric puts up a long three and nails it. The crowd explodes. The Fairview players all glance up at the scoreboard. 24–37. They've still got a comfortable lead, but I know they're starting to sweat. The momentum's shifting.

Fairview forces the shot on their next few possessions and manages to hit a couple. But each time we get it back, we stall and find the open man.

The quarter ends with Fairview only up 39–47.

Eight points behind. Eight more minutes. Even though I'm burning with anger that I've got to make sure we lose, I'm going to scare the hell out of them.

Right off the inbound, Santos fakes left, spins right, and powers it into the lane. I step in the way and plant my feet. He smashes into me, and we both drop to the ground.

Whistle: charging.

Drew helps me up and then we bump chests. That's Santos's fourth—one more, and he's done. The crowd instantly realizes this, and half of them cheer while the other half start chanting, "Bullshit."

Play stops as Fairview's coach and Santos argue with the ref. Things get heated, and a moment later, the ref signals a tech on Fairview's coach. Oldhead's face flushes red. He tosses his clipboard to the ground and steps right up in the ref's face, shouting up a storm. The ref starts to walk away, and then the coach grabs his shoulder. The ref blows his whistle again and jabs his finger into the air, ejecting the Fairview coach from the game.

Veins bulge in the dude's neck as he continues screaming even as he heads out of the gym. He kicks over a chair before he disappears into the locker room, and the Fairview players exchange lost looks as we clap it up.

One of the Fairview assistants — a young-looking dude with glasses — picks up the clipboard and shouts at everyone to get back into position.

Because of the double tech against their coach, we get four free throws. Coach Baum chooses Eric to take them. He misses the first but sinks the last three, cutting the lead to five.

Santos stays in the game and calls some play as he crosses half-court. The other guard sets a pick, and he flies around it. Instead of driving, he fires a pass through the lane to Yurevich — but I'm right there and taking it downcourt in the blink of an eye. Santos and the two-guard backpedal to stay with me, and I can see them trying to figure out if I'm going to kick it back, pull up, or take it all the way. Feeling unstoppable, I fake like I'm going to pop it back but instead take it all the way and tomahawk it so hard the backboard shakes like it's going to shatter as the crowd lose their minds and cameras flash like lightning.

Santos laces his hands behind his head, looking up at the ceiling. Yurevich yells at the shooting guard. The young assistant coaches stand on the sideline, jaws clenched and arms folded across their chests, looking like they're in over their heads.

We don't let up. Press so hard that Fairview can't even inbound. They get called for five seconds, and the ball's ours again. Our guards shave some time passing around the perimeter, and then Eric cuts into the lane and dumps it to Drew, who gets an easy two. Just like that, it's a one-point game at 46–47. If I can keep it like this until the end, maybe there won't be too much shame in taking the L.

Fairview uses their last time-out, a thirty-second one. We huddle up, Coach talks some more about keeping it slow and staying in control, and then we hustle back onto the court at the ref's whistle.

Santos breaks the trap on the next possession and ends up finding Yurevich posting. He tries backing me down, but I'm not giving up any ground, so he picks up his dribble. He looks to the outside like he's going to pass but then pivots, swinging his elbows — clocks me right in the nose.

There's a flash of red.

Everything goes blurry.

I stumble backwards.

Nothing and then a rush of pain at the center of my face. My eyes tear up, and I feel something warm leaking out of my nostrils. At first I think it's snot, but I touch it and my fingers come away bloody.

I drop to one knee and cover my face with my hands. But the blood won't stop. It leaks through my fingers and onto the court. Coach Baum and the trainer rush over and start talking to me. But with the noise from the crowd and my head ringing, I can't make out a word they're saying. I hear someone snapping on latex gloves. A moment later, the trainer moves my hands away and then presses thick gauze to my face.

Once it turns red, the trainer tosses it aside, tilts my head back, and shoves a rolled-up piece of gauze into each nostril. She helps me to my feet and then the crowd applauds as she leads me over to our bench.

My head starts to clear up, but the pain holds steady. The center of my face feels bright and warm.

"Tilt your head forward," the trainer says.

I follow her instructions.

"Good. Now pinch the bridge of your nose. Like this." She does it on herself to show me, and then I copy her. Pain flares soon as I do. I clench my teeth. "Good. Now tell me how it feels."

"Great," I say, even though I'm pretty sure this shit is broken because it feels the same as it did when I broke it playing on the courts by my house a few years ago.

I hear the whistle blow. Sneakers squeaking. The thud of the ball against the court. I start to look up, but the trainer holds my head in place. "They start again?"

"We should take you back for x-rays."

I shake my head. The movement brings more pain, but I don't let it show. "It doesn't hurt."

"Right. Just keep holding it like that," she says at my side. "Let's see if we can get this bleeding to stop. Then we'll see how you feel."

I clench my jaw and keep my head down. The pain pulsates, like my heart's beating inside my nose.

I hear the crowd roar. My teammates groan.

"What happened?" I ask.

"You don't want to know," the trainer says.

I sigh. Close my eyes. Take a deep breath. Try to will away the pain, the blurriness, the fog, the blood. I listen to the game and try to guess what's going on by the sounds. There are a lot of whistles, a lot of stopped action, making me glad the last few minutes of a close game almost always get stretched out.

"I'm ready to go back in," I say.

The trainer kneels in front of me. "Let's see." She slides the pieces of gauze out of my nostrils and they come away dripping red. But I don't feel anything running down my nose. She nods. "Good."

"So I'm cool?"

She shakes her head. "We're trying to keep you safe, okay? It's swelling. Let's get some ice on it and see if that helps."

"The game will be over," I say. "Can't you give me one of those facemasks and let me go back in?"

She ignores me. "Can you sit straight up?"

I do, but as soon as I lift my head, it swims with pain and my stomach clenches with nausea. I don't even manage to catch the score before my eyes get blurry again, so I close them. But I get a bit of relief a moment later when she presses the ice pack to my nose.

I keep my eyes closed and continue listening to the sounds of the game. The cheerleaders. The ball. The sneakers. Guys calling for the pass, the pick, the shot. The coaches shouting. And, over it all, the sound of the crowd, welling and swelling like the ocean.

The ball clangs as it hits the rim. Grunting and yelling. A whistle. The crowd goes wild.

"What happened?" I ask the trainer, my voice muffled by the ice pack.

I feel her shift to look at the court. "Santos fouled out."

I smile. It hurts. "What's the score now?"

"44–49. Fairview. A little under two on the clock."

"Thanks," I say, thinking about how happy Wallace probably is about now.

The pain starts to fade, numbness taking its place. I open my eyes just in time to see Yurevich back Drew down and drop two. Coach calls our last full time-out.

"I'm good now," I say, putting down the ice pack and standing.

"Hold on," the trainer says. She peers into my left eye with a penlight, and then my right eye. She clicks off the light. "Follow this," she says, and starts moving the pen back and forth. I concentrate on that thing real hard. I must have passed because she nods and slips the pen into her back pocket. "Do you feel dizzy at all?"

"No."

"Nauseous?"

"No."

"On a scale of one to ten, how much pain are you in?"

I touch my nose, and it feels swollen as hell. "Zero," I lie.

She gives me a skeptical look.

The ref blows the whistle. Time-out's over.

"So? Can he go back in?" Coach asks over her shoulder.

The trainer stares at me for what feels like an hour but is really probably a couple seconds. She glances at the scoreboard. "If you don't feel right, pull yourself out right away, okay?"

"For sure," I say.

"Get out there," Coach says.

"Don't fuck this up," Clay says as I sub in for him.

If only I didn't have to. I step back onto the court, the whole place going wild. Everything's thundering and vibrating. I can barely hear myself think.

Luckily, I don't need to think. This right here is instinct.

"Welcome back," Yurevich says, grinning. "Looking good."

I ignore him. Rub my eyes carefully and glance at the scoreboard as I head to the sideline to take the ball from the ref. My movements feel slow and my head foggy, but I push through. The scoreboard reads 48–55, Fairview. One minute and fifty-seven seconds left to make this loss as close and as respectable as possible.

Right off the whistle, I fire it to Eric and then move like

I'm cutting to the hoop but then step back, shaking Yurevich. Before he recovers, Eric swings the ball back to me, and I launch it from behind the arc.

There's silence — and then the crisp kiss of the ball finding the bottom of the net. The crowd blows up.

Next play, the kid who subbed in for Santos at point ends up dribbling into a trap and then stepping out of bounds. I inbound to Eric, who whips it to Drew down low. Since Yurevich is sticking to me, Drew's got a mismatch. He backs his shorter man down and then kisses it off the square for two. Just like that, it's 53–55.

Next time down, Fairview's shooting guard bricks a three. Eric bricks it at our end, but I get the put-back to tie it up. Fairview's point throws it out of bounds. I shake Yurevich and bank it off the glass to add two more to give us the lead for the first time tonight, 57–55. I know I can't let it stay like that, but I wanted to feel good for a moment.

So next time down, I give Yurevich some space and let him hit a deep three from the baseline, making it 57–58. I inbound to Eric and then glance at the clock. Eleven seconds.

Eric gets caught in a trap immediately, and gives it back to me. I take it up court, stutter step right, fake left, and then cross over back to the right. Yurevich slips, and I breeze into the lane. Every green jersey on the floor gets in my way, so I kick it behind me to Drew.

I spin around just in time to see him lay up an uncontested two.

The buzzer wails before Fairview even brings it across half-court.

And that's it — 59–58. We're state champs.

My teammates crash into me. The crowd swarms the court. Cameras flash. I smile so wide, feeling like my heart is about to burst.

We won!

Oh, shit.

We won.

52

NASIR

Bunny's family, Keyona, Anna, and all the others in our section are going wild. They're hugging and high-fiving and hugging again. They're clapping and dancing and snapping pics and taking videos with their phones.

But I'm standing there stunned, a terrible feeling in the pit of my stomach.

What did you just do to Wallace, Bunny?

53

BUNNY

On the bus ride home, as everyone else is talking excitedly about the game and passing the trophy around, I'm sending Nasir text after text. All variations on the same theme: I'm sorry. I didn't mean to win. I fucked up. I'm sorry. Have you heard from Wallace?

But he doesn't answer a single one of them.

He was with my family and Keyona when I met up with them. Told me, "Great game," like everyone else, but I could tell he was just keeping up appearances. We both knew what that win meant, what it might cost.

It's a strange thing to feel so upset about something that was supposed to give me so much joy, something I've worked so hard for.

Someone palms the top of my head and shakes it around. It's Eric.

"Buuunnnnnyyyy!" he shouts, and the entire bus starts shouting my name in the same way. The trophy gets shoved into my hands, people press their faces next to mine, and someone takes a picture. I try to smile.

It hurts, and not because of my busted nose.

54

NASIR

Bunny won't stop messaging me with his apologies and excuses, but Wallace hasn't responded to any of my texts or answered any of my calls. Soon as I get home, I ask my parents to drive me over to his place, but neither of them will do it, since it's snowing pretty hard now and it's already late.

So there's nothing for me to do but wait.

I can't sleep, so I try playing some video games, wasting time online, watching some TV—but none of it distracts me enough. I'm checking my phone every second for a message from Wallace and standing up all the time for no reason. I'm not feeling an ounce of tired.

Just after one in the morning, I hear a couple of soft knocks at the front door.

I bolt down the steps as quietly as I can and open it up to find not Wallace, but Bunny. He's got his winter hat on and hood pulled up, the bridge of his nose all swollen. The snow's coming down real hard in the darkness behind him.

"Can we talk?" he says.

I start to shut the door, but he plants his boot in front of it. "Please."

"It's late, Bunny. My parents are asleep," I say. "And I'm guessing your family is, too."

"Let's go somewhere, then," he says. "The courts?"

Bunny's the last person I want to see right now, but getting out of the house seems like a good idea. I'm starting to go crazy.

"Fine," I say.

I slip on my winter gear and join him outside a few minutes later, making sure I've got my phone in my pocket. It's wild out here. A couple feet of snow blankets everything on our block, and more is falling. It's beautiful. Almost bright, in a way. Plow hasn't come through yet, so it's all perfect and untouched. Not a single tire track or footprint. The sidewalk, the stoops, the cars, the streets—covered until they've become simply suggestions. It makes the world feel clean and fresh, hiding the trash and broken bottles. I try not to think about how the snow will eventually melt and mix with the dirt to create a muddy mush that will make things even worse than they were before.

The best part of it all is the perfect silence, like someone hit Mute.

I dig my hands into my pockets, taking it all in and ignoring the hell out of Bunny standing next to me. It's cold, but not freezing. My breath puffs up in little white clouds in front of my face. I look up, wanting to see stars. But of course, there aren't any. Just an uninterrupted sheet of gunmetal clouds dumping all these fat flakes down to earth.

We start walking, taking huge steps to plow through the snow. I feel kind of bad ruining the perfect sheet of white, but there's also something satisfying about making the first tracks. Then again, fresh snow will probably have covered it all up by the time we return.

Neither of us speaks. We walk. The only sounds in the night are our breathing and the soft shuffle of our feet plodding through the powder.

To break the monotony, after some time I ask, "Is your nose broken? That was a lot of blood."

"Probably. I'm going to get it checked out in the morning."

I nod, thinking about how it serves him right for messing up that game.

"Any word from Wallace yet?"

I don't answer.

Eventually, we reach the courts. The street lamps are off, but the world is glowing. The hoops stick up from the smooth plane of white, looking youth-size with how high the snow is.

Bunny follows as I walk across, taking slow, long strides. I make my way to a raised mound marking one of the picnic tables, the same one I was sitting on with Wallace when he found that kitten. I start pushing snow off the bench and the table so I have a place to sit, Bunny doing the same next to me. Some snow gets in between the bottom of my gloves and the cuff of my coat sleeve, but the bright points of wet cold actually feel kind of nice.

Once we've cleared enough off, we sit down, our butts on the table part and our feet on the bench. We both wince.

"That's cold," he says.

I don't say anything as I shift to try to find a position that's not going to end up with me having a frostbitten ass. I give up after a few moments and deal with it. Gaze at the evening. It's as quiet and perfect as when I was standing on my stoop.

But I'm not cold. My anger at Bunny's keeping me plenty warm. And the more I think about it, the angrier I get. Only thing keeping me in check is worrying about Wallace.

"I'm sorry, Nasir," he says.

I keep my mouth shut.

"I meant to lose for you. I really did. But I thought if I had to, I'd at least keep it close, you know. Go down swinging." He sighs, examines the palms of his hands. "But in those final seconds, I guess instinct took over. Drew did the rest."

I stay quiet.

"I know you're mad at me for messing that up, but it's not like it was fair of you to ask me to throw the game. I tried, but at the end of the day, I'm not responsible for Wallace."

"Then who is?" I ask.

"Wallace."

"Yeah, okay."

He shakes his head.

A plow rumbles and scrapes down a side street somewhere

close by, and then the world's quiet again. I consider hopping down and making my way back home, but for some reason, I don't.

"Please, Nasir," Bunny says after a few moments, "you have to believe me. I meant to lose tonight. Not for Wallace, for you. I want us to be cool again."

"Then you shouldn't have been trying to keep it that close," I say.

He sighs again. "Yeah, I know that now."

There's so much regret in his voice when he says that, I feel my fists unclench. "It was stupid. Real stupid."

"I know," he says.

I look down. Scrape the soles of my boots across the bench to clear it off again. "So how was that team dinner?"

Bunny smiles. "Dr. Dietrich hooked it up, man. Steak for the entire team. Can you believe anyone has that much bread? If I was that rich, I wouldn't be using it to buy a bunch of teenagers steak."

"You'll be richer than that in a few years," I say.

Bunny doesn't deny it.

"So what will you spend it on?" I ask.

"Easy," he says. "First, I'll buy back Word Up."

"Obviously. What else?"

He answers right away, like he's already thought this all out. "College funds for everyone. Even my mom. She always talks about going back to school after all of us move out."

"Third?" I ask, helping Bunny spend imaginary money even if I know it's kind of dumb.

Again, he doesn't hesitate. "Maybe donate a whole bunch of it."

"Cool. Fourth?"

"Fourth?" He laughs. "This is getting out of hand, man. I don't know. Maybe a nice car to take out Keyona in."

I nod. "So everything's good with her? She was at the game."

He raises his eyebrows. "Did she say we were cool?"

"Nah. She ignored the hell out of me the entire night."

"Damn," he says. "At least she came."

"Well, I hope it works out," I say, finding that I mean it.

He shrugs. "Me too."

"But you realize that after tonight you could probably have any girl you want," I say, because it's true. Most girls have always looked at Bunny like they'd be all over him if he said the word. And now he's a state champion. "To be honest, it's always made me kind of jealous."

"Nah," Bunny says, looking down. "You know me, Nas. I'm not like that. Neither are you."

I nod. "True. But I got to admit part of me wishes I was."

Bunny laughs. "Why?"

"I don't know," I say.

We watch the snow fall until it covers up what we just said. I stick out my tongue and catch some flakes.

"I'm sorry about tonight," he says again.

But there's not much of my anger left. "Don't be. I shouldn't have asked you to throw the game," I say. "It wasn't right."

"You were trying to help Wallace."

"You deserved to win, Bunny," I say, and I know it sounds corny. But I don't care. Sometimes the corniest things are the things we need to say the most, the things people need to hear the most.

Bunny drapes one of his long arms around my shoulder and pulls me closer until our heads bump together.

Even though someone watching might get the wrong idea if they saw two dudes hugging like this for as long as we do in the playground in the middle of the night, I don't care. We stay like that, the snow falling on us, and it feels good. Peaceful. It makes me feel better, like I matter to someone. Like I have a brother. Whoever decided that guys can't hug too much must have been a real bitter, lonely-ass person.

Eventually, we pull apart. Then we sit and watch the world again, even though everything is so still and quiet there's not much to watch. I drop my gaze and stare at the snow on the ground in front of us.

Beneath the bench, I notice a basketball. I hop down, reach underneath, and pull it out. It's that cheap orange rubber kind, half deflated.

"Bet you can't make it from here," Bunny says.

I look at the court. The nearest rim's probably a good thirty or forty feet away. I draw back my arm and launch the deflated basketball overhanded like a baseball. It wobbles through the air before dropping into the snow with a small *poof* about ten feet short of the hoop.

We laugh.

Bunny pushes off the bench and trudges to the spot where the ball disappeared. He digs it out, squares up, and sinks the bucket without even grazing the rim. Only, the net's frozen, so the ball gets stuck inside it. We both laugh again.

"So you told me how you'll spend all that money," I say, "but we're getting ahead of ourselves. First you got to go to college. And every team in the country will be knocking on your door come June fifteenth."

He digs his hands into his pockets and shrugs. "I don't know. That still seems like forever away."

"Just three more months, man. If you had to decide today, where would you go?"

"I don't know. I don't think I could be that far away from my family, so I think I'll probably end up somewhere close by."

Then he scoops up a handful of snow and throws it at me. I duck, but it doesn't matter. The powder scatters soon as it leaves his hand, and it all blows right back in his face. I laugh as he brushes it off.

"Stick to balling, man," I say.

"Whatever. So what about you: Princeton? Yale? Harvard?"

I laugh. "Yeah, right. My grades are good, but not that good. I'll probably end up at Rutgers or Temple. Maybe Penn State."

"We always talked about going to the same college. You still down with that?"

The fact that he still thinks about that makes my heart

feel full, like it's about to lift me into the sky. "It'd be nice, but I don't want to hold you back, man."

"Nah, it wouldn't be like that," Bunny says, and then checks me with his shoulder.

"Look who we've got here," a voice calls from the other side of the court, breaking the evening's peace. I know who it is straightaway, and I'm filled with relief as I turn around.

"Wallace!" I say.

But as soon as I see his tall figure making its way toward us, kicking up the snow like a playground bully kicking over some kid's block city, I know something's not right. He's swaying, clutching a bottle in a paper bag in one hand and a lit cigarette in the other.

"You okay?" I ask. "What happened with those guys? Everything cool?"

Bunny draws a bit closer to me like he's closing ranks.

Wallace stops short a few feet away from us. Glaring and grinning, he takes a drag on his cigarette and a pull from whatever's in the bag.

"The real question is," he says, slurring, "what the fuck happened with this guy?" He points at Bunny.

55
BUNNY

E ven though I'm glad to see Wallace is okay, I've got a
bad feeling about the way he's acting. But I try to play it
cool. "What's good, Wallace?" I say, closing the distance
between us and holding out my fist for a pound.

But he just laughs and stares at my hand hanging in the
air. I shove it back into my pocket.

Wallace continues glaring at us and takes another swig.
It's so quiet I can hear him gulping it down. After several seconds, he lowers the bottle, sighs with satisfaction, and wipes
his mouth with the back of his hand.

"Where you been, man?" Nasir says. "You didn't answer
any of my texts."

He doesn't answer.

I look at Nasir, who looks at me and then back at Wallace.
"You all right? Need a place to sleep tonight?"

"Hell of a game, Bunny Boy," Wallace says, ignoring Nasir and glaring at me.

"Thanks," I say, even though I know he doesn't mean it.

He doesn't take his eyes off me. "You fucked me over,
though. You know that?"

Nasir steps between us. "Chill, Wallace."

"Ha."

"I know you're upset," Nasir says, "but Bunny didn't place those bets to put you in the hole. And he didn't sell that tip to try to dig you out. You did."

Wallace looks from me to Nasir, back to me, and then lets his eyes settle on Nasir. He takes an unsteady step toward him. "Why are you taking his side? He doesn't care about you." Wallace pauses, then says, "He knows, doesn't he? You told him."

Nasir doesn't say anything.

"He did," I say. "And I meant to lose—for real . . . It's just . . . I'm sorry, man."

Wallace laughs as he stumbles toward me. "Oh, you're sorry? In that case, everything's cool! I'll tell the dudes looking for me right fucking now that *I'm* sorry, and then everything will be cool with them! I should have thought of that earlier. Gee, thanks, Bunny Thompson!"

"They're looking for you?" Nasir asks.

Wallace spits, staggers through the snow toward us a couple more steps.

"Come home with us, Wallace," Nasir says. "We'll figure something out in the morning. I promise, man."

"What was your line?" Wallace asks me.

I don't answer.

"Come on," Nasir tells him, his voice quiet. "It'll be okay. Let's get you somewhere safe."

Wallace laughs again, shaking his head. Takes another drink. "Fuck you, Nasir."

I step forward. "It's my fault, Wallace. I'm sorry that—"

"Stop apologizing," Nasir interrupts, the compassion gone from his voice. "He brought this on himself. He was dumb all on his own."

I wait for Wallace to react, but he stands there, grinning.

"Yeah," he finally says. He takes one last drag and flicks his cigarette away. "By the way, your buddy Nas tell you how I got your phone?"

"Yeah, he told me." I keep my eyes on Wallace. "It's cool."

"Is it, though?" He spits.

"Wallace," I say, "we're going back right now. Come with us and stay with Nasir like he said."

He narrows his eyes and points at me with his hand holding the bottle. "Fuck you," he says, his sarcasm replaced with raw anger.

Nasir looks at Wallace for a long time, like he's trying to make up his mind about something. Finally, he sighs and turns to me. "He's a lost cause. Let's go."

He turns his back on Wallace and starts heading back. I wait for a few seconds and then follow. But we don't even make it off the court before something whips through the air overhead. Whatever it is bursts against the metal backboard of the nearest hoop, and shattered glass rains down around us. I cover my head, but Nasir whips around and steps to Wallace.

"Come with us or leave us the fuck alone, Wallace," he says, craning his neck upward to stare his much taller, much bigger cousin in the eyes.

Wallace steps forward and bumps chests with Nasir. He doesn't say anything, but Nasir keeps his ground.

I stand by, mind racing, trying to figure out what to say or what to do to calm things down. I can't think of anything.

But then Nasir takes a step back and puts his hands up in surrender. "I've tried to help you, Wallace. But if you're not going to accept it, then I'm done." He walks away for a second time.

But soon as his back's turned, Wallace tackles Nasir to the ground. In a flash, he's on top of him, fists swinging.

I rush over and drag Wallace off Nasir. We fall into the snow together and wrestle for control. But I end up on top, trying to pin his arms down while he keeps trying to hit me. Most of his punches are thrashing and wild, glancing off my sides or my shoulders. He's strong, but he's drunk. I finally manage to grip his wrists up so he can't hit me anymore. But I'm not sure what to do from here.

"You okay, Nas?" I call over my shoulder, panting.

I hear him breathing heavy, sucking in the cold air as he tries to get back to his feet. "Yeah, I think so."

"Get the fuck off me," Wallace growls. Eyes wild like he's completely lost control of himself, he starts bucking and twisting, trying to shake me. Then he spits into my face.

I let go of one of his wrists so I can wipe it off, but soon as I do, his fist slams into my already broken nose, filling my head with a burst of fresh pain. I cry out and roll off him, onto my hands and knees, the snow crunching beneath me. My vision blurs. Blood leaks out my nose and drops onto the white.

I hear a click.

I look up.

Through the tears, I see Wallace standing there, holding something and pointing it at me—he shifts, and it glints, catching the light from one of the faraway street lamps.

It's a gun.

"Wallace, you don't have to do this. Don't—"

56
NASIR

Wallace," I say, stepping in front of the gun with my hands up before I even realize I'm doing it. The barrel's pointed straight at my chest, and I know this is probably the stupidest thing I could do right now. But now that I'm here, there's no way I'm moving. "You don't have to do this."

"Move," Wallace says through clenched teeth while gesturing with the gun.

"No."

He sidesteps to get a clear shot, but I stay between him and Bunny. "Wallace," I repeat, trying to keep my voice calm even though my heart's hammering in my chest. "You really don't have to do this, man. Put the gun down. We can figure something out."

He sidesteps again, and again I follow. I try to make eye contact, but he's glaring past me at Bunny.

"I'm not here to hurt you, cuz," he says, "but if you don't move . . ." He doesn't finish his threat because he doesn't need to.

"Get out of the way, Nasir," Bunny says from behind me. "Don't be stupid."

"Yeah, Nasir," Wallace says. "You heard your girlfriend. Don't be stupid. Get out of the way." Wallace laughs for some reason. Then he keeps laughing. Drags the back of his free hand across his eyes like he's wiping tears away—but I don't think he's crying from the laughter.

I don't know what to do, so I keep my hands up and stand my ground. I can't see Bunny, but I hear him getting to his feet, and I shift to make sure I stay in front of him.

"Wallace, man, I'm not moving," I say. "Come on—put it away. It doesn't need to go down like this."

Wallace takes a step forward and raises the gun so it's aimed at my head. My breath catches and my eyes close, waiting for the click of metal and the crack of the shot.

But it doesn't come.

"This is the last time I'm going to say it, cuz. Get out of the fucking way."

I open my eyes. Exhale. Try again. "What do you think this will solve?"

Wallace finally looks at me, but he doesn't say anything. He doesn't need to. In his eyes, I see a lifetime of rage, of desperation, of hopelessness. I see he isn't trying to solve anything. He's out to destroy.

My mouth goes dry. I'm out of words.

Bunny comes up beside me. "Wallace—"

57
BUNNY

The blast shatters the silence like the world just ripped in half. The sound rings through my brain, drowning out everything else and even making it hard to stay on my feet.

I look up. Nasir and Wallace are staring at me, eyes wide and faces pale.

And then I notice the gun's still in Wallace's hand. A thin line of smoke snakes upward from the barrel.

I look down.

There's blood on my chest and my arm. Dark splotches on the snow at my feet.

Someone calls my name, but it sounds muffled and faraway, like the person's shouting from the other end of a long tunnel.

That's when the pain arrives. I try to cry out, but it's hard to breathe. I'm suddenly cold. My strength drains away, and I fall backwards.

Nasir's face appears above.

His lips are moving, but everything is slipping away . . .

58

NASIR

rush to Bunny's side as he falls. Let Wallace shoot me, too, if he wants. I need to help my friend.

"Bunny," I say. "Bunny—you all right? Can you hear me?"

But he doesn't answer. His mouth opens and closes, opens and closes, as he struggles to breathe. His eyes gaze upward, unfocused, losing their light. The snow is stained dark all around his body, a stain that's spreading like ink soaking paper.

I look him over, searching for the wound. I find it—it's at his arm below the shoulder, pouring out his life. I press my hands to the spot to try to stop the bleeding, because I think that's what I'm supposed to do. But the blood soaks through my gloves to my fingers, hot and infinite, more blood than I've ever seen in my life, more blood than it seems like fits inside a body.

I'm shaking, hyperventilating. I don't know what to do. I continue putting pressure on the wound, and I press my forehead to his.

No, I pray. *Please, God—No.*

"Bunny," I say. "Bunny. You're going to be okay. You hear me? You're going to be okay." I turn to Wallace to tell him to call 911, but he's gone.

The ringing in my ears fades. Sounds return in a rush. Bunny gasping. Me sobbing. Dogs barking.

Keeping one hand on Bunny's wound, I use my mouth to tug off the glove on my other hand, then I grab my phone out of my pocket and dial 911, hands slick with blood and shaking. I hear myself tell them my friend is dying, tell them to please come quick he is my only friend and he is the best person I know and the best person in the world and he does not deserve this. I tell them where we are and they say help is on the way and keep talking but I'm shaking so bad I drop the phone into the snow and can't find it so I put both my hands back over the wound again and my mouth tastes like copper.

I don't know how long I stay like that—minutes or hours or days. The dogs even stop barking.

An immense hush settles around us. The dark stain grows. The snow continues falling. Large flakes catch in the lashes of Bunny's open eyes.

59
BUNNY

60
NASIR

I do not remember how I got here. In the hospital. I am in the waiting room. It is bright, so bright it hurts. My clothes are stained with red. Bunny's blood.

But I am here.

Me. My parents. The Thompson family. Keyona, her dad, and stepmom.

We are all here. Except for Bunny.

We are crying and taking turns holding each other. But I know that each of us is alone.

Time passes.

A doctor walks out, a mask pulled down under her chin. Her face is worn and sad. We gather around, holding our breath and hearts and hope, knowing this is probably not the face of good news but wishing so badly we are wrong. I am somewhere inside of myself — collapsing, falling, fading — preparing to hear the worst, preparing to hear that my friend is dead.

Because of me.

She scans our group. "Mr. and Ms. Thompson?"

They step forward, and she leads them aside to deliver the news privately. I watch, out of earshot, heart in my throat.

She says something to Bunny's parents, more than I expect. And they hug, tears streaming down their cheeks. Then they return to the rest of us, arms wrapped around each other.

Mr. Thompson swallows. Removes his glasses and wipes the tears from his eyes. Then puts them back on. And smiles. "He's alive."

Everyone lets out a collective sigh of relief.

I cry.

I thank God.

I cry some more.

And I am not alone.

61
BUNNY

My eyes open. Barely, but enough to see through the fog to find faces looking back at me. My family, I think. And Keyona. And Nasir. They're all smiling and crying, and I'm wondering what's happened, what went wrong.

They're speaking to me, but I can't make out a single word. I'm so tired.

I feel like I did when I'd fall asleep in front the TV late at night as a kid and then half wake to my dad carrying me upstairs to my bed. Just like I'd do back then, I let the tiredness overtake me as I feel myself floating upward, safe.

62

NASIR

———————— **NASIR** ————————

Jess takes Justine and Ash home after a couple hours. Keyona and I decide to stay, but her father and my parents head out also. We promise to let them know what's going on as soon as Bunny's out of surgery or there's an update.

He was lucky, the doctor had said. I'd called 911 quickly, the park was close to the hospital, and the plow had just gone through the area where we were. Bunny had lost a lot of blood by the time he got to the hospital, so if it had taken just a few minutes longer, then he probably wouldn't have made it.

As we wait, Mr. Thompson paces around while Mrs. Thompson downs cup after cup of vending machine coffee. Keyona and I sit in those uncomfortable chairs, not saying a word to each other. At one point, I drift off and dream of Bunny's funeral.

We're in a church. Everyone who came by the hospital tonight is there, packed into the pews, even the doctor and nurses I've seen flit past.

We pray and cry and share memories. Jess and Keyona give beautiful, heartbreaking eulogies, but when it's my turn,

I'm too wrecked to make it all the way up front. I stop at the open casket, feeling like I'm about to curl into myself — but it's not even Bunny inside.

It's Wallace.

Before I can say anything, the pastor shuts the lid, an old lady starts playing the organ, and the pallbearers lift the casket and carry it outside and into the hearse waiting out front like it's all happening in fast forward. We get in our cars and follow in a long, slow procession all the way to the cemetery. Then we watch as they put the body into the earth. All the while, I'm wondering who we buried.

63
BUNNY

I wake to the sterile smell and bright lights of the hospital, the steady beeping of a heart monitor. No pain. I'm light-headed and groggy, probably thanks to the IV connected to my left arm.

My parents don't notice I'm awake at first, and I don't say anything. Partly because my mouth's so dry it feels stuck closed and partly because it's kind of nice. They're sitting in the two chairs against the wall, and my dad's holding my mom as she rests her head on his shoulder. They're watching *The Fresh Prince of Bel-Air* on the TV mounted near the ceiling with the volume turned down low. Neither of them is laughing at the show's funny parts, but I let out a weak chuckle at something Will says.

"Bunny?" my mom says.

"Hey, Mom."

She rushes over to my bedside and gathers me in her arms. "Are you okay, baby? How are you feeling?"

"I'm . . . I'm all right."

"Careful, Sharon," my dad says.

But she doesn't let me go for a while, and I'm cool with that. And when she finally does, she keeps my left hand in hers. My dad hugs me next, squeezing me harder and holding me for longer than my mom.

"We love you, Bunny," he says.

"I love you guys, too." Then I remember how I got here and sit up a little. "Is Nasir all right?"

My mom and dad exchange a look.

"He's fine," says my dad. "Right outside with Keyona."

"Wallace?" I ask, wondering how much they know.

My mom exhales. "Gone."

I drop back into the hospital bed and close my eyes, nose still aching. It all starts replaying in my head. Hanging out with Nasir at the court. Wallace pulling the gun. Firing. My world fading to black.

I thought I died.

I open my eyes and turn my head to look at my right arm, which is in a cast from my shoulder to my wrist and a sling.

Before I can ask about it, my mom says in her nurse voice, "The bullet went straight through. It hit the brachial artery on its way, but they were able to repair it. That's why you were in surgery. It also grazed the humerus and fractured it a bit, which is the reason for the cast. It's going to take some time to heal, but it will."

"How long?" I ask. I figure I'm going to miss spring and summer ball, but I'm wondering if I'll have to sit out next season as well.

"Doctor said it should be as good as new in a few months," my mom says. "Of course, you'll have to go to physical therapy for a while."

"Think of it as some time to rest," my dad says.

I try to feel thankful that I'm still alive. But I'm not going to lie, I'm wondering if it's going to mess up my game. I'm right-handed, after all. And even if it doesn't—even if my arm heals perfectly—scouts might still be afraid that it could cause problems later on.

"I can see on your face you're already worrying about recruiting," my dad says, interrupting my thoughts. "But the doc said they expect a full recovery, so try to relax."

I nod, though that advice is a hell of a lot easier said than done.

"The police are here," my dad says. "They want to talk with you about what happened once you're feeling up to it. I'm guessing they want to see if what you tell them matches up with what Nasir said went down."

"Can you and Mom stay?" I ask.

"Of course, baby," my mom says, and squeezes my hand.

"And then can I see Keyona and Nasir?"

My mom's jaw tightens when I say Nasir's name. Dad touches her arm, and her face softens a bit. "Sure," my dad says. "I'll go tell everyone you're awake now."

He dips, leaving me alone with Mom.

After a moment, I ask, "Nasir tell you everything?"

She nods.

"Please don't be mad at him."

"He almost got you killed, baby. None of this would have happened if it wasn't for him." She squeezes my hand.

"I know, Mom. But he's, like, the only friend I've got."

"So I should just let it go?"

"Yeah."

Before she can respond, my dad returns with two cops. One's a skinny young dude and the other's a tall, athletic-looking woman. I tell them exactly what I remember happening. The guy cop jots things down in a notebook the entire time, and the woman cop interrupts me to ask follow-up questions every now and then. Everything must line up with Nasir's story, though, because they don't seem to doubt anything I tell them. Eventually, I run out of words, and they run out of questions. They assure me the police will find Wallace soon, but that they'll stick close by since he's still at large.

That should scare me, but I don't think Wallace is going to try to come back to finish me off or anything like that. Those guys he sold the bad tip to were already after him, and now the police are, too. My guess is he's in the wind.

When I think of Wallace, I find I'm not even angry. Maybe I would be if he'd shot Nasir instead. More than anything, I'm sad for him. I'll heal, but his life's over. Even if it is his fault, that doesn't make it any less tragic to me.

After the cops leave, my mom and dad hug me again. A nurse comes in and checks my vitals as she chats with my mom. She says everything looks good, then congratulates me on the state championship—which I almost forgot about—says the doctor will be by shortly, and leaves.

My parents hug and kiss me, like, a hundred more times, my mom tells me we'll talk more about Nasir later, and then they head into the waiting room. Keyona walks through the door next, Nasir trailing behind her. She comes right over and starts kissing me. The beeping of my heart monitor speeds up, and we both start laughing at that even as we're kissing. Finally, we break apart, but keep our foreheads touching, both of us with tears in our eyes.

"Bunny," she says.

"Keyona," I say.

"I thought I lost you."

"I know."

She laughs. I laugh. She runs her hand over the top of my head and then kisses me once more, and it tastes like the salt of our tears.

"Sorry," I say over Keyona's shoulder to Nasir, who's been leaning against the door this entire time.

"Nah, it's cool," he says. "Really."

"Come over here, man," I say.

Keyona scoots over so Nasir can stand beside me. He goes to give me a close-fisted dap, but I pull him in for a hug with my left arm. My other one may be broken, but my heart feels stronger and larger than ever. It feels so wide it could swallow the world.

"I'm sorry," he says.

"Me too," I say.

And we don't need to say more than that. We both understand what we're apologizing for.

"I'm glad you're okay," he says.

"Me too," I say. And then I laugh, because I am alive and it's clearer than ever now that I really need to spend more of my life laughing.

EPILOGUE
June 15

NASIR

I put on khakis and a nice shirt, and my parents drive me to the County Correctional Facility. Nobody says anything along the way, but my mom and my dad keep glancing at me in the rearview mirror. I ignore their worrying and try to think of what I'm going to say to Wallace. I thought I'd know by now, thought I'd have a speech ready to go. It's been a few months since that night. But every time I sat down to write something out, my mind went blank.

The jail's downtown, only a few minutes' ride from our place, not too far from where Wallace used to live with his grandma and where Word Up used to be before Mr. Thompson sold it.

We park in a gated lot across the street, and then my dad turns in the passenger seat to face me. "You sure you want to do this?"

I take a deep breath and try to steady my shaking hands. "I'm not sure I'd say I want to, but I think I need to."

"We'll be right there with you," my mom says from behind the wheel. "If you want to leave before the time is up, just let us know."

"It's only half an hour," I say.

"Still," she says.

I nod.

We step out of the car and into the warm summer morning. The sky is a perfect blue, which contrasts with the jail, which is a series of tall, blocky buildings the color of sand and with windows like knife slits. The facility is surrounded by a red brick wall topped with coils of barbed wire. We cross the street and join the clump of visitors waiting in front of the gate. The crowd's a mixture of people, all different ages and races. Some are smoking and chatting quietly, while others stare at their phones. Some look like this is about as routine as going to the grocery store, and some look as nervous as I feel.

I check the time on my phone. We're half an hour early.

My parents stand on either side of me as we wait. My dad's reading a book, and my mom's gazing into the distance with her arms folded over her chest.

I close my eyes. I try thinking through what I'm going to say, but words won't come. Instead, images fill my mind.

Bunny holding a trophy, hoisted onto his teammates' shoulders.

Bunny at my door in the middle of the night.

The courts covered in snow.

Bunny's shot with the deflated ball getting stuck in the frozen net.

Wallace appearing with a bottle and then busting it on the backboard.

The snow against my face as Wallace shoved me to the ground.

The jolts of pain as he climbed on top of me and punched me over and over again.

The glint of metal.

The thunderous crack and burst of light.

Bunny bleeding.

The snow falling.

All of it like a silent movie playing in my head. No words. No thoughts. Just images, pure and painful, flickering against the backs of my eyelids.

I start crying. I'll never forget that it was my fault Bunny came so close to never playing ball again or worse. Or maybe it's because I could have stopped Wallace from firing the gun in the first place if I had only said the right words in the right way. Or maybe it's both reasons.

Anyway, my dad notices, hugs me, and offers a tissue. I shake my head. It's not a snot-running-down-your-nose kind of crying. It's the quiet kind.

Eventually, a couple of guards appear. One of them gives instructions I can't hear and then opens the gate. He leads the way as the other guard brings up the rear like they're shepherding us. We follow the crowd into the building and then stand in a line in the vestibule while they wand each person. After that, each of us signs this big-ass book, and they check our names against the computer. They put all of our belongings in these little lockers and then we wait around for the elevators.

It's a quiet, awkward ride down a few floors. The guard cracks a joke, but nobody laughs. He repeats a few of the rules, and a moment later, the doors open and we all follow him to the visiting area.

It's like in the movies. A row of booths, each one with a stool, a phone, and a glass wall that separates the mirrored situation on the opposite side. The thing I don't expect is that the prisoners are already seated and waiting. I walk down the row, my parents lingering behind me, until I find Wallace sitting at the second-to-last booth. He looks like a faded photo of his former self. He's in one of those traffic-cone-orange jumpsuits with a number stenciled on the front. His head is shaved, the lopsided fade gone. His face is gaunt. Eyes cold.

He doesn't smile when he sees me. He just lifts his chin in recognition.

It's a strange thing, seeing him again. In my mind, he's been as good as dead all this time. Having him in front of me in real life feels like being with a ghost.

My hands are shaking again. I take a seat. Wallace is inches away. He picks up the phone, and I do the same.

Neither of us says anything for a minute. We hold each other's gaze, a static silence crackling on the line. And then he speaks.

"Bunny didn't want to come with you?" He laughs.

I don't.

"Just kidding, man. What's good?" The phone makes his voice sound small, but it's the same low mumble I remember.

"Not much," I say. But that's not true. Bunny's arm is

healing well, and he texted me earlier that college coaches have been blowing up his phone all day since he's officially a junior now.

But it's not like Wallace needs to hear that.

"I wasn't sure you'd ever visit," he says. "Nobody visits."

I try to gather my thoughts. Any hope I had that they'd magically form in the moment is dashed. My brain's a mess of images from that night and raw emotion. Anger. Hatred. Sadness. Exhaustion.

"You don't look like you want to be here, cuz," he says.

I shrug.

"How's life on the outside? I know the Sixers still suck."

"I tried to help you," I say. "I did everything I could."

He looks away.

"Everyone says I should forget about you. That you're a lost cause, you know?"

"Yeah, I know."

"They right?"

He shrugs. "Looks that way."

I wait for Wallace to say something else, but he doesn't. He just sits there, looking down with the plastic phone pressed against his ear.

I think about how he turned himself in a couple days after the shooting. How he pleaded guilty to the attempted murder charge. How that means by the time he's out of here, Bunny and I will be out of college, maybe even have careers and families of our own.

My parents, Keyona, and Bunny all say that I tried and

that that's enough. They say that at the end of the day, Wallace isn't my responsibility.

Logically, I know they're right. But there's something in me that keeps on asking if he is, that keeps on saying that if he continues believing he's nothing, then nothing's going to change.

The night everything went down, I wish I could have spoken something so true, so powerful, that it would have caught in his soul and forced him to take his finger off the trigger. Or maybe there was something I could have said before it even got to that level. But I didn't.

So right now, I don't hang up on Wallace. We sit with the silence and glass between us. I continue to search for the right words, hoping they're out there somewhere.

ACKNOWLEDGMENTS

Much love to the team that helped bring this story to life:

To Kathryn—thank you for pretty much everything. I am a better writer and a better human being because of you. Thank you for reading so many drafts of everything I write, for board game date nights, for weekend hikes, and for season one of *The Amazing Race*.

To my parents—thank you for believing in me throughout the years. To my brother and sister—thank you for being excited about my writing even when I wasn't. To all my family—thank you for the love you send across borders and oceans. From your kind words to the selfies with my first book you posted online when you found it in the store, your support makes my heart explode.

To all my students, past and present—thank you for inspiring me and for continuing to give me hope in the next generation. I truly believe you are more aware and more compassionate than any other.

To Margaret Raymo and the entire HMH crew—thank you for believing in this story, whipping it into shape, and sending it out into the real world. It would be grossly obvious to say this book would not exist without you all, so I won't.

To Kaylee Davis, Kimiko Nakamura, and Dee Mura—thank you for your editorial feedback and moral support, and for handling all the business-y type stuff so I can focus on playing make-believe.

To Paul Davis—thank you for giving me insight into what life is like for a high school basketball star. Though, I'm pretty sure I beat you one-on-one when we were kids in that little court in your backyard. If not, I'm still going to tell people that I did.

To Aaron Kim, who read the very first version of Nasir and Bunny's tale when it was just a short story—thank you for your critique notes and encouragement as I turned it into a full novel. I still remember the exact moment when you told me you knew you'd see it in a bookstore someday.

To my early readers; RJ McDaniel, Xavier Berry, Shahmar Beasley, Miles Burton, Brendan Kiely, Patrice Caldwell, and others—thank you for your honest feedback. This story is better because of each one of you. Of course, all mistakes are my own.

To Dr. Kate Delaney—thank you for answering my weird medical questions. Book-related and otherwise.

To Kendrick Lamar, Kid Cudi, Blue Scholars, and Tupac—thank you for your music. Your songs played as I wrote much of this book, and I know my words would not have been the same without yours.

To Loki and Arwen—you can't read this because you are dogs, but thank you for making sure I wake up in the morning. Also, you are very soft, which I like.

To my YA communities in Philly, the Bay Area, and online—thank you for the panels and Twitter chats, the advice, the writing sessions, the companionship, the conversations, and the commiseration. Thank you for making me feel included, and thank you for the stories you tell.

Thank you to the teachers and counselors and coaches who care, to the teammates who know they need to look out for each other on and off the court, to the librarians and booksellers and bloggers who know that stories can save lives, and to anyone who fights for careful representation because they know how much it matters.

Finally, thank you, dear reader. You are why I write.